The Returners

Praise for The Returners

"To put it completely blunt, 'The Returners' is a work of art—a harmonious blend of science fiction, humor, action, history, and a hint of romance."

-ScienceFiction.com

"The Returners by Mikey Neumann is an action-packed page turner, filled with a memorable cast of characters, some great humor, and more historical references than you can shake a World History 101 syllabus at."

-Word of the Nerd Online

"'The Returners' is full of wit, action, history and humor! Author Mikey Neumann's talent for storytelling makes one wonder if his own past lives were once literary legends!"

-Bonnie Burton, Columnist for SFX Magazine, Host of Geek DIY and author of "Star Wars: The Clone Wars: Planets in Peril"

The Returners

Season One Omnibus

Mikey Neumann

Published by "BOZ." 2013

THE RETURNERS

"BOZ." Publishing

www.bozpublishing.com

ISBN 978-0-578-11621-1

Book layout and editing by Timothy Hudson

Cover by Mikey Neumann

Season One Introduction

They say the best writing comes from a place of experience. While I cannot step forward and claim to know what it is like to be a famous historical figure born back into their body hundreds or thousands of years in the future, I know a thing or two about feeling lost.

Life spoiler alert; don't read any further if you haven't read my autobiography that doesn't yet exist—or if you're someone that gets really uppity when someone writes the words "spoiler alert" in an internet article—which I do, so I won't be reading anything I've written beyond this point. I would expect all kinds of misspellings and grammatical errors to follow.

In Octobler

Ahem.

In *October* of 2011, a number of strange things happened to me. I lost feeling in my side, lost the use of my right eye for the most part, needed to get around on a cane. This landed me in different hospitals for the better part of a month, and, though the theories of what was wrong seemed to be all over the map, the growing consensus was a) that I had suffered a stroke and b) it was caused by a hole in my heart called a PFO (Patent Foramen Ovale.) This did not account for all the symptoms, but seemed like a reasonable enough thing for a twenty-nine year old to experience (accent on the nope.)

As time went on, and more doctors were brought into the fold, a nice man from Johns Hopkins called me out of the blue on a lovely January day to tell me he had been forwarded my chart and information and wanted to talk. He went on to say something akin to: "Yo Breezy, real talk. You should come up to Maryland so I can run some tests and get Mercedes up in this bitch." (Or something more doctor-sounding. I tend to form memories through hip hop-tinted glasses.)

I don't generally turn down any opportunity to get Mercedes in Baltimore, so I went up North expecting to wallow in the Hpnotiq and Hennessy flowin' like a Ludacris album, but like anything in life, was not treated to the results I so selfishly expected.

What follows is an excerpt of an actual conversation we had.

"You have Multiple Sclerosis."

I paused. "Are you sure it isn't Singular Sclerosis?"

The doctor looked at me as if I had just shot a puppy that did amazing tricks at the circus. It turned out, much to my limitless dismay on the subject, that I was not the first person to make that joke. I know, right?

And this is where The Returners comes from.

After months upon months or searching for answers, wondering on certain nights if I would even wake up again in the morning, I had my answer and it wasn't exactly the sexiest of the Scleroses.

So I started writing.

There was this peanut of an idea that I had been knocking around in my head one day in Los Angeles and I decided to start putting it down on paper as a short story. It was a really sticky idea, I thought. Take historical figures like Alexander the Great, Joan of Arc, Genghis Khan and pit them against each in a modern setting where they each have no idea who the other one is; just that they're trying to kill each other.

Upon finishing the story, which ended up becoming the first chapter in the novel, I realized that I had just started a new novel. There was simply no way I could let it go as a small glimpse at this universe. The problem was that I was already shopping around my other novel, and there was so much work still to be done on that one (and at the time of this printing, is still not finished.)

So "BOZ." Publishing was born out of this. The book (or tablet) you're holding was an experiment in publishing I decided to take on. When I started, I had no idea that it would grow so much, nor attract the amazing fans to the experiment that it did. Every single chapter in this book was published one at a time, in a serialized format, on the website for "BOZ." I knew from the beginning, that someday I would be able to collect the entire first season into a book and share the emotions of my journey with as many people as I could.

These characters were lost and so was I. The joys of writing and getting an audience reaction right in the moment were the things that kept me moving forward. The Returners helped me find my way through physical therapy and the nights where the lights at the end of the tunnel were just a bit too dim to continue onward. Depression is a hell of a thing and I'm sure there are many in the audience that know what I'm talking about. It can wrap you up in chains and drop you into the ocean because sometimes life will just try and drown you.

So don't let it.

Pick yourself up and find the thing in life that gives you drive and meaning. As it turns out, it's not all Hpno and Hennessy until the sun comes up.

In the strangest of ways, Alexander the Great saved my life. I think there's a beautiful message hidden away in there because we all have to set our course and discover the meaning of existence on our own.

With that, I hope you enjoy reading Season One of The Returners as much as I enjoyed writing it. A lot of love went into this book and I greatly look forward to continuing the adventures of these characters well into the future. I hope we meet again in Season Two.

Mikey Neumann

Author of The Returners, all-around swell guy and breakdance fighter for great justice

Season One Foreword

I don't know how Mikey Neumann does it.

Keep in mind that I didn't know the man personally until we met at the Penny Arcade Expo East in Boston in March of 2012. Which means I've not known him very long at all; In the Geological sense I mean. As far as normal human life spans go I've known Mikey for something like one or two percent of what a lot of us spend on the Earth. I'm not making my point very well. What I suppose I mean to say is that I feel like I have known him a lot longer than I have. Part of that is how we met.

The story of our meeting is much like an arranged marriage. Here we were, two people who somewhat obliquely ran in the same circle of friends. Somehow it was discovered that despite his work on various amazing projects involving the, and pardon me for industry speak here for a moment, Interactive Entertainment Industry, and despite my work in same, we had somehow never crossed paths.

It's a weird feeling to tweet something like "Wow I just saw *Aliens: Colonial Marines* and it's amazing!" and get a couple of replies saying "Tell Mikey I said hi!"

My mistake, to my benefit it turns out, was tweeting back "Who's Mikey?"

Turns out Mikey didn't have any clue who I was, nor me him, and yet all our many Twitter followers and friends were saying "THIS IS RIDICULOUS YOU GUYS WILL BE BEST FRIENDS FOREVER STOP EVERYTHING AND GO TO GEARBOX BOOTH NOW DO IT NOW DO IT NOW" which is kind of a long tweet but represents what most people were screaming.

From the moment we were finally thrust into each other's arms at the behest of, like, a hundred thousand twitter followers, we knew we were going to be those wise old BFF's later who at one point didn't know each other existed then proved the odds wrong and became friends and by the way one of my weak points is stretching a metaphor so far it results in a weirdly structured run on sentence that extends into the distance like a simile does something across a long stretch. (Ed note: I can't even hyphen that). Since then we've written a couple of things together, hung out, sang Karaoke, I played a game he worked on called *Borderlands 2*. Then I discovered he was writing something called *The Returners*.

Which brings me back to my initial point: I don't know how Mikey does it.

I read fast. I don't mean in the speedread skip-over-words sense. I read fast and I still can't keep up with how much of a world Mikey is creating with *The Returners*. This, along the other amazing work he does in the video game world, astounds me. Sometimes he'll post a chapter a night in *The Returners*. And I'll read it and wonder who his broker is for selling your soul to the devil for good stories. In Neil Gaiman's *Sandman* universe there's a library in the world of dreams for all of the unfinished books author's either never completed or are still working on. I fear the section on The *Returners*, being a serial story, might take up most of Fiddler's Green at the moment and it's getting smaller with each chapter getting released.

The Returners is the perfect playground for a writer like Mikey. He weaves history and humor, mystery and action, a touch of Sci Fi and a sense of fun in such a way that I simply don't know what to call the genre. I'm thinking of calling it AltSciFiHistFunFic with a twist of lemon and some bitters. The best part is that he's followed the Internet style of providing the content for free in some forms, and charging a small price for other forms such as putting it on Kindle, etc. This is the great thing the Internet has brought us, the ability of authors to get their stories out quickly in a variety of formats and locations, generate a following, and get compensated for it.

It's a model I use myself, but as a reader *The Returners* is one of the first ideas in a long while that I've been so thankful I can get it anytime, anywhere when Mikey releases a new chapter.

I assume if you're reading this you're passing familiar with the premise but if not, allow me to divulge: Various historical figures are reincarnated into alternate people in the present time. I KNOW, RIGHT? By the way, I mean reincarnated in its strict sense and not in a spiritual sense. The easiest way to describe it is that these individuals are incarnated again. To explain it any further would be to assume too much. But here's the interesting part: not only is the oddity of various historical figures being reborn and retaining their memories an interesting premise, there's the fact that someone is trying to kill them, their returning itself might threaten the world, and it features the single most unpleasant birthday party a 13 year old Albert Einstein could possibly experience. And that's just the beginning part of what Mikey is calling "Season 1"! I don't know that I want to tell you any more because things go whack-a-doodle pretty fast.

Whack.

A.

Doodle.

I do know I don't want it to end. I have my favorites amongst the various chapters, from the opening story that hooked me involving text messages, Alex the Great, and Genghis Khan to my favorite story so far *Adagio for Helio 31*. You're lucky in a way, dear reader. I had to read *The Returners* in chapter sized chunks when Mikey released them, which was fun but agonizing despite how quickly he writes. But you? You get this big ole' Omnibus. All *The Returners Season 1* in one go.

Oh you're going to have fun. I don't want to keep you from it any longer.

One day I'll figure out how Mikey Neumann does it.

-Stephen "Stepto" Toulouse

Author, Former Xbox LIVE enforcement Director, part time PAX and w00tstock performer, a geek of pure pedigree.

Season One is dedicated to everyone that has been there along the way. From numerous family members and friends offering encouraging words to keep moving forward, or worthwhile critiques that helped shape what this story was to become. Most of all, I'd like to thank Timothy Hudson whose tireless work at my side during this book is a big part of why it exists at all. You are an artist, editor, and most of all, a friend.

We did this together.

(Ckk totes foxed.)

The Returners

Season One Part One

CHAPTER ONE
Text Messages

Sunset Boulevard
Hollywood, California

Relying on the belief that horrendous acts of violence only happen to *other* people, nine out of ten persons will not correctly identify a gunshot upon hearing one. The more common reaction is to explain it away as a car backfiring, a random bit of construction noise, or for the truly desperate: a clap of thunder on a perfectly sunny California day.

He never made *that* mistake and knew a damn gunshot when he heard one. He froze in place as the sound reverberated in and out the hilly offshoots of Sunset Boulevard past small groups of people showcasing their knowledge of car-backfires, toiling construction projects, and the rolling thunder of Southern California. Based on the number of times it echoed, he knew it had been fired less than two blocks away as the curvature of the boulevard would stifle the crack of the bullet from echoing too much.

Who was trying to kill him?

Alex Heton tipped the brim of his ragged fraternity cap tightly over his blonde curls and slipped a phone from his pocket, checking on his girlfriend. The inebriated patrons bounced from his shoulders as he pushed further down the street. There was little doubt in his mind that the next shot would be traveling in his direction. A successful escape, to the untrained eye, would not register as an escape at all but as a young man attempting to make a phone call.

Chloe wasn't picking up.

She never picked up, he cursed to himself loudly and *blandly* enough to draw no attention from the people surrounding him. As with any twenty-something girls prowling the hedonistic streets of Los Angeles on a Friday night, Alex had a higher probability of running into Wes Anderson rocking a football jersey than his girlfriend answering his call. Texting would have to suffice despite his objections to that particular form of communication.

"It's me, Alex. Are you close?" He typed out to 'Chloe Freimont,' careful to punctuate and capitalize his message as if it would someday hang in the Museum of Modern Art.

"u dont have 2 say ur name babe. it says it rite on the phone," she rebutted with less careful attention to the urgings of Strunk and White.

Did Chloe still have the phone out from ignoring his phone call just ten seconds earlier? He knew she had and angrily typed out another message. "Okay, apologies. Seriously, I need you to get here as soon as possible. We're in". The message was not completed as he accidentally mashed the send button in lieu of the "D" key. The next word of the text was to be "danger."

"where r u?"

"I'm going into that taco joint on San Vincente. Come here NOW."

"b there soon k? <3"

Alex put the phone away and casually strolled into the restaurant. He grabbed the table closest to the counter, supplying him with full line-of-sight to both entrances and every window in the shop. He leaned back in his chair and pulled the collar of his jacket up, just above his ears. He knew he was presenting the world an erroneously douche-like exterior, but any assailant would have to take a moment for target recognition on such a high traffic avenue—a moment that gave Alex identification of his target first, and the upper hand.

Twenty minutes went by and no tacos were ordered.

The dented bell above the main door clanked twice as Chloe entered the taco diner and sped across the floor to the table against the wall. "What the hell is going on, Alex? You texted that we were in danger," she barked in a hushed tone at her boyfriend.

His head dipped back as he raised an eyebrow, "I never said the word danger."

Chloe rolled her eyes before taking an unwelcome sip from his glass of water. "Honey, you text me that we're in danger, like, four times a month."

"We *are* in danger like four times a month."

She gently placed her hand over his, growing desperately tired of this familiar paranoia, and looked him square in the eyes. "Maybe it's time we talk to somebody about this. Karen has a friend in Burbank that specializes in delusional—"

"This isn't a delusion, Chloe!" he cut her off, raising the ire of the man behind the counter. "This is going to sound like a bad spy movie, but there's so much I wish I could tell you."

"The girl always dies before the bone-headed asshole comes clean in those movies. Alex, are you into something bad? Drugs? Seriously, you can talk to me," she urged while gasping back tears from falling on half-price taco night. "This isn't a movie, Alex."

The nightshift manager walked over to their table. They were the only two customers in the restaurant and their argument quickly aroused suspicions that something was amiss unrelated in any way to half-priced taco night. "Is everything okay over here?" His voice was soft and kind.

Alex leaned forward in his chair and gave Chloe an eyeful before turning to the manager on duty. "Yeah, we're fine, thank you. I'll have another glass of water."

"Apologies, sir, but I wasn't asking you," the manager spoke before turning back to Chloe, his attention piqued.

She wiped a tear before it collected enough to fall from her eye. "Yes, thank you. We're just having an off night."

Alex snapped his head to the front of the diner. Had someone just been looking through the glass? He was almost certain a face had disappeared just before he turned to see it.

"If you don't order something, I'm afraid I'm going to have to ask you to leave," the manager said flatly, aggravated he had just been lied to twice.

Alex did not turn to speak face-to-face this time, steeling his gaze instead to the four massive panes of glass at the front of the store. "What do you have here?"

"The name of the place is 'Taco Baron.' We serve," the manager sarcastically paused for a moment before completing the thought, "tacos."

"Why Baron?"

"What?"

Alex slurped the icy puddles of water from the bottom of his glass. "Why Baron?" he repeated with unchanged condescension, eyes still fixed on the glass by the doorway.

Chloe kicked him under the table, "just order some damn tacos, Alex."

He was on autopilot, completing thoughts and speaking words as a means of distraction. "The Baron is the lowest member of English nobility. If I were naming a restaurant, I would choose something that spoke prestige or power."

"Hey man, I'm just the night manager." A pause. "Is there someone outside the window?" The man spoke back now more puzzled than angry that the young man could not return his eye contact. "You're starting to freak me out a little."

Alex ignored him. "Barons were generally fat assholes that were given land from someone of much greater nobility. They were also never referred to as 'barons,' but as 'lords.' So technically, the name of the establishment should be 'Lord Taco,' but returning to my earlier point, that's just one step above 'Taco Serf.'"

She kicked him a second time.

The manager squeezed the two sides of his forehead together and let out a long sigh. "The Barbacoa is pretty good. How about four of those?"

"Sounds," Alex sarcastically paused for a moment before completing the thought, "awesome."

The manager skittered back behind the counter, which left the two alone to return to more serious topics. Chloe grabbed both of his hands and gave a loving, though admonishing, squeeze. This snapped his attention away from the window and back to her beautiful face. He loved the way she smiled when she was mad at him.

The bell above the door clanked the moment Alex looked away.

Chloe did not turn before the shot.

The bullet screamed past her right eyebrow, searing the flesh before shattering the window behind them. She grabbed her forehead and fell to the ground screaming in pain before her brain could make sense of the cacophony or the blood.

A second bullet ripped through Alex's collar as he lunged down toward a table in between him and the assailant. He bent low on his knees to gather the maximum amount of force before lunging back up from under the table, sending it tumbling at the man near the doorway.

Alex took account of the attacker's dark skin tone and long black hair in the fleeting moment before impact. With a rushed consideration, he intuited the man to be a Filipino with poor taste in goatees.

The Formica surface smashed into the gunman's face, sending him hurtling off balance into the swing-door trashcan behind him. A bucket of ketchup packets fell off and spread out across the tile.

Alex moved swiftly on his feet and formed a tense two-handed grip around the pistol still in the grasp of the attacking man. It fired twice into the tiled floor of the restaurant as the two combatants fought and struggled over the weapon.

He took two steps to his left in an attempt to leverage the grip he had over the Filipino man's arm. He leaned back and threw the gunman with incredible force into the corkboard behind the counter, sending work schedules and hasty reminders floating down onto the front desk.

The gunman dazedly pushed up from the ground as a cash register collided into his face, sending the Glock-17 skipping across the kitchen floor. He gasped as a hand crushed down on his esophagus and picked him up from the ground. The next thing he knew, he was being slowly dragged across the kitchen.

Alex looked back toward Chloe who helplessly glared back in his direction with one astonished eye that she was refusing to blink. He returned his attention to the man who had just tried to kill both of them and tossed the concussed heap toward the dishwasher.

"Don't move." Alex leaned forward and recovered the pistol from the floor. Without breaking eye contact, he popped the slide back and caught the ejected bullet in midair. He mashed the clip release and tossed both the remaining ammo, and the pistol itself, into a nearby deep fryer. The ejected bullet was carefully placed onto the flat grill where burned chicken and steak continued to sizzle around it. He turned the temperature control as far to the right as it would go.

He grabbed the man on the ground by his long black hair and forcefully shoved his face as close to the upward-facing bullet as possible. The heat coming from the grill was already causing the man to sweat profusely.

Muted pops began to send errant molten vegetable oil into the air a few feet away. The bullets were going off in the deep fryer. Alex could hear Chloe on the phone with someone in the other room. It was most likely the police, so it was in his best interest to make this interrogation go quickly.

The gunman looked down at the tip of his own bullet one inch from his retina as the metal casing began to redden on the four hundred degree surface. Alex spoke with barely audible menace. "At first glance, I thought you were from the Philippines."

The gunman refused to answer his question or speak back in any way. He was simply waiting for the powder to blow and imbed the shrapnel of the bullet deep into his skull. *That would be a good death.*

"But when I picked your ass up off the floor, it became pretty clear that you are Mongolian." Alex grabbed the Mongol and tossed him to the floor. The attacker landed on his back and desperately looked around the kitchen for something to kill Alex with. "So, please forgive me if my racial acuity is low in life-threatening situations. I meant no offense when I thought you were Filipino."

Ruptured shards of the bullet, and its casing, ripped through the air and ricocheted off pots and pans that hung over the stoves.

"I know who you are," Alex sneered but remained careful to speak softly out of earshot of the nightshift manager curled up in the fetal position under the front desk and repeating Hail Mary's ad nauseam.

"What do you know of who I am?" the Mongolian snarled back at the blonde youngster who had bested him, unarmed. "The vehicle may have changed, but we are all still part of a wheel." The man spit in Alex's face.

Alex leaned down into the face of the man on the floor of the kitchen. "Did someone send you after me?"

The man's eyes dropped toward the floor in confusion. "Your arrogance survives to a new generation. What makes you think I was coming for you?"

Alex grabbed the Mongolian and slammed the back of his head into the dishwasher. "Khan, you will tell me of your aggressions or you and I will begin fishing for the remaining ammunition in the deep fryer," he soured through gritted teeth.

The Mongol smiled, "you desperately cling to our titles of a bygone generation. I am no more a Khan than you are Great, Alex."

Chloe's ears perked up from the other room. The phone call no longer seemed relevant to her.

Alexander again slammed his attacker into the dishwasher. "Why are you coming after the ones who have returned?"

Genghis Khan looked back through his concussion into the eyes of a man who did not understand what was happening. "Alexander, you are trying to play from three moves behind—"

A blast sent Alex to the ground and left a deafening ringing in his ears.

He grimaced and slammed his eyes shut at the realization that a gun had fired at such close range. When he allowed his eyes to open once more, he could hardly stomach the sight of what was left of the face of a once great warrior.

Someone was speaking in muffled tones to his right.

Alex turned slowly enough to avoid startling the second gunman. His eyed widened.

The one holding the smoking gun was Chloe.

He realized the people on the phone with her were surely not the cops. This meant they were still five to ten minutes from arriving on the scene and Alex would be dead before they turned up dusting for prints on a gun they would wish he had not recently deep fried.

She slid across the counter and landed with a graceful thud a few feet away from the man she had just murdered. Alex could feel her eyes looking him over and deciding whether or not to put a bullet through his skull as well.

How had he missed it? Thoughts became a flurry in his mind. She was late because *she* had fired the bullet down the street, but into whom, and why? There was a strong possibility he would throw up momentarily.

Alex recoiled again as two more bullets were fired under the counter into the night manager's chest. He died tightly clutching his wallet as photos of a widowed family crumbled in his other trembling fist.

Chloe rotated her gaze back to her startled boyfriend on the floor. "Can you hear me okay, Alex?"

He could make out what she was saying well enough but the deafening ring was showing little sign of dissipating. He attempted to stand up.

She raised the gun toward his face, "Please don't move. There's more going on here than you realize."

He acquiesced and returned to the ground, never breaking eye contact with whoever the hell was pointing a gun at his face. "Chloe, what is—"

She cut him off. "Surely your arrogance has divined that my name is not actually Chloe, dude."

"You used me."

Chloe laughed. "You treated me like a hot young slam piece. Which doesn't matter because I kept you alive, Alex."

He thought back to all of the times he became annoyed that his girlfriend was not up to the conversation at hand. How stupid could he have been not to see it before this moment? So many people had died, some of them for the second time, and it was entirely of his error. "You know what I meant."

Chloe walked past Alex to the back door of the kitchen—she kept the gun trained on him at all moments. She paused before exiting, "You guys took it upon yourself to find everyone that returned. Did none of you stop to think it was you leaking the information that lead to their deaths? The returners are more than you know."

"So what happens now?" he prodded her decision on whether or not the fourth corpse of the evening would be his.

She smiled, "I never saw twenty. There's so much to see and do in Los Angeles, you know? "

"Who are you?"

She kicked the door open and back peddled away, "Soon."

Minutes passed and Alex sat idly between two corpses in the Taco Baron kitchen dwelling on the events that had transpired. The red and blue flashes of police cars shone through the front window and he elected not to think on it anymore.

His pocket buzzed twice.

Alex pulled the phone from his pocket and saw the name "Chloe Freimont" dishonestly blinking on the lock screen. He slid his thumb over to find that she had texted him a single word. A name he had been chasing for months and never realized that this person was sleeping over three nights a week and consistently refused to eat Chipotle with him. He smiled like he was angry with her and said the name out loud.

"Joan."

CHAPTER TWO
The Stack

Minutes Later
The Taco Baron

It was as if the sweat running down Alex's face was trying to crawl back in through his pores. The information he received moments before would be of little use should he have any desire to appear innocent or victimized when law enforcement came crashing into the Taco Baron.

Though, in that moment in time he didn't have the power to discern if he was innocent or victim in the events of the evening. It had been a night of heavy realizations and near-death experiences.

The dancing red and blues of police sirens were colliding in a dizzying array all throughout the small taco restaurant (soon to be under new management.) Alex slid his back up the wall as the officers ran through the door screaming things rife with cliché.

"Up against the wall. Spread 'em!" The first officer yelled as he ran through the door, his hand looked to be one false move away from a Grand Jury shooting investigation. Alex complied and turned to the wall, spreading his fingers down the textured wallpaper that smelled of cumin and sadness. The policeman frisked him up and down his sweat-soaked clothing before allowing the blonde witness a moment to explain what had occurred there.

"I was in here when it happened," Alex sheepishly offered to the man continuing to search his clothes for hidden contraband. "Gun's in the deep fryer."

The man stopped patting him down and looked to three fellow police scanning the Taco Baron for any surprises. "You wanna say that again?"

Alex sighed and motioned with his head toward the kitchen. "I threw the gun into the deep fryer."

"Put your hands behind your head, careful to interlock your fingers one after another."

"Wait. No. The guy on the floor attacked my girlfriend and I. The dead Mongolian guy!"

The officer continued his arrest oblivious to the foul cries of the man he was arresting. "You have the right to remain silent. Anything you say, can and will be held against you in a court of law."

"So, that probably includes that bit about me throwing the attempted murder weapon into the deep fryer, huh?" Alex blurted. Words were escaping his face faster than he could think and stop them.

The officer wrenched Alex's right hand down the back of his shirt and shoved him into the wall with a considerable force. "You have the right to speak to an attorney. If you cannot afford an attorney, one will be appointed for you," the policeman continued his well-rehearsed Miranda warning as he clasped the second cuff on Alex's other hand.

He felt his phone buzz in his pocket but could not figure out a way to check his messages without the use of arms, be it his own or a charitable donation. "Hey, I said *attempted* murder."

"If you are not a United States citizen, you may contact your country's consulate prior to any questioning."

"That's a loaded issue."

The now familiar clunk of the dented bell above the door rang twice and Alex felt the pressure being put into his back lessening immediately as this person entered. He knew the voice of the man speaking straight away.

"Everybody make tracks." The voice said with a quiet resignation.

One of the other officers looked up from examining the body in the kitchen to object. "Sir, this is our suspect in the shooting—"

"Leave the cuffs on then." He rephrased once for clarity. "But everybody get the hell out."

Alex turned to meet the detective he had been in sporadic contact with for just over a year. Detective Stack looked him up and down through tinted 1980's bifocals and refrained from speaking as the first responders stutter-stepped toward the exit. His unkempt and graying goatee concealed whatever smile or grimace he was currently bestowing on Alex. Every little detail about Stack said 'career cop' loud and unflinchingly clear.

As the last patrolman left the room, Stack let out a rare smattering of laughter before returning to his comfortably gruff exterior. "The deep fryer, Alex?" The detective unlocked the handcuffs ensnaring his friend only to turn around and lock them again in the front.

"Eliot—"Alex began.

Stack cut him off. "You know the rules. *Do not call me by that name in public.* Did you not get my text?"

"What text?"

"The one I sent you before I walked in about not calling me Eliot."

Alex bit his lower lip and glared down at the handcuffs around his wrists. "Yeah, sorry, Mr. Ness."

Detective Stack shoved Alexander into a booth near the door with the familiar bell and sat down across the table, checking once more into the kitchen that all police personnel had vacated the restaurant. "Listen greaseball, I know you think you're safe but all it takes is some Bruno with a heater and it's lights out for either one of us," he punctuated with a finger-gun.

"I'm older than you, *Stack,*" Alex iterated sarcastically.

"I'm thirty-two, you're twenty-four."

His lips pursed, "you know what I'm saying."

Stack's eyes darted out of the window at the gathering crowd of suspicious officers congregating around a box of stale donuts. "Kid, just remember photographs of me actually exist and there are a number of people I knew back then that are still *alive*—some even live in this city."

Alex dropped his gaze and nodded to himself. "Got it, boss."

Stack pulled a few napkins from the dispenser under the windowsill and tossed them across the table to Alex. The young man had no idea there was still a great deal of blood and brain matter from a once great conqueror splattered across his face. "Before I take you out in cuffs, I need the low down on what went down in here. Who's the pill?"

Alex stared blankly at Stack, completely unaware of what he just said.

Stack dropped both of his hands to the table in mild frustration. "Come on, kid. A *pill*. A *corpse*. The dead guy who walked in here with a gun and shot at you! Who is it?"

Alex tossed his ball cap aside to run fingers through the matted gold mess underneath. "He *was* a returner," he trailed off.

Stack leaned in and hushed his voice even further. "You met another returner tonight?" The detective's eyes grew wide with curiosity.

"Met two actually."

"Spit it out."

Alex motioned his head toward the stiff in the kitchen. "Dude on ice in there is Genghis Khan. Took one in the dome from my ex-girlfriend."

The detective raised his eyebrows with concern, "Alex, that's impossible."

Alex cocked his head to the side with bewilderment. "She played us, Stack. I found our her real name is *Joan* right before you and the cavalry showed up." He checked out the window and snapped back immediately. "We better hurry up."

Stack stroked his beard for a moment as he weighed the information spinning around in his mind. "I will assume this Joan to be the Maid of Orleans?"

Alex nodded. "Correct—you ever wonder why they called her a maid? I mean, what did she clean?"

"The English." He looked at the floor for what seemed like a few minutes. Something was troubling Stack and he was having

immense difficulty putting it into words. "None of this fits together, kid."

Alex smiled politely before putting his hat back on and leaning across the table toward the detective. "Eliot." Alex watched the eyebrows go up and down in disbelief before continuing. "*Eliot*, she has your list. The killings are from your list!"

The bifocals lowered to the table as he rubbed the bridge of his nose. "Khan wasn't on my list. That doesn't add up. I didn't even know he was a returner at all."

"Who was the other body, Eliot?"

Stack bit his lower lip and again failed to grapple with the words he was attempting to string together in his mind. "I need you to talk me through the timeline."

Alex could feel his annoyance growing in the base of his chest. "Stack!"

"I'm thinking! Give me a second. Walk me through the damn timeline."

His eyes grew large as he slammed his body back into the booth. "Okay. I was walking down Sunset to get out for a bit—get some air, you know? I told my girlfriend to head on out of her place and meet me somewhere on the boulevard. Have you ever had that feeling that somebody is following you?"

Stack blinked twice.

"Oh, right. I respectfully rescind the dumbest question ever."

"Keep going," the detective said abrasively.

"So, I start booking it east past all those artsy hotels and there was a gunshot. Maybe two blocks west?"

He put a fist to his chin and continued to run the scenario through his head over and over. Stack mumbled, "That's where the body was," and trailed off. His head jerked up and startled Alex. "And you met your girlfriend—"

"*Ex*-girlfriend."

"And you met your ex-girlfriend *after* the first gunshot, in this restaurant?"

Alex stood up from the table, causing concerned movement from the police officers on the other side of the glass. Stack waved them off and cautioned Alex about sudden movements like that. Alex stared the detective down, "Eliot, what the hell are you going on about?" His tone was rising quickly. "Gunshot. I ran the hell away. Taco Baron. Girlfriend shows up. Genghis Khan shoots at us. She blows his friggin' head off in front of me. You guys show up. That is what happened. That is the goddamn timeline!"

"Alex!"

"What?" He screamed back at Stack.

"I just came from the other crime scene. The other body—the shot *you* heard—the body was Chloe's."

Alex could feel the cold sweat of denial returning to his brow.

Detective Stack stood up from the table, placed his hand on his pistol and motioned the kid to come outside with him. "Alex, your only proof that you didn't kill this man was dead thirty minutes before the murder even occurred."

For the second time in the same evening, Alex was read his Miranda Rights in full before being put into the back of a squad car.

Stack leaned into the doorway of the car and looked at Alex with exhaustion. The tinted bifocals could not hide the bags under his eyes. He took a deep breath and looked around to make sure the rest of the officers were at a fair distance before turning back to Alex. "We'll figure this out, Alex." He took another breath in. "Sorry about Chloe, kid."

The detective closed the door and jumped into the front seat of the squad car.

CHAPTER THREE
Six Words

Evening
Los Angeles County Morgue

Alex rubbed his arms and shivered in the frigid storage room. It was located just beyond a pair of swinging doors and a security guard failing at Angry Birds. Despite being in handcuffs and warned to say nothing, he yelled to the guard reclining in a chair, "you gotta wait to split the blue birds until the last possible second!"

As a show of courtesy, and the knowledge that there was a round in the chamber of his .45, he took the cuffs off of his prisoner. It was freezing in the mortuary—much colder than Alex expected. He delighted in muttering curse words and watching them freeze into vapor when they contacted the air around them.

Detective Stack pulled back the sheet on a nearby corpse to reveal the face of Chloe Freimont, or based on recent revelations, one Jeanne d'Arc. He caved backward, hoping to give the kid a moment to soak this in.

Alex recoiled and darted his glance angrily back to Stack. "Warn me before you do that next time. God damn, man." His eyes dropped back toward the corpse and his face collapsed with woe. "Wow—that's her." Looking down upon his deceased ex-girlfriend, he steadied himself against the gurney and forgot his inability to make sense of the evening. In that moment, Alex was a twenty-four year old man longing for another late night game of Scrabble over Cabernet with the woman lying dead on the table. He couldn't bring himself to look at her eyes for too long, they were traumatized with fear.

"Did she have any birthmarks or tattoos to your knowledge," the detective asked crudely.

Alex looked back up toward his arresting officer with welled eyes. "Um, yeah. She has a tattoo of Saint Barbara on the inside of her right arm."

Stack shot up, "you're kidding me."

Alex cocked his head in confusion. "No, I'm not. What is she the Saint of?"

The detective lifted the sheet over her right arm and turned it outward to confirm. "Barbara," he paused examining the tat, "is the Patron Saint of artillery."

Alex deadpanned, "that would have explained a lot."

"Well, I'm afraid it explains very little."

"What was Joan the Patron Saint of again?"

Stack let loose a long lapsed-Catholic sigh, "France, obviously. She was martyred when the English burned her at the stake."

"How do you know all this stuff about Saints, man?" Alex stared back at the detective inquisitively.

"Spent my entire childhood in a Catholic school, even thought I might go into the Seminary when I got out of High School." He stopped for a moment to examine dirt under Chloe's fingernails. "Then I realized I wanted to be a cop."

"So you switched religions but kept the same profession?"

Stack furrowed his brow. "Yes, in my, dare I say it this way, *previous* life I was a Presbyterian. What does it matter, Alex?"

"I think for starters, it means we're both Buddhists; reincarnation and such."

Detective Stack dropped the sheet and turned back to his young friend. "Let's assume for a moment that you aren't completely out of your mind and murdered five people tonight."

The kid raised an eyebrow. "Thanks for that vote of confidence."

"Stick with me for a moment. We have to run through as much we as can before I toss your ass in holding." He waited for an agreeable nod from Alex before continuing through his train of thought. "Let's also assume for a moment that Joan did not shoot

Khan a good thirty minutes after she miraculously murdered herself in an entirely different location."

Alex held up his hand to stop for a moment. "Wait, you said there were five victims. I only count four: Joan, Tycho Brahe, the Taco Baron manager, and Voltaire."

Stack smiled. "Good catch. Old cop trick."

"You're an asshole! Eliot, who else is dead? Our numbers are dropping here!"

The detective's smile melted and was replaced by his usual enigmatic lack of emotion. "Einstein."

Alex's eyes widened with anger and shock before slamming his hands onto the table. "Albert was only twelve years old! What the hell happened to –"

Stack grabbed the kid by the shoulder and held his finger to his lip to remind him there was a security guard on the other side of the doors. "Alex, calm down." He made sure to make soothing eye contact to sort him out as much as he could non-verbally. "Okay, *that* was actually the cop trick. Albert is fine, he's *fine*, Alex. I did not want to do that to you, but I had to be positive you weren't concealing any knowledge about these killings."

Twenty-four year old Alexander the Great reeled back and punched the thirty-six year old Eliot Ness as hard as he could in the shoulder.

He watched as the detective stumbled helplessly back into a metal case and made quite the racket upon impact. "You just punched an officer!"

"You were being a miserable asshole!" Alex retorted.

"Don't ever do that to me again." The detective collected himself from the cabinet and got back to his feet. He began to speak in an urgent whisper. "I had to know for sure. Do you know how much I put my ass on the line just to get you in here for twenty minutes? You were at a murder scene sitting on the floor *after* tossing the murder weapon into the deep fryer. The victim of the other murder was your girlfriend, and it was at in a location you admitted to being at this very evening! Alex, do you understand how incredibly screwed you are at the moment?"

Alexander stood up straight, careful to lend serious weight to everything his friend was saying. "It wasn't the murder weapon."

"What."

Alex spoke in even tones. "The gun in the deep fryer wasn't the murder weapon. They'll match ballistics to the few shots he got off in the restaurant, but the bullet that went through Khan's skull won't match." He paused. "I quite imagine they won't find that gun any time soon."

Stack lowered his eyebrows. "Alex, are you sure?"

He shrugged back. "As sure as I am that Joan of Arc shot him in the head."

"We'll run the ballistics. I believe everything you're telling me, but you gotta understand something that I'm going to tell you."

Alex nodded in his direction, "oh yeah, and what's that?"

"That whoever has been going around and killing the returners is still on the loose, and it might possibly be more than one person. I can't even wrap my head around tonight," the detective trailed off in confusion.

Without warning, Stack spun Alex around and placed the handcuffs back around his wrists. He was about to put him in a twenty-four hour hold back at the station in West Hollywood. With the evidence unable to produce a weapon, an alibi, a fingerprint, or usable ballistics, he could cut the kid loose and get back to finding the real killer. Stack had been doing this for two lifetimes and it was rare that he felt this lost with a case. Not even Al Capone had been this confusing.

The next morning, Alex awoke in a cramped holding cell with a tiny window letting in the barest rays of sunlight. He scratched his head and looked around at three other beds, all completely empty.

There was a piece of paper on top of the pile of his clothes he pulled off to get a good night's sleep. He let out a yawn and reached down to grab the folded note. There had been no one sharing the cell the night before, and surely he would have noticed if a guard or Detective Stack had come into the cell and left a piece of paper six feet from his face.

Something was wrong.

Alex slowly opened the note and saw six words scribbled in permanent marker that made him freeze as the goose bumps formed on his forearms. Before he could make sense of it, a burst of gunfire rattled off somewhere else in the station.

Instinctually, he crammed the note into the pocket of his jeans and slipped on only his shoes. If he was going to have to run, there was no need for anything else.

He crashed into the door and began to scream. "Help! Hey, help me out in here."

For a few uncomfortable moments, Alex did not hear anything except for the air conditioning unit cycling on and off in the complex a couple of times.

Then he heard a few muffled voices coming from somewhere in the station. It sounded very much to him like two men arguing back and forth. The muffled shouts of the arguing men continued to escalate over each other until there was they were abruptly cut off and silence once again filled the air.

There was another eruption of gunfire.

Alex shoved off of the holding cell door and looked around for any point of weakness within the room.

The gunfire continued to echo off of every bare cement wall in the strikingly empty holding area. In point of fact, Alex realized that he was the only person in the numerous cells that neighbored his own. *What's the likeliness that even the drunk tank would be empty*, he thought to himself.

A door slammed behind him and he heard someone running directly for his cell. Alex spun around just as Detective Stack crashed into the door, fumbled with any number of keys, and ripped the door open.

He was covered in blood, none of it his own, all of it fresh and dripping with immature death.

Stack tossed a police issue semi-automatic pistol to Alex without hesitation. "We're in trouble," he coughed out, ejecting shells and popping a speed loader into his own .45. "Do you know how to use that?"

Alex Heton looked over the Beretta, checking the 9mm cartridges in the clip before popping it back in and chambering his first round.

Stack raised his brow; "I will take that for a yes, then."

"Eliot, what the hell is going on out there?" He asked as they put their backs to a wall looking around for the best exit.

The detective was out of breath and out of shape. His eyes danced around the different doors as he breathed heavily from his mouth. "Ten, maybe in the teens. All masked with fully automatic rifles. Two of them might be dead, at least another wounded."

"How many did we lose on our side?"

Stack turned back to Alex and gave him a look that read clearly as *please don't ask me questions like that right now.* The detective turned back to the door, readying his sidearm to take down whoever was unlucky enough to check the holding area first.

A loud siren began to blast through the hallways of the entire station. Stack could not make sense of what he was hearing until he turned to Alex and saw that he slid down the wall and pulled the fire alarm.

The sprinklers popped on and began to blast the entire station in hundreds of gallons of water. It began to collect on the floor almost immediately.

"Why would you do that?" Stack yelled back to Alex over the cacophony of water and deafening sirens.

The back door swung open—a man dressed in body armor and riot gear readied his weapon as he charged through the doorway.

Alex fired twice into his chest and dropped the man to the ground. He knew the gunman was down because of the ballistic impact on the vest, not an actual wound. He rushed through the water bouncing in every direction, and slammed his tennis shoe onto the riot helmet of the man on the ground. He fired two shots into the unprotected area between the helmet and the vest, directly into the sternum and lower throat of the attacker.

Wasting no momentum, Alex slid his foot down, kicked the helmet off the attacker's face, and put a third round into his forehead. He pointed the Beretta into the next room and scanned quickly for any further.

Stack came running over, having missed that entire exchange pass by in less than four seconds. Alex grabbed the assault rifle from the ground and tossed it to the detective.

"We got at least three down. Leaving this room or trying to escape means we could take fire from doorways, hallways, windows, and stairwells. There are two points of entry to this room we can both cover at angles they would be unlikely to look first."

The detective chambered a round in the rifle and yelled back over the noise. "Are you suggesting we stay in this room and wait for them? Alex, we can get out of the window in that room and jump to the roof next door. God dammit, this isn't our fight."

Alex pushed the detective into a nearby cell; the two of them were struggling with their drenched clothes as they churned through the two feet of water collecting on the floor. "They're here for us, Eliot!"

He pulled out the note and held it up in the light from the window. Even though the scribbled marker was running down the page, it was clear what had been written was a message to the returners.

SOME WERE NOT MEANT TO RETURN.

CHAPTER FOUR
Enlightened Conversations and Soured Whiskies

Twelve Hours Later
Maryland

This particular dive bar off the 795-north was mostly empty, save for the usual alcoholic fathers nervously boasting of imaginary soon-to-be successes and drunkenly pulling out wallet photos of children they had chronically ignored. This bar was called 'The Rowdy Screw' and on any given week night, would not be particularly rowdy. The ordering of drinks were the most common conversations, exchanged over pleasantries and tightfisted tips. For the most part, this was a bar people went to for an opportunity to drink in silence.

In a booth toward the back was a lonely man, whose hair grayed at thirty-one, seated in a tweed Coppola hat and sipping on his fourth Whiskey Sour. The straw crackled in the bottom of the glass and he motioned to the waitress to fetch him another round.

She finished the text to a man she met on a dating site and dropped the cherry into another glass. The waitress walked the beverage to the table at the back of the bar and dropped it off. "Is there anything else I can getcha, friend? Last call is in twenty," she trailed off as she realized he was transfixed on the television over the bar.

On the program were four talking heads shouting over each other about whatever political brouhaha they had manufactured to fill the hour. He straightened his cap, stood up from the table, and brushed right past the waitress toward the television over the bar. He punched the button to turn it off, turned about face, and began the journey back to his table.

The older gentleman in the Coppola hat froze.

Someone was seated in the space he had vacated. The woman was familiar, and although not *unwelcome,* this was certainly not the best time to have a conversation. The woman was African-American, around twenty-eight, and sported a closely cropped hairstyle. She smiled, "How are you doing, John?"

John took a seat on the opposite side of the booth, frowned, and began to work his way down the fifth Whiskey Sour. "Don't call me John, you know the rules."

The woman laughed. "Yes, dare I refer to you by the most common name on this planet."

"Mohammad."

"What?"

He set the empty glass down on the table and replied grumpily, "Mohammad is the most common name in the world, not John."

She leaned in, hushing her voice from the drunken idiots twenty feet away, "or would you prefer Quincy?"

"One more," he shouted over his shoulder rather rudely to the waitress, who was once again busying herself by texting at the bar. John returned his gaze to the woman across from him. "Harriet," he paused. "You're just about the only one of 'em I can stomach in all of this, but I believe I made myself clear, with crystalline clarity, that I want to be left alone. I want no part of this."

Harriet frowned, "who knew the sixth president was such a loner?"

He grabbed the drink from the tray upon arrival and sipped directly from the glass. "Literally everyone that knew me knew that. Now, Mrs. Tubman—"

"I'm obviously a widow now."

John upended his glass and annihilated what was left of the drink before slamming it back down onto the table. "Aren't we all, love. Now if you'll excuse me—"

She stood and shoved him abruptly, sending the tipsy man tumbling back into the booth. "You're not excused. Pull yourself together, John."

A crease came across his brow. "You know, I don't think I'll do that. I will continue treating this farce *without* the respect it *doesn't* deserve."

"We are all going through the same thing."

"I spent the twilight years of my *real* life fearing this country would fall into a war with itself because a pack of ignorant dung-beetles could no more establish the value of human life than they could fly to the sun in a hang-glider."

Her face became deadly serious. "Do not misunderstand who you are talking to, John."

"Apologies, madam, but I do not misunderstand. The country *did* fall into a civil war after my death and I am most aggrieved to learn we haven't learned a damn thing since that moment," he leveled, motioning toward the television he had just turned off moments before.

Harriet reached across the table and grabbed for the saltshaker. She slowly unscrewed the top and set it aside near the napkin holder. There was a moment where she sat there holding it, as if making a lesson for John from it, before throwing the whole bottle in his lap, sending him into the air in a fit of rage.

"What the hell did you do that for?"

A smile once again crept across her face. "To prove a point, obviously."

The annoyance had not subsided. He brushed at his pants to remove the salt and barked back angrily. "Which was?"

"That you cared more about me dropping salt down your trousers than continuing that childish tirade you were trying to hide behind."

He finished brushing the seasoning from his zipper and took a seat once more. "Now who's misunderstanding?"

"People are dying."

"Well, I certainly hope it goes down easier the second time. People are always dying, Harry. They were dying then, they're dying now and tomorrow when another war starts for insipid god damned reasons, they'll be dying for that too. We were all born to die; some of us just have the indecency to try it twice."

Harriet stood up and dropped a twenty-dollar bill on the table in an effort to leave. "For the drinks."

"Harriet, sit down."

She did not.

"Harriet, *please* sit down."

She did.

John took a deep breath in and tried to relax as much as possible before beginning to speak. "From what I've heard, the killings were Mr. Brahe, the insufferable Mr. Voltaire. That's hardly proof that anyone knows that we—"

"There's more."

He felt the hair on the back of his neck stand up. "Who?"

"Joan of Arc and Genghis Khan."

"I didn't know either one of them had—wait, did you notice that all four victims are not American?"

"No. There's more," Harriet mumbled with a grave tone while shaking her head. "Alexander and Eliot were both at a police station in Los Angeles when it came under attack by around ten masked men carrying automatic weapons."

His eyes widened when he heard what had just been said. "Say that again."

She did not.

John leaned across the table, realizing the gravity of the conversation at hand. "Were they killed, Harriet?"

"Maybe," she said, her fingers shaking. "That's why I came out to talk to you. We are all in very real danger."

"Then I welcome it." He paused and motioned to the bartender that they would be leaving shortly. John turned back to Harriet and grabbed her hand, "I've lived two childhoods, two puberties, two first loves, and I have wonderful memories of two completely different sets of parents. There is no great miracle here, no great mystery. Some of us returned and *some* of us are already old enough to die of natural causes *for a second time.*" He took a sip of her water. "I've no desire to entertain anymore of this foolishness. Four of us, possibly six, have been brutally murdered and even *that* is beside the point of all of this."

Harriet wiped a tear from her eye. "And what is the point of all of this?"

"That we might be trying to understand something we can't. Look at it this way, Harriet. We have all been granted an amazing miracle, the gift of life for a second time—and yet, we are all miserable. We all lived remarkable lives and have nothing to try and accomplish with a second one. We are useless husks of former glories toiling away on borrowed time. I think *that* might be the point of this."

"Break that down into English, John."

He laughed and stood up from the table to leave. "I'm saying we all might want to start entertaining the idea that this is Hell."

CHAPTER FIVE

The Great Escapes

Twelve Hours Earlier
Los Angeles Country Lockup

Stack wiped a watery mixture of blood and water from his forehead and slowly scanned the flooded lockup for signs of danger. The nightshift had been miraculously small the previous night; he counted only five stationed officers in his head—all of which he was now sure were dead.

Alex fired twice as he leapt out from behind a door toward the unlucky clod that had just burst through. Both bullets entered through the top of the gunman's spinal cord by ramming the Beretta under the back of the helmet. He returned once again to darkness.

"What's the count?" Stack screamed across the lockup, coming increasingly to the belief that Alex was using him as bait.

"Five down total." He glanced through a doorway and down onto the street below. "SWAT's here with what looks like the whole damn force."

"Why wait to breach," the detective called back again, already knowing every reason a SWAT team would hesitate to clear a hostile situation. He paused for a moment before answering his own question. "This building's wired to blow isn't it?"

Alex smiled. "That's my guess." He stopped and noticed something about the man he had just killed. There was a faint mumble about eye color before he crouched down and removed the helmet of the assailant. "Hey Stack!"

Stack was pushing a bed up against the door to the station lobby. "Kinda busy!"

"Drag one of the other bodies over here!"

The bed was firmly in place. He began with an exasperated breath, "Wait, what?" Although it was not the time for dragging corpses around in a foot of water—water that was turning opaque with blood—he did it anyway. "Okay, here you go."

Alex ripped the helmet off the second lifeless attacker and became too stunned to move.

Having noticed the same thing, Stack stomped through water to a third attacker floating facedown in the murky water. He flipped him over and knocked the helmet off. His body fell back into the water and took a number of deep breaths before bothering to speak. "Yeah. They're all the same person," he yelled back only to find that Alex was nowhere in sight.

Stack jumped to his feet and scanned the flooded prison cells for any sign of his friend. Someone shuffled through the water to his rear and he spun around, rifle at the ready.

This new attacker arched his back in agony as two bullets ripped through his esophagus before lifelessly plunging into the water below. As the body fell away, it revealed Alex smiling behind the door once more, "I figured if they're all the same person then they would all fall for the same thing."

"You freak me out, Alex."

Alex flipped the bird. "You're just mad you didn't think of it."

The detective pulled the fresh body out of the doorway and off into a nearby cell as to arouse no suspicion should they use the trick further. He walked over to Alex who was slinking back into the shadows behind the door.

"Get your own spot," he whispered.

Stack slung the rifle from his shoulder and attempted to hand it over to Alex, who refused.

"I don't want that." He motioned to the pistol, "I can slip this right under the helmet."

"I know. That's why we're switching."

Alex turned back entirely confused.

The detective swallowed and again shoved the rifle toward Alexander. "There are a lot of people in more danger than us. I'll stay here, but you need to get to Albert and start rounding everyone up."

"You think they'd go for the kid?"

"I think they're going for everyone."

Alex put his ear to the door to make sure no one was coming before relenting. He grabbed the rifle and handed the Beretta back to Stack. "Two to the top of the spine; don't get fancy."

They finished switching firearms and Stack grabbed Alex by the shoulder. "There's a hundred cops out there that think you perpetrated a double murder last night."

"So don't shoot them?"

"I was going to say don't get caught, but I'll go ahead and amend that to also not shooting them."

Alex turned to the door and checked the adjacent room before stopping cold. "So does this mean you think I'm innocent?"

Stack slid behind the door and whispered back to Alex. "No one is innocent, but I know you're not going to shoot that kid."

"Until next time, then."

"Until next time," the detective murmured with a smile before disappearing completely from view.

Alex moved swiftly into the next room raising and lowering the rifle as to not alert any shooter he was about to come around a corner. The water shut off a few minutes earlier, so it was far quieter in the police station. Anyone moving through the shin-deep water would telegraph his or her movement a mile away. He climbed up on one of the desks and began quietly leaping from desk to desk to silence his advance through the second floor of the station.

He heard a series of splashes down a nearby hallway and knew that someone was upstairs trying to flush them out. As quietly as possible, he leaned over and pulled a drawer of office supplies from the desk he was kneeling on and slid silently into the water behind the desk, waiting for the splashes to come around the doorway.

There were four full boxes of staples in the drawer and he carefully unloaded row after row into the barrel of his rifle. He knew that he couldn't get much distance out of this, so he was going to wait until the assailant drew near.

Alex pushed low into the water so he could see under the desks between them. He pointed the gun straight ahead, and would have to wait until the armored attacker was within four feet of his location.

Screams through a megaphone could be heard on the other side of the window. If Alex did not get out of this building before the SWAT breached, there was no way he was getting out of there alive. Returning his attention to the situation at hand, he held his breath as the target moved within a few feet of the opening under the desk. The first boot sloshed into view. Another boot followed.

Alex fired.

The scream coming from the man with four hundred staples and a 7.62mm round lodged in his legs was enormous. The man fired his gun around wildly before dropping it into the water and falling into a piteous whimper.

Alex leapt over the desk and bolted for a nearby staircase. The man he had wounded was certainly not dead but would provide no threat, as the pain would surely knock him out momentarily. It also stood to reason that the police officers would find use in a suspect to interrogate.

He crashed through the stairwell door and headed up to the roof as fast as his tired legs would carry him up three more flights of stairs.

The roof was surprisingly quiet except for the sound of helicopters approaching in the distance. He turned his gaze to a much taller building with a fire escape facing his roof. With the rifle slung over his shoulder, he took a few paces back. The jump between them must have been fifteen feet and his pants and shoes were soaked.

He begrudgingly tossed the shoes aside and made peace that he was about to jump onto rod-iron, barefoot. Alex lowered to the ground and took off in a sprint, planting one foot on the raised ledge of the roof, and jumped as hard as he could across the expanse.

His stomach collided with the railing, knocking the wind out of him hard enough that he almost forgot to grab the ledge. Alex wrapped both arms around the railing and slowly began to pull himself up and onto the landing.

A bullet struck him in the shoulder and he fell back into the open window of somebody's kitchen, losing blood onto whatever the family had just fixed for dinner.

The pain was enormous but he managed to sling the rifle from his wounded shoulder and fire a few shots back at the two men on the roof laying fire on his location. He knew he would be no match for two shooters firing from a raised position.

Alex dove through the window and over the dinner he had recently ruined before rolling across the kitchen. He got to his feet and ran into the living room where a family of five had just finished washing up for supper. He did not want to do it, but he had no choice.

"Cell phones, out of your pockets and toss them on the ground by me," Alex ordered carefully keeping his finger far from the trigger.

The family did as they were told. Five cell phones slid across the ground to where Alex was bleeding on the carpet. He motioned to the smallest boy among them to pick them up. "Grab those and toss them in the garbage disposal. Now!" he ordered.

Tears were falling down the face of the boy but Alex knew there were lives actually at stake. The boy gently slid the phones into the sink one at a time, before turning back to Alex for the next set of instructions.

"Turn it on."

The noise coming from the sink was deafening—tiny pieces of plastic and silicon flung wildly around the kitchen. Alex turned back to the family and lowered the rifle toward the floor, blood dripping all the way down his hand.

"Alright, I need the strongest alcohol you have and a sewing kit. And somebody find me some clothes."

CHAPTER SIX

The Unfounded Dollar

Afternoon

The Rural Outskirts of Broken Arrow, Oklahoma

There is an elder Comanche saying that states, "All who have died are equal." Some interpret this to mean that no matter the strength of one's decency or iniquity, they will return to the Earth from which they came, an equal, for there is no escaping the act of birth or the act of death.

This, naturally, does not include those that cheated death by returning for a second birth. It also stands to reason that, "All who have died are equal (except for a smattering of confused historical figures who find themselves ill-content with a second go of it)" does not fit neatly onto a bumper sticker.

Janey Baptiste was not born a Comanche, though her return to the Earth lead her to find acceptance among people she felt most comfortable calling her own. Janey was known around her small outcropping of hand-built homes and ramshackle shops as a kind-hearted young Native American woman who enjoyed her two dogs and the occasional bit of company to play board games and listen to Roy Orbison records. The quiet seclusion was of comfort to her as the nightmares of a previous life were burrowed far too deep to simply ignore.

In a previous life, she gave birth to a boy as an unwed teenager, lost her only daughter in infancy, and traveled with two men across thousands of miles of terrain acting as both an interpreter of the Shoshone language and as a guide across the rough terrain. She had trouble recollecting the last time someone had called her by her given name, Sacagawea. Janey found a source of laughter in watching numerous historians, and a counterfeit tombstone proclaiming her death in 1884; butcher the spelling of her name across the century. Janey also kept a pot full of her own golden dollars, oftentimes marveling at the chubby-cheeked portrait as anything *but* what she looked like.

She did her best to ignore the frustration and concentrated instead on baking artisan breads and selling them to larger suppliers around the great state of Oklahoma. She had little use for local friends; the people around her always seemed to take too much advantage of her.

There was a pounding at the door.

She burned her finger on the peanut butter bread pan and turned to the living room. It was not often that anyone would show up at the house unannounced that wasn't feigning ignorance at the "No Solicitation" signs and trying to sell her a vacuum, lawn service, fundraiser baked good, paint service, or *some damn thing.*

Janey trolloped her way across a sea of unwashed clothes and opened the old front door a crack to peer out into the unkempt wilderness some people mistook for a front yard. She was always mindful to leave the chain in place on the door.

Through the crevice, she could see a young woman in a hoodie carefully rotated to conceal everything but her svelte silhouette. "Can I help you, ma'am," she called out sheepishly through the sliver.

The silhouette tilted her head in the slightest of manners and took a mammoth breath in, which she held for around a minute.

Having lost her patience, Janey tried to push the door closed before she flew backward as the door was kicked in with substantial force. She landed on her back and struggled to find something resembling a weapon nearby. The basal wood sailboat on the coffee table would not suffice.

The figure pulled a pistol from her sweatpants' waistband and closed the door carefully behind her. She pulled the hood back, and although unfamiliar to Janey, there was no mistaking that Chloe Freimont was standing in the living room pulling the hammer back on a .45 special.

"I–I don't have much of value. Take whatever–"

Chloe stepped forward. "Shut up, *Shoshone.*"

"How the hell–," trembled Janey. There was not a soul on Earth that knew who she really was.

"You will listen carefully or I will bore a hole in your face and *then* fail to take the muffins out of the oven before they burn. You can decide which would upset you more. Nod if you understand, Baptiste."

Janey Baptiste nodded.

"Good. Have you told anyone of your return?"

Janey Baptiste shook her head.

"There are many who have returned. No one knows of you and no one *will* know of you. "

Janey pushed up onto her knees, she could feel the blood dripping down her back. "There are others like me?"

Chloe tapped the barrel of the gun onto the young lady's forehead. "Not to you, Shoshone."

"Don't call me that."

"I'm not sure you understand how gun negotiation works. You see, I have the gun, so *I* negotiate."

Janey sprang to her feet and ripped a gun from a concealed waist holster and had it cocked, pressing against Chloe's cheek before she even managed to the finish the sentence. "Is this bartering?"

Chloe's eyes narrowed, "I'm not afraid to shoot you."

Janey lowered her 9mm and fired a shot into the top of Chloe's foot. She raised the pistol back to her face in less than a second.

Wounded and screaming, Chloe pushed herself backward across the floor to a nearby wall. "You bitch!" She screamed.

"You threatened to burn my muffins," Janey growled with a sarcastic flare.

Chloe glared back, knowing that she underestimated Sacagawea by a generous margin. "You best shoot me now. If you leave me alive I swear—"

She shut up as the 9mm pressed firmly into her forehead.

"I think I'll talk for a minute, thank you," Janey smiled. "What's your name?"

"Chloe," she said as she wrapped her hands around her bleeding foot, checking for any missing toes.

"What's your *real* name?"

There was a hesitation. This was exactly what she was trying to prevent. "Joan."

"Care to finish that, Joan?"

She rolled her eyes. "Of Arc."

Janey took a moment to herself; staring down at the poor woman that was desperately applying pressure to a foot she just took a bullet through. "Why don't you want any of the people like me to meet up?"

"Can I have a rag or something for this," Chloe chirped as she motioned to the half-pint of blood that was oozing out across the wood floor.

The pretty Native American smiled and removed her purple flannel over-shirt before tossing it to down the wounded French woman. "Wrap it up and answer my question, please. I need not remind you that I have every legal right to kill you."

"We weren't supposed to return."

"Who is 'we?'"

"I can't tell you that."

Janey aimed the 9mm down. "You know you have another foot, right?"

Chloe pushed against the wall and began to slide back up to her feet as a show of intimidation. "If the returners get together, this whole universe could cease to exist."

There was silence in the room.

"I don't believe you," Janey broke the silence.

"I don't care."

"You wouldn't have traveled from God-knows-where out to the middle of rural Oklahoma to scare a poor American Indian girl into doing something she was already doing. Nah, there's more to your game, Joan of Arc."

"Please, call me Chloe."

"No."

Chloe laughed. "And you are correct, there is something else."

Janey kept the gun trained on Chloe and opened the door next to the visitor bleeding against the wall. "Then tell me what it is and get the hell out."

"Stay away from Alex."

She raised her eyebrow. "Who the hell are you even talking about?"

There was an awkward silence as Chloe's answer to the question was to raise an eyebrow and wait for her to figure it out. Janey looked around at the photographs on her wall: there was a photo of Janey and her childhood friend Alex that grabbed her attention. The two were around the age of six and running through some silly sprinkler toy with bright wiggling-arms.

"Wait. Do you mean Alex Heton? I've been friends with him pretty much my whole life." She took a moment to herself. "What does he have to do with this?"

"He has everything to do with this."

Janey took a menacing step toward the girl that broke into her house. "Bitch, I already shot you once."

"Alex is dangerous."

"*No shit,* he's a dude."

Chloe smiled and turned to the open door. "I like you, *Shoshone.*"

Janey kept her sidearm in firing position as she watched Chloe limp painfully down the driveway and into a vehicle of questionable repute.

After the car had pulled out of the driveway, all that remained was the trail of a single bloody-footprint that disappeared in the middle of the driveway.

CHAPTER SEVEN

The Stodgy Inquisition of Waylan Dwight Jessup III

Evening

Hollywood Police Station

Detective Stack put the bag of frozen peas to the knot swelling on his forehead. He glanced around the frigid room for any would be allies, but came up empty. "So do I get to find out who's been holding out on everyone with the peas?"

Detective Ransic gently placed his sidearm across the table from Stack and took a seat, sighing heavily. "It was that or a Healthy Choice Lobster Cheese Ravioli."

"Sounds delicious," Stack replied.

"Shut up."

"Have you tried the Lean Cuisine Butternut Squash Ravioli? I feel like you get more pasta when you—"

The Chief walked in.

"Shutting up."

The Chief's name was Waylan Dwight Jessup III, but everyone knew to call him "The Chief" to further blur the lines of fiction and mythology. Had the Chief really broken a man's hand with a can opener during an interrogation at a creamed corn factory? It didn't matter as long as the rookies coming in believed it enough to fly right.

Stack put his hand out and offered Chief the chair that Ransic was currently sitting in. "Have a seat, sir."

The elongated six-foot-five frame of Ransic stood up and glowered his untidy unibrow back in the direction of Stack, who was smiling through a bloody visage of deep cuts and frozen peas.

The Chief slowly maneuvered about eighty pounds of excess weight into the seat across from Stack. "No, please, go on about low-carb microwaveable meals in light of six of your fellow officers losing their lives today—with one more in intensive care that won't last the night."

Stack glared at Ransic before turning back to his superior officer. "Totally out of line, sir. My apologies. I had a hell of a day."

His superior motioned to clear the room. Ransic put up a stink for a moment before deciding to go outside the door and wait. When all personnel had left the two alone, Chief spoke in hushed tones. "You did have a hell of a day, didn't you?"

Stack nodded, knowing he was not about to be portrayed in a positive light.

"Now, you're going to have to connect the dots for me as you're not just the only credible witness we have to this PR nightmare, you're also the *only* witness we have period," the Chief inquired.

"Mulkey didn't make it?" Stack asked in disbelief.

The Chief took a moment to respond, "that kid put up a hell of a fight. Once his liver failed, the kidneys followed. There was nothing the doctors could do."

Detective Stack looked through the observation window at Ransic standing on his tiptoes, trying to glean information from the conversation. He turned back to the table, "how bad is it out there?"

"Well, you know the Feds. They were here with actionable intel before I knew which next of kin to notify—the bastards," Chief often said of the FBI. "Homeland Security showed up after. Then the jurisdictional circle-jerk began. I believe the phrase they were parlaying was, 'an act of domestic terrorism.'"

"I can't say I disagree with that assessment, Chief. They came in with a purpose—and that was to kill everyone in the building," Stack responded with a swallow.

Chief grimaced and tightened his fist on the table. "I will not stand by when my men were murdered and let the Department of Homeland Security point at whatever they want and call it 'terrorism.'"

"Sir?"

"Well think about it, Detective. What the hell is 'domestic terrorism?' We're not talking about religious zealots halfway around the world, we're talking about anyone committing a crime at home."

Stack took a moment to consider the words of a man he trusted with his life. "Well, sir. I think the difference between murder and terrorism is preparation. These men were stacked and ready to kill everyone in the building."

The look on the Chief's face took a turn for the bitter. "And these men were *so* well-prepared that you managed to kill every single one of them?"

"I had help."

"You mean you released a murder suspect from his cell and armed him with your sidearm—the same gun he used on one of the attackers, whose rifle he also took, before jumping to a neighboring building and holding an innocent family at gunpoint?"

The Detective bit his lip and checked to see if Ransic was watching from the door and relishing every moment of this. "Yes, sir. I mean that."

The Chief slammed his fist onto the table, "Come on, Stack! I got you on felony aiding and abetting a fugitive charges—that's not even calling into account the line of cops around the block ready to take you down!" he fumed. "Give me something, here."

Stack sighed and knew there was no way to talk his way out of everything that had occurred the night before. "I found myself in an extraordinary situation that required the use of unusual tactics. I would be dead if not for Alex's aid—"

"I would leave the casual first-name basis stuff out of your report, lest you desire Home-Sec putting you in a tiny cell in Cuba for the rest of your life."

"Sorry, the *suspect* was my only hope of survival and the only reasonable way to stop the attackers once they had entered the police station."

Chief made a face, there were at the station that referred to it as 'that face.' "You know the next thing I'm going to ask you."

"Yes sir, I do." Stack took a deep breath and knew that the moment he answered the Chief's question, his days as being a police officer in the country were over. To protect the returners, he did what he thought he had to.

"The ten assailants that you two killed."

"Alex escaped after the sixth went down. I believe he killed the seventh in his getaway."

Chief put his hands through his hair in disgust. "Which leaves only you with all ten bodies before we were able to gain safe entrance to the building."

Stack was sweating profusely. "Yes, sir, that's accurate." *Here it comes.*

"We are still waiting on basic forensics to return, and it *will* return, but care to explain how all ten attackers had all of their teeth knocked out, their finger prints burned off and their faces so badly disfigured that we can't correctly identify a single one of them?"

Because they're all the same person and you'd shit an entire house worth of bricks, he thought to himself. "I can't answer that, sir." Stack said instead.

Chief went ballistic. "You're going to have to do a god damn lot better than that, Stack!"

He felt the Eliot Ness he used to be stand up in the back of his mind and start pushing. Detective Stack stood up from the table and leaned across the table to his portly Chief inspector. "It's not going to matter."

The Chief's face turned so red that Stack thought he might suffer a third heart attack. He was cut off before speaking.

"Before you blow up, Chief, you need to understand how this is going to go down. I understand that you are dealing with a logistical nightmare with a seemingly endless array of questions—these questions seem to all hit a brick wall at me. Would you say this is a fair assessment?"

Chief nodded. He looked like a tomato that was about to faint.

"I'm going to keep my mouth shut that you failed to send in SWAT for a whole twenty minutes after they knew there was no explosives wired into the building."

"I knew of no such thing," his boss stuttered out in furious disbelief.

"Doesn't matter if the press gets a hold of it."

"That would never stick."

Stack began pacing around the room in far better control of the situation. "You will hold me for three days, announce an extended debriefing period, and award me the Los Angeles Police Medal of Valor, which I'll accept on stage in crutches–for effect."

Chief threw his chair across the room in revolt.

The detective ignored the aggression and continued, "Before the ceremony, you will cremate all ten terrorists on suspicion of exposure to lethal chemical weapons. While it was certainly a close call, the people of Los Angeles have been spared a terrifying attack on US soil thanks to the tireless efforts of officer Stack—"

Stack felt the last word slip out as a burly forearm smashed into his windpipe, knocking him against the wall. "Why the hell would I do any of this?" the Chief spit out in utter disgust.

Choking the words as they escaped, Stack could feel the room going lighter. "Listen. We both know your job depends on a controlled situation here."

"And?"

"*And* if you plan on escaping this with your pension and your job intact you're going to need something."

The Chief pushed harder, barely containing his fury. "What? What the hell do I need from a traitorous piece of crap like you?"

"A way out."

CHAPTER EIGHT
Since We Were Four

Evening
I-40E near Santa Fe, New Mexico

Alex glowered at the fuel gauge as he surrendered the afternoon, and the road trip, to an unwelcome detour in the key of 'E.' Being a federal fugitive made it difficult enough to find wheels to get halfway across the country, but every stop he made increased the chances that someone would recognize him from the news. He got lucky at a Grandy's; a restaurant he believed no one would eat at if they owned a television. He was taken aback when a man wearing two flat-brimmed baseball caps walked up to him and exclaimed, "Yo! You're that dude with the dude that did that thing!" before running off with a plastic sack full of biscuits.

It was actually fairly correct. He was, in fact, the "dude" that did "that thing," if you were referring to killing a few assailants while being held on suspicion of a double homicide—and then escaping.

He pulled over to the least technology-savvy gas station he could find—one that advertised cash-only pumps—and parked the car he had procured from a rental facility he used to work at. He knew from experience that the economy sedan row would be lined with keys already in the ignition. It would be days before any of the morons he used to work for would even notice it missing.

After he hooked up the pump and walked inside, he had a careful look around to ensure he wouldn't need to make a hasty exit. The station was vacant except for the woman behind the counter reading some novel called "The Ending" with what looked like horses on the cover. Alex dropped sixty dollars in wrinkled bills onto the counter and walked off to grab a drink and some variety of high-fructose corn syrup candy pretending to be made of fruit.

He held them up to the lady at the counter, knowing he was overpaying by about seventeen dollars, and walked back outside without getting close enough for the lady's suspicions to be raised.

It was a nice day outside. He raised both arms to stretch and screeched before doubling over from the pain in his recently shot and shoddily repaired shoulder. *Surgery at gunpoint is just so damned unreliable,* he laughed to himself.

His backpack vibrated.

Alex remembered tossing his phone into a parked convertible somewhere around Reno, so it was unlikely he would be getting a phone call without his original phone. He rifled through the pack and came across an old flip phone he kept around for emergencies—a phone that four people on the planet had the number to. One of which he strongly believed was now murdering his friends, so it was unlikely he would be returning Chloe's phone calls.

The text read: CALL ME. NOW. –JNY PS. NOW MEANS FKN NOW!

Janey? What could she possibly consider an emergency when he was on the run for first-degree murder among a laundry list of significant felonies? He momentarily considered not returning the phone call, but Janey was one of his oldest and dearest friends in the entire world. She could lend sanity to his unstable situation. Alex typed her cell number from memory and ducked behind the gas station to gain concealment from the highway.

It rang once and she picked up instantly.

"Alex! I've been trying to get a hold of you for a day. Where the hell are you?" She did not sound pleased.

He looked around at the barren desert surrounding the hidden gas station. "I'd say I'm about thirty miles outside of Santa Fe. Give or take." He continued sarcastically, "also, hello, Janey. It's so nice to hear the sound of your voice. I hope the world finds you well."

"Oh, stuff it, Lex. I had a long chat with a friend of yours."

Every hair on his body stood to attention. "Janey. Which friend?"

"Who are you?" she replied coldly, ignoring his question.

"What do you mean who am I?" He was aware he this conversation was about to make him feel incredibly strange.

"I *mean*, why didn't you tell me you were a damn returner?"

Alex could feel the blood sound the retreat from his head. He sighed heavily before speaking, "Do you know what that means?"

"Of course I know what it is you moron. I am one."

He did not intend to scream the word "what" so loudly back into the phone but he was unable to control his volume. "Who are you?"

"Alex. I asked you first."

In that moment, Alex felt about as lost as when he realized he was a returner in the first place. He spent his entire life around Janey and never shared his deepest secret. How was it even possible that she had done the same? "Alexander the Great. Who are you?" He replied flatly, as if he was disappointed this was how she was finding out.

There was a long pause and the faint sounds of crying on the other end of the phone. "Sacagawea," somehow managed to escape her lips on the back of a whisper.

He dropped the phone to his leg and felt like he could lie down and weep behind the gas station that time had forgotten. Alex took a bite of a powdered donut and brought the phone back to his ear. He replied, "Janey, how could you never tell me?"

"That street goes two ways you clueless Greek bastard."

"Fine, equal fault. Janey, we got a hell of a problem," he blurted, smiling and trying to prevent this from turning into an argument.

She blew her nose on the other end of the line. "Would this *problem* be a five-foot-seven dusty redhead with a gun control issue?"

He closed his eyes. "What happe—"

"I shot her."

Alex's eyes flew open. "You did what?" he screamed back into the phone.

"Calm down, Colin Ferrell. I only shot her in the leg. She pulled first and I put her down."

Alex thought he must be in an episode of The Twilight Zone as he struggled with everything being volleyed around.

She continued on the other line, "Who else is out there? Why can't we meet them?"

"Wait. Who told you that we couldn't meet them?"

"Your *girlfriend* was saying —"

"*Wait*, how did you know she was my girlfriend?"

"Oh my god, Alex! She was really your girlfriend?" she screamed back in disbelief.

He needed to take a moment and make sense of the conversation they were having. Like any conversation with Janey, it could get out of control a little too quickly. "Okay, let's hit the pause button. Can we slow down for a second?"

"What are you doing in New Mexico?"

"I am on my way to Kansas to pick up Albert."

"Prince Albert?"

"Einstein, actually," he said with a laugh.

"*Both* German. But, wow, Einstein. Is he really a kooky old man in person?" He could hear her excitement brimming through the receiver of the phone.

"To be honest, I have no idea. He's about to turn thirteen and he's never met any of the returners."

"Who are the other returners?"

Alex gave genuine thought to smashing his phone on the ground if she did not stop answering ever reply with another question. It had been like that between them their entire lives. "You should meet me in Kansas, Janey. I have to keep moving. I'll text you the address."

"What if I decline?"

Was she serious? He kicked a plastic jug across the sandy nothing that spread out for miles behind the gas station. "Then I'll come get you. I need you to be safe."

"Oh, are you worried about Ms. *Of Arc*?"

Alex rolled his eyes. "No! Clearly you can handle yourself in that department—I must say though, I am quite worried about the group of men carrying assault rifles."

"What about—"

"Stop asking questions, Janey!"

She started laughing on the other end of the line. "I was wondering when you would freak out."

"I will freak out right *now*. Will I see you in Kansas? You're closer than I am, so I wouldn't leave for a few hours from—what does everyone call Oklahoma again? The Sooner state?"

"America's toothbrush."

He laughed. "Yeah, I don't think that's it."

She smiled on the other end of the line—he could always hear her smile. "I'll see you Kansas, Lex."

He hung up the phone and suddenly felt alone—standing in the middle of a desert hoping he could avoid getting shot for longer than a week.

Alex sat down against the cinder block wall and slid to the ground. *God, my shoulder hurts,* he thought to himself as he pulled out the pistol he had tucked into the back of his pants. His bottle of stolen prescription pills fell from his loose jacket pocket and rolled across the ground. He pulled a couple of Vicodin and an assortment of antibiotics he did not recognize and knocked them back. Turning back to the gun, he counted eight bullets and knew that was not going to be enough for whatever came next. Even as he tried to clear it away, his mind was wandering with so many questions.

Why did Joan of Arc say that the returners couldn't meet?

How had Janey not told him the truth? How had he not told her the truth?

He picked himself off the ground and casually strolled to his stolen rental car. He hopped back into the front seat. Alex turned the ignition and winced as he carefully placed his wounded shoulder onto the leather seats.

The temporary phone buzzed again. He opened it expecting to see Janey's number but found himself disappointed.

The message was from Chloe and it read: You don't want to go to Kansas. <3

Alex tossed the phone onto the floor and put the car in drive. It was only a few more hours to Kansas and he wasn't going to stop for anything.

CHAPTER NINE
Einstein's Birthday

The Next Morning
Lawrence, Kansas

A gathering of brightly colored balloons proclaimed a thirteenth birthday and fluttered from the mailbox in the morning mist. The birds were eerily silent, and the street was lined with far too many cars to be occupants of the few houses in the neighborhood.

Alex knew something wasn't right.

He parked against the curb in the only available spot. As he got out, he checked the address hurriedly inked into his palm one final time. *Looks like it's about seven houses away.* He began to walk softly down the sidewalk toward the house he believed Albert to be in.

"Alex! Over here," said a hushed whisper from behind a tree. His gaze shot to his peripheral. He smiled when he met eyes with Janey, or to his recent surprise, *Sacagawea.* She was standing behind a tree four houses down and across the street from the address he texted her roughly twelve hours prior.

"Why are you out here, Janey?"

She ran over and gave him a quick and welcome hug before turning back to the house. She continued to converse in a heightened whisper. "I got here seven hours ago. No one has gone in or out of that house."

He looked over to Albert's house. "It was probably a sleepover."

Janey shot back an incredulous look. "And all the parent's stayed over too? Look at all these damn cars, Lex. Does that not seem just a little strange to you?"

She was right. It was incredibly strange. Alex did a quick count of the cars and noticed they were all situated around the birthday boy's house. "Are you ready to go inside? Wait. I mean, are you armed?"

She shook her head 'no,' and he tossed her the pistol he had been carrying for some time now.

"What about you?" she snapped back.

His eyes widened. "Well, if you find me about to get *murdered* go ahead and put one or twelve in their skull." Alex grabbed her hand and led her across the street to the silent house at the end of the block.

The door to the house was slightly ajar. Alex slowly pushed it open and stepped into the foyer. "Don't come in," he called back over his shoulder to Janey, who wouldn't have obeyed such an idiotic command in a million years. "You gave her the gun," Alex quietly scolded himself for giving such a stupid order in the first place.

She pushed past Alex and stopped dead in her tracks, almost slipping in the blood that covered the white tiles in the foyer.

There were bodies everywhere. Men, women, children; no one had been spared from the carnage. Janey doubled over. She desperately wanted to vomit but could generate only heaving and sobbing in the face of such a massacre.

Alex slowly knelt down and put his arms around Janey. He did his best to comfort her but could not make sense of what he seeing. This wasn't someone attempting to kill the returners, this was a mass grave disguised as a birthday party.

"This is my fault," she started to say in between breathing that bordered on hyperventilation. "I had my chance to kill her. I should have killed her!" Janey buried her face in the tile entryway.

"This wasn't her," he said in a barely audible grunt.

Janey looked up in disbelief. "How the hell could you possibly know that?"

He doubled-checked his reasoning against the tattered massacre in front of them. "She's too controlled for this."

She remained silent and stared at the bodies strewn around the living and dining rooms for what felt like minutes. Janey grabbed Alex's ankle as he tried to move through the room. "Please, don't leave me here."

He turned back and gave her a convincing look of comfort. "I need to check the rest of the house."

"For what?"

"Anyone else."

Alex walked carefully in between the corpses and made his way back into the kitchen, his shoes squishing into the bloody carpet and making a horrible noise with every hesitant stride. The kitchen was bathed in a vile odor. The cake remained uncut, and all of the candles had melted down to waxy circles all across the frosting.

There was someone else in the room.

He stopped moving completely, not wanting to startle the boy kneeling beside his slain parents in the middle of the linoleum. The boy was covered in blood up to his shoulders with crimson fingerprints painting his face.

"Albert." Alex said quietly not to startle him, inching closer to the birthday boy kneeling on the floor. "Albert, my name is Alex."

"I know who you are," said the boy without looking up from his parent's bodies. "You used to be known as Alexander the Great and you came here to gather me up. You thought you could protect me. I am remiss to inform you, Alex, but you are just a little bit late."

Alex felt a knife press into his throat from behind. His neck tensed up at the realization of such an amateur mistake. He had not bothered to secure the location before letting his guard down.

He swallowed and wondered if this was how it was all going to end for the second time. For a master tactician, Alex made a grievous and amateur mistake.

Albert rose to his feet and begrudgingly waved the person holding the knife from of the table and over to where he was standing.

Alex was shocked to see a little boy land with a joyous thud and come running into view next to Albert. He was holding two kitchen knives caked in a considerable amount of blood. He now had no idea what was going on.

Janey stumbled into the room and recoiled from the site of Albert and the little boy with knives standing over so many bodies. "What the hell is going on?" she asked.

"I was just about to—"

Albert cut him off. "This is Richie. Say hello, Richie."

"Hello," said the little boy named Richie in a distinctly classic French accent.

"I would be dead right now if it wasn't for my pal here," Albert said as he placed a friendly hand onto Richie's shoulder. A tear ran down his face before he continued. "He is a brave young man." He turned to Alex with gravity. "There were eight men, but they were all the same person. Does that mean anything to you, Alexander?"

"It does."

Albert motioned to the young boy standing tall, still on alert for any further confrontation. "I found him by creating a worm that illegally sources child psychologist's encrypted data world wide. The algorithm cross-references the data against phrases from my own file. Dreams of another life, delusional identities, expertise in unlearned mechanics; you know, that sort of thing." Albert paused and checked the perimeter of the house before popping open the fridge and pulling various food items from it like fruit, meats, and breads. "I don't believe we have much time."

Janey took a knee and put a hand on the birthday boy's shoulder. "Albert. Are you okay?"

He stopped and gave her a surly look. "Of course I'm not okay." Tears filled up the young man's eyes. "Richie, can you grab your backpack and," he sniffled, "pack all of that up for the road?" Albert then embraced Janey and began to cry full out on her shoulder. She gently ran her fingers through his hair, like her mother used to do when she was that age, doing her best to calm him down.

Richie bounced back into the room and began throwing all of the food items into his Darth Maul backpack. He was a boy of staggeringly few words, but given the existing circumstances was a beacon of efficiency.

Alex turned to the sobbing Albert and put his hand upon his shoulder. "Who is Richie, Albert?"

He sniffled in return. "Isn't it obvious?"

"No?"

Albert turned to the young boy in the Star Wars backpack. "Richie, what do you remember from the *other* life you had. Remember? The one before you were a kid for the second time?"

Richie got a face resembling that of a child ordered to eat something healthy and green before responding, "I remember knights and horses. I had two older brothers" He stopped and shuddered. "There was also a bunch of weird stuff with men." He did not pause before asking, "What's an Aquitaine?"

Alex's eyes swelled with amazement. "Richard the Lionheart?"

"Correct," mumbled Einstein as he secured the backpack to Richie as best he could and led him toward the front door. "And now we must depart."

Janey returned to her feet and carefully stepped over Albert's parents. She returned to where Alex was standing. There was a look of concern plastered all over her face. "Are we really about to add kidnapping to the list?"

"I don't think we have a choice," he motioned around the house at the aftermath of what had occurred. "Look at what happened here. In an ordinary situation, I'd surely listen to what you're saying but we are not in anything resembling an ordinary situation. This is going to happen to all of us."

"Right, until we get some clue as to who cloned us in the first place—"

Albert cut her off, loudly. "We're not clones."

Janey was startled by how quickly the young man hurtled between differing emotional states. "I didn't—then what are we?"

"It's the *memories*. A clone is simply a rebirth of the same DNA—like an identical twin, really. Beyond the physical, there is no similarity."

Alex stepped forward. "Perhaps we could talk about this in the car?"

Albert ignored him. "If we even had the knowledge to back up a human brain, which using rudimentary math would be in upwards of a thousand terabytes of data, there is simply no available technology to map said data back to the trillions upon trillions of signals bouncing around at untouchable speeds along your synapses. Think of it like trying to map the entire known universe with a pencil and a piece of paper—to the micrometer."

Janey sat down in one of the kitchen chairs and gave Alex a tired glance.

"Well, common sense would suggest that there is another possibility," Alex suggested to Albert.

He sneered back, "common sense is as useful as any other voluntarily inaccurate data you might feel like throwing out."

Alex smiled. "I simply mean, if we're to sit around and debate the impossibility of what is *clearly* possible, that is a waste of time."

"Then what do you suggest?"

"I suggest get everyone to Kansas and find who or what is coming after us."

"And our families." Albert curtly amended Alex's statement.

Richie jumped, literally, into the middle of the conversation, "can we get hamburgers on the way?"

Janey smiled, "of course."

With that, Alexander the Great, Sacagawea, Albert Einstein, and Richard the Lionheart grabbed what was left of their things and walked out of the house and hopped into Janey's car.

Albert hobbled to his knees in the backseat as the car began to pull away. He looked at the balloons still fumbling about in the breeze over his mailbox. He did not bother wiping his final tears away as he whispered one final goodbye to his parents and his friends.

CHAPTER TEN
If I Just Lay Here

The Middle of the Night
I-70W near Dayton, Ohio

Harriet Tubman lived through hardships that a vast majority of the world's population could not accurately fathom. While she appreciated that historians adopted her into the lexicon of America's obsession with the word "freedom," it was rare they could accurately capture the *emotions* behind the dryly-depicted events. The memories were always vivid, still very much alive. Nothing would ever eclipse the frozen terror of hiding, unmoving, for hours in the dense brush of America's southern woodlands. Every day was a courageous acknowledgement of certain death. Survival was in the hands of luck, only after the fear was choked back in whole.

That was all before she drove a Prius and listened to the Dixie Chicks.

As she sang along to "Travelin' Soldier" in whichever key of the three part harmony felt most comfortable, she felt her eyes begin to float heavily. Harriet was driving alone down the long and empty stretch of highway as the rhythmic pounding of the tires against the damaged pavement played like an unwelcome lullaby.

Harriet was accustomed on long trips to playing digital music from her phone until it ran out of battery. Given the amount of time she spent on the road that day, she was about an hour past "10% of battery remaining."

A casual glance up to her rearview mirror gave her pause.

How long had that van been driving behind her? The headlights were distinctive in that she remembered a few companies experiment with a uni-light spread between the two headlights in the early nineties. *Were those Mercuries that did that?* The brand did not seem as relevant as the fact that vehicles that supported such a feature haven't been on the road in well over ten years.

As she traveled back and forth across the country trying to gather as much information about the returners as possible, she made a habit of doubling back at every tenth exit—which added fifteen percent of additional travel time, but gave Harriet an added sense of security in such unsure times.

Her glance darted to the unoccupied passenger seat; again filling with disappointment that Quincy had refused so heartily to have any contact with the returners. There was a significant history between them, in this lifetime, and she knew all too well what a stubborn curmudgeon he could be. She knew that he was aware of the dangers they were facing, but would not be party to facing them together—or in the open.

Harriet pulled off the highway and turned into a gas station to see what the car trailing her would do in response. While a second traveler in the car would make for better protection, she would plant a rusty pair of house keys into the skull of anyone that dared attempt something.

The gas station was unfortunately quite dark, save for a few lights to allow people to use the pumps in the middle of the night should the need arise. She left the car running but removed her car key from the ring and slid the remaining keys between her fingers. Harriet looked into the driver's side mirror as the mysterious hunter green Mercury pulled in behind her to an adjacent pump.

Harriet's fumbling arm patted around on the seat, trying to grab her phone without breaking eye contact with the car across the station. As she lifted it to her periphery, she already knew that gluttonous sing-along with the Dixie Chicks was going to mean a phone with no remaining battery.

"Call Alex Heton," she spoke aloud, never breaking sightline with the green Mercury.

"Calling Al-ex He-ton," it proudly spoke aloud in a broken robotic female voice and began to connect with what precious few bars the outskirts of Dayton, Ohio had to offer.

It rang once and died; its death rattle a spinning circle of white against black.

Harriet threw the phone into the passenger side door and gruffed a choice expletive. She heard the car door open and spun to look as a man got out of the car behind her and bolted out of the grasp of the station's neon lighting. His steel-plated Beretta glistened twice when he loaded a round into the chamber and ran off into the darkness.

With one hand she popped the cigarette lighter down to prep and the other simultaneously slid the sunroof open and let in the cool night air. She pulled herself halfway out of the roof and into the chilly breeze, hoping to provide spatial awareness in all directions.

The first shot screamed past and sent up sparks as it skidded across the roof. She discerned from the flash that the attacker was just under a hundred feet away. With that pistol, he would need a few shots to drop a target unless tonight was to be a very unlucky night for Harriet Tubman.

A second shot ripped through the fabric of her leather jacket and made just enough contact with her bicep to get the adrenaline pumping through the body.

The dashboard made a popping noise and she slid back into the vehicle before grabbing the cigarette lighter from the console. She grappled for the door and rushed out into the night, knowing that she would have to be quick, carefully concealing the lighter in the palm of her hand. There was little question her assailant was watching from close proximity for any strange movements she would be attempting.

Harriet cleared the distance between the cars and ripped the door to the gas tank open on the aging Mercury. She pushed the thin piece of metal that separates the fuel line from the outside air inward and lodged the cherry-red lighter into the opening—she knew that any movement would send it tumbling down into the tank.

She turned and ran back to her car, hearing the footsteps approaching from behind her. The door to her vehicle smacked her in the chin as she ripped it open and jumped inside. The cool blood dripping from her chin felt strange, as the pain was yet to register.

Wiping the blood on her shirt, she popped the transmission into drive and the Prius's tires chirped as they spun against the cold asphalt. Harriet floored it and was soon moving back up the access road toward the highway onramp. A glance into the rearview showed the man jumping into his car from the opposite side of the gas tank. *He didn't see it;* she exhaled at the realization.

Her gunman's Mercury peeled out and took a sharp turn onto the access road, sending the tail end of the vehicle sliding out across the blackened pavement.

She recoiled.

The fireball was enormous and eclipsed all three of Harriet's mirrors in a blinding light show that was more than likely heard for miles in all directions.

Harriet drove for another hour before she pulled over into an empty parking lot at a fast food joint to take triage of the her wounds. She pulled her jacket off and saw her white blouse caked in blood from both the bullet wound to her arm and a busted chin that was going to need more than a few stitches. "That's going to need more than a dry clean," she quietly joked to herself before realizing it hurt to move her jaw. The driver's side door popped open and she walked around the exterior of the car to the trunk.

The key jiggled in just the right way to open the trunk. A rustling was heard beyond the door. Harriet popped the trunk and held up her hands in a defensive posture, not wanting to have *that* argument right now.

John Quincy Adams' eyes swelled to the size of quarters as he struggled and tried to speak all matter of curses through the duct tape wrapped tightly around his mouth.

"Now, I know what you're going to say!" She argued to the man who could not argue back.

His brow furrowed, enraged. Quincy sniffled in the cold and realized that Harriet was covered in blood. As he relaxed, she took the tape from his mouth. "Mother in Heaven, what in God's name happened to you, Harry?"

She smiled and wiped half a pint of blood onto the back of her hand. "One came after us, friend. We have to find the other returners lest we allow ourselves to be picked off one by one."

His anger returned as he struggled with the tape binding his legs and arms, "This is of no consequence to me. Did I not make this clear to you, Harry? I've as much use for this second life as—"

"Is this going to be another condescending metaphor? Tell me, Quincy, how little use do you have of this life? Like a toad for a tractor? Like an ant for a magnifying glass? Oh yes, shower me in your simile, friend."

Quincy was taken a back. "I was—I was going to say like a wallet has for a credit card."

"That does not even make sense."

"Well, think of it from the perspective that a country run on credit is an unstable fit of bother."

Harriet punched him in the arm with playful annoyance. "So while I was taking bullets out here, you've been in here thinking of ways to voice your displeasure with the nation?"

"When phrased like that—"

She cut him off. "Look, *John*, I understand that you want nothing more than to shove off and ignore this life ever happened, but you know there's more value to it than that."

"What value would that be, Harry?"

"You're a dummy."

"You stifle me with your transcendent vocabulary."

Harriet pursed her mouth, "I'll punch you again, old bat."

"So tell me, what value have I on this ancillary plane?"

"To me, John. *I* value your company and your companionship. You are a friend, and I would be most upset if you died. I did this to save you — and because you're valuable to the returners," she quickly spilled out when she realized she might be overstepping her bounds.

He smiled.

She reached for the tape binding his hands behind his back. "If I let you out, can you drive for a while? I need to dress these wounds."

He nodded.

Harriet helped Quincy out of the hatch of the Prius and put the keys in his hand. They stood for a moment as their breath danced in the cold before walking past each other and hopped back into the car.

He put the car into drive and she piped up immediately. "Oh, do you have a phone charger on you? I really wanted to listen to Snow Patrol for the last leg of this trip."

CHAPTER ELEVEN
Death Threats and Tartar Sauce

Dinner Time
Motel Estándar, outside of
Lawrence, Kansas

Richie rammed the door open and took in the fresh breeze as he held the door ajar for everyone to make his or her way onto the roof of the motel. This was the third time in a week they were partaking in the finer avenues of take-out seafood from a fast food joint. Alex took a whiff from the bag before tossing it onto the ground in disgust.

"Look, I know you guys like this crap—I'm begging you for this to be the last time," he pleaded with the pair of boys who were already tearing through their fish planks.

Albert looked up from shoveling nondescript fried bits into his face, "you don't like the fish?" he asked innocently enough through a mouth full of food.

Alex took a seat on the blanket Janey was busy straightening out across the patched and tarred surface of the roof. To break up the monotony of bouncing between hotels in Kansas, they agreed to have a rooftop picnic—where the boys once again chose the dinner of the evening would be from Pirate Mike's Fish Hole ("If it isn't Pirate Mike's, it's not real fish!") He was not a fan of that particular food oeuvre but knew that the boys had been through more than he could imagine in the previous few days and let them eat what they wanted.

"Which part of the fish do you suppose this was?" Albert inquired as held the fried diamond aloft.

"I imagine it's *every* part of *many* fish," Alex said under his breath.

Janey smacked him on the arm and widened her eyes in disapproval. "Did somebody take all the tartar sauce?" She called out to everyone on the blanket, looking around for the missing sauce.

Richie ran back across the roof to a lone paper sack resting the door. It appeared someone had dropped it on the way up, so he grabbed it and ran excitedly back to Janey. "I think there's more in here."

Without thinking, she lunged her hand into the bag and made a disgusted sound at the realization that one of the sauces had spilled in the bag. She pulled her hand back, preparing to make a witty statement, when she froze her gaze at the blood all over her fingers. Janey tossed the bag to the ground and grimaced, "Oh my god."

Albert grabbed the bag with his inquisitive demeanor and peeked inside. As if describing his meal, he muttered "there's two fingers in here."

"Which two," Alex asked without considering how morbid they were being.

"Index and middle."

Alex held his arm and motioned at his fingers, "which hand?"

Albert's top lip sneered for a moment. "*Different* hands. There's a note in here too."

Richie piped up. "So is there tartar sauce or not?"

"There is not." Albert spoke back dismissively to the younger boy struggling with his failure to secure sauce. He pulled the note from the bag and stared at it for a lingering moment. "That's unpleasant."

Janey snatched it away. "What does it say?"

"The savage will die in pieces," he spoke softly, knowing that was going to strike a chord.

Silence.

Janey stared back in utter disbelief; she grasped for Alex's hand to calm her down. "I'm gonna throw up," she ran to the edge of the building and leaned over the edge.

Alex stood quickly and ran across the rooftop to her. He put his hands on her shoulders and rubbed her back, "nothing is going to happen to you."

She spun back with swollen eyes. "It already did—or perhaps you forgot when your main squeeze, Chloe, burst into my house and tried to kill me!"

"Did she?"

Janey sniffled, "What?"

"Did she actually try and kill you, though? She broke in and could have fired right away."

She puked over the side of the building, perhaps in rebuttal but all in fear, and wiped her mouth before turning back. "Alex, are you defending the woman that put a gun in my face?"

"Chloe put one in my face too. We're both still standing here."

"You watched her put a bullet through Genghis Khan's face!" She brushed his arm off her back.

"Who admitted he was there to kill her!"

She glared into his eyes. "Why are we even having this argument? I didn't say the first god damn thing about her being the one killing the returners!"

"Because she didn't," he trailed off.

Janey rolled her eyes. "Can we get back to the two fingers we found in a bag of tartar sauce with a vaguely racist note threatening to *dismember* me?"

"Yeah, sorry about that."

She punched him in the arm, returning to their usual playful demeanor. "Just stop being a dick, Lex. Not everything is an argument you need to win, okay? I'm on your team—and I'm not Chloe." She took a moment to gauge his reaction and then took a step closer, placing her hand on his chin. "Damn, that chick did a number on you didn't she?"

Alex looked up sheepishly. "I identified the body at the morgue *before* she put a gun to your head. I have literally *no* idea what she is attempting to accomplish. I can't think about her because that's the only thing I can think about once I do."

She faked a laugh. "Remember when I shot her in the leg? I miss the good old days."

He smiled back and gave her a quick hug, whispering into her ear. "Almost there, Janey. Whoever wants us dead, we'll fair better in a group."

Albert walked over to them with the bag of fingers. "Should I throw this away or put them on ice or what? Won't somebody be needing these?"

Alex nodded to the boy, "we'll grab a bucket of ice on the way in. Let's hope they were severed recently—add that to the list of phrases I never thought I'd say."

They had been severed recently.

Across the street, in an abandoned department store, a man and a woman were tied down and being held against their will.

Paul Revere looked downed at where the index finger on his left hand used to be. The pain had been increasing over the hour as he struggled with his ropes.

The man that abducted both of them spread his knives and prods across what used to be a perfume counter. He had not spoken and his identity was unknown to his hostages.

Paul turned to the woman on his left, nodding comfort, as he was unable to speak with the tape over his mouth. The woman's middle finger was severed from her right hand and she had been unable to stop crying since they woke up in the department store.

The man grabbed for a small ice pick and walked over to the woman, she recoiled in his presence, screaming under the tape as loud as she could. "If you tell me what I want to know, you get the bullet," he spoke in an icy growl, motioning to the pistol on the counter. "If you withhold information, you get this." He slowly drove the ice pick into her shoulder and left it put as he turned his attention toward Paul.

She tried to scream, but was unable.

"Do we understand the rules?" He grabbed for one of the larger knives. "I do detest having to repeat myself, even when used for dramatic effect. Understand? *I hate having to repeat myself.*"

The last thing Marie Antoinette saw before passing out was Paul Revere taking a four-inch blade through his abdomen.

CHAPTER TWELVE
Precious Medals

The Next Morning
City Hall of Los Angeles

Stack shifted his weight on the crutches to sell his fictional injuries to the cheering people of Los Angeles. He caught the eyes of the Chief, who was midway through a fabricated speech about honor and duty in the face of 'domestic terrorism.' *Jessup must be crawling in his skin right now,* Stack laughed to himself.

"And it was thanks to the fast thinking and ingenuity of Detective Bob Stack, that all ten of the attacker's plans were thwarted with just precision. He sent a message to terrorists, domestic and abroad, that we will not stand idly by, regardless of whose favor the odds are in, and let them take our rights and lives away." He wiped the sweat from his brow and darted another painfully awkward look toward Stack. The crowd roared with approval of the speech—a speech that Chief wrote in the car ride over as if it were a Mad-Lib children's activity book. "We lost seven of our finest officers that day, but they did not get eight. In the war on terror, every inch is a mile—and Detective Stack," he paused for the audience uproar. "And Detective Stack moved that mountain a mile."

Stack laughed into his clenched fist as Chief continued to get more lost and his metaphors began mixing in a dizzying array of bad symbolism. He waved to the crowd and recollected the conversation they shared two days before that moment.

He remembered finally getting out of holding and reporting for duty in the Chief's office—Ransic posted at the door cleaning whatever two thousand calorie abomination he had for lunch out of his teeth. Stack brushed past and slammed the heavy door behind him. "Chief," he said flippantly.

"Stack," he growled with disapproval.

"You wanted to see me?"

The Chief took a badge and a revolver from the top drawer of the desk and set them on the thick oak desktop, the badge rocking back and forth across the surface. "I believe these are yours."

Stack raised an eyebrow but made no eye contact, "thank you, sir. Will that be all?"

"No. Please, have a seat so we can discuss some things."

"All things being equal, I'd prefer to stand, sir. Though I'm sure you've heard, I have been in a holding cell for three days," he finished, again not making eye contact with his superior officer.

"Oh cut the crap, Stack. There are no cameras in here. *You* chose to stay in holding for three days."

Stack looked directly toward the lens of at least one camera he knew was in the bookshelf. "Sir, I'm quite sure I have no idea what you're talking about. My understanding is it took three days to corroborate, I wish a had a better word than this, but the *heroics* of my actions when the SWAT team did not, for whatever reason, gain entry and attempt to save those officers we lost in the conflict."

The Chief's eyes widened at the brazen disregard on display before him.

The detective brought his eyes down, finally making contact. "In further, I hope the knowledge that I brought those murderers the justice they deserved, even when exercising the use of non-standard tactics, brings some comfort to the spouses and families of those brave men and women that lost their lives."

Chief stood up and walked over to his detective. He spoke in hushed and threatening tones, "look. I'll play ball with you on this, Stack, but we need something from you in return."

"The knowledge that I have served my state and my country are all the gratifi—"

"I can't award you the Medal of Valor without a promotion. We lost Mulkey and Schiefer, and if anyone else was awarded that promotion there would be a public outcry."

Stack tilted his head, actually confused by the new information. "You want to make me Detective Lieutenant?"

"No, I *really* don't."

"It would be an honor. I *humbly* accept the responsibilities being asked of me by my country."

"Oh, for the love of god," the Chief mumbled under his breath, clearly fed up with the Boy Scout routine on display before him. "You know I'm still a Police, right? I actually care about this badge and what it stands for—regardless of whatever mockery you're attempting to make of it right now."

It was Stack standing in the office and reciting rhetoric, but it was Eliot Ness who turned to his officer and spit fire. "This badge means more to me than you could possibly know. You need to understand, I didn't ask armed assailants to burst into *your* poorly defended Police Department to try and destroy everything we've built here together. I'm glad they're dead. I'm glad that Alex Heton was here on suspicion of murder charges, because *without* his help, you would be hanging by your dick right now. So how about showing just a little respect for the only guy standing between you and the front door, *sir.*"

The Chief took a seat behind his desk and bellowed in silence for a few moments, reflecting on everything Stack had just said. He reached once again in the top drawer and pulled out another police shield, this one an entirely different metal. This one was a Detective Lieutenant badge.

Stack grabbed it and slid it into his pocket; he couldn't contain the momentary smile that crept across his face.

"You know what has to happen, right?"

Detective Lieutenant Stack laughed back at the Chief, "I knew what had to happen when I walked in here. I just wanted to hear you say it."

"Will you do it?"

He looked out the window at the cars rushing around on the busy streets of Los Angeles. "It's all we got."

Stack snapped back to attention, still standing on the stage in front of the Los Angeles City Hall building and accepting the reward for his bravery. The Chief walked over, pinned the Medal of Valor to his uniform, and went back to the podium as the roar of applause overtook the stage. "Before we conclude, I know that the Detective Lieutenant has prepared some words of his own to say on this historical day for the Los Angeles police force. Bob?"

He walked up to the microphone, his throat drying instantly and his hands beginning to shake. Stack flipped through his note cards nervously, but knew in moments he would set them aside and never once refer back to them. It wasn't within his ability to stay on script. "I am still piecing together the part I played in stopping the attackers that attempted a takeover of the West Bureau Hollywood Precinct." He swallowed hard and looked out across the sea of flashbulbs going off in his face. "The last few days have been the most trying of my life as I waited for clearance of any wrong-doing in the attack. I humbly thank all of the people of Los Angeles for the honor of earning a medal in defense of the citizens that live here. I know it would mean more if my seven colleagues that perished in the attack could be standing by my side, but I know they would want to get back to work because that's just the kind of men and women they were. They were heroes all, and I stand graciously in the shadow of their selfless sacrifice. I beg of the media to ignore my actions as best they can, and focus on the courageous men and women that lost their lives defending this great city."

Stack wiped a real tear away from his eye and took a quick sip of water as the press snapped shot after shot of the 'Hero of Hollywood.'

Almost got through it, he thought to himself. *Just a little further.*

"The injuries I sustained in the attack were not only physical, though those have played a role in my decision, but there has also been a significant amount of mental trauma inflicted during the tense standoff. I have not slept through the night since the ordeal and at current I believe I am unable to fulfill my duties on the Los Angeles Police Force."

Gasps echoed around the group of parasites holding tape recorders. Stack looked around and thought that they must all be thinking about local Emmy's for whatever poorly cross-faded bit of garbage they would edit together from childhood photos and third grade music teacher interviews.

"With a heavy heart," he looked over at the Chief trying desperately not to smile, "I announce my indefinite hiatus from the service. I stand tall knowing that my final act as a Police was an honorable one. I ask for your privacy as I return to my home and try to battle back from this unprecedented attack on our state and our country. Thank you."

He stepped down from the podium and the roar of questions that were hollered up to the stage was deafening. Perhaps they had missed the part about respecting privacy, Stack thought to himself. He turned to the Chief and shook his hand for real. "You know, I'm going to miss this," he projected over the cacophony around them.

"You did the right thing, Stack."

Was Jessup being nice to him now that he held up his end of the bargain? "I sure hope so, Chief."

The portly Chief of Police leaned in closer, putting his mouth as close to Stack's ear as close as he could. "I think we both know you have other things on your mind, *Eliot*." He gave Stack a wink, turned both of them toward the crowd, and raised his hand in a celebratory show.

The applause washed over Stack as he stood dumbfounded that the Chief just referred to him by his *real* name.

CHAPTER THIRTEEN
Nature Versus Nurture

Twenty Minutes Later
Abandoned Department Store outside of Lawrence, Kansas

Paul Revere dazedly peered at the knife protruding from his abdomen—and despite the number of times he blinked — it did not seem to go away. His head fell onto his shoulder; his mouth completely full of blood from his taped mouth. He checked on how Marie was doing with an ice pick dangling from her shoulder. She looked terrified but alive.

The man with the knives was humming the theme to Little House on the Prairie as he double-checked the equipment he brought along for the ride. He did a simple dance as each knife was carefully tucked back into the purple velvet tool holder in a tidy array of tortuous implements. His gaze turned to the pair he had tied up. "One of you will be dead five minutes from this moment. Now, before you get *too* excited, I have not yet decided which of you it will be. Would you say that's more scary or more comforting that the decision is still up in the air?"

Marie and Paul shared a long look, neither wanting to turn back and face the monster gently arranging a menagerie of knives before them.

He continued, "I would guess that the vast majority of major scientific breakthroughs are a result of completely unrelated experimentation. Case in point my little baby birds, in the battle of nature versus nurture it came down a controlled experiment. We are all quite special, the *returners,* "he laughed, or at least attempted to. It came out more like a sarcastic cough. "We all got to live twice through in two different timelines, and *surprise,* there were dramatically different results. I'm sure under that layer of duct tape you're asking yourselves, *now, Marie and or Paul, wouldn't that mean that our upbringing decides who we are? Nurture is the correct answer.*"

He kicked hard into the knife protruding from Paul's stomach. The chair fell backward and he screamed as he collided with the ground and the tape came off his mouth.

"You would be *wrong*, Paul!" the man screamed as he grabbed for a strange blade no longer than an inch in length. "Explain to me how in one life, a man can be one of the most revered men in history but in his *second* life—no pun intended on the *revered* thing, by the way—but in his second life, he became a psychopath. Such divisive paths can only be the result of nature! My brain did not form the same way twice. It's so strange; I remember the feeling of remorse clearly, but I no longer feel it."

The corner of the tape on Marie's mouth had come up enough to breath. Instinctively, she whimpered, "please."

The man sliced through the air, leaving a gash from Marie's ear to her nose. It was so deep that the skin had come off the bone.

"You will *speak* when *spoken* to. Now, Marie, we won't learn from our mistakes without proper punishment. It kills me to do it, it really does. There is a difference between speaking *to* and speaking *at*. I am speaking *at* you, darling."

She lifted her gaze, spitting out the blood rushing across her lips, and stared into his eyes. "Permission to speak, then," she said breathlessly.

The man with the knives grimaced, biting his tongue. "Granted."

Marie watched as the blood continued to drip down to her chin and onto her pants. She glanced to her left and saw Paul trying to right himself in the chair so the dagger would be resting and not moving through his body with every breath. There was no question he would be dead in a few minutes with no medical attention. "Who are you?"

The man passed the tiny blade between his fingers like a quarter. "We both know I won't be passing that information along. I am saving that for when it will do the most damage." He did not break his gaze with Marie as he curled his lips in annoyance. "Is that your only question, love?"

"No."

"*Yes?*" He responded, correcting her answer. "Delightful!" The man tossed the small blade over his shoulder with abandon and grabbed a makeshift mace from his spread. He put it up to Marie's face so she could examine it at a close distance.

She noticed it was nothing more than two hammers duct taped together with somewhere in the ballpark of twenty corn-holders super-glued to it.

The man with the knives smiled, "you see Marie; this is my point. I'm sure among the myriad of emotions swimming around in your head right now, the one sticking out the most is *déjà vu*. To quote the great John McClane, "How can the same shit happen to the same guy twice?"

"I was scared the first time," she replied coldly, oblivious to the Die Hard 2 reference.

"And how do you feel this time?"

"That it better go quick."

The man smiled for an uncomfortable number of seconds before bringing the strange mace down with enormous force into Paul's shin, who awoke from blood loss just enough to scream and pass out again. "Gosh, Marie, I'm just not sure Paul is going to make it."

She didn't waver. "You can't scare me."

The man put on his best fake frown and skipped back over to the chair Marie was taped into against her will. "Now who is being a Grumpy Gary? If I wanted to scare you, I'd probably just start talking about eating cake."

"I never said that—"

He punched hard into the cheek he had already sliced deeply into. She recoiled and returned her gaze, trying to focus on his face through the blinding pain. "Here's a funny thought, do you have a Facebook, Marie?"

"I had a MySpace."

"Marie Antoinette, always doing it backwards."

She spit out some more blood onto the floor. "It's been over five minutes."

"Now, if you rush me cake-face, I will have to kill you both and find two more returners to conduct my little experiment." He gave her a kiss on the forehead and walked back over to Paul who was unconscious on the floor. "Poor guy. He's just tuckered out from all the blood loss." The man with the knives tussled his hair as he dropped Paul into Marie's lap. "I warned you guys to eat a big meal before coming, and did you listen?"

Paul's eyes blew open.

He swung his taped hands under his legs like a jump rope. He grabbed the man with the knives around the throat and ran forward into a nearby counter top. They crashed through the display case that used to house watches and back down onto the floor. The two of them rolled around trading blows on the dusty department store tile.

Paul kicked the man with the knives in the stomach and lifted him, tumbling over his head. With only a split second to make the decision, he screamed at the top of his lungs as he pulled the knife from his abdomen and turned back to his attacker. He managed to get all the way to his knees, still holding the knife as he tried to steel himself to take him down the kidnapper. "Unlike Marie, I don't really care who you used to be."

The man with the knives swung up behind the counter, wiping blood from his lip with a deranged smile. "All you had to do was ask nicely, and I would have told you. Gosh!"

Marie leaned around Paul so she could see the man. "Who are you? Uh, please?"

The man stood up straight and dusted himself off. "I'm Abraham Lincoln."

Stunned silence came over Paul and Marie. Paul figured it out first.

"No you're not."

The man with the knives laughed heartily. "Oh, *god no*. Had you going there for a minute though, didn't I?"

Paul switched the hand the knife was in, he could feel the world growing dim around him from blood loss. He needed to make a move soon or he wasn't going to be able to make one at all. The blood could not be blinked from his eyelid.

The man with the knives took three steps forward, talking as he made his way down the path to Paul. "What's that he used to say about a house divided by itself?"

Paul Revere fell over onto the floor.

"Yes! Thank you for reminding me, Paul." The man grabbed him by the lapel. "Now, if you'll excuse me, I need to have a private conversation with Marie, here. If you wouldn't mind waiting outside."

The man with the knives threw Paul out of the plate-glass window on the second story of the department store. He landed on the ground and rolled over into the street, most of his bones having shattered on impact.

Marie looked up as the man walked over to the knife that Paul had recently removed from his gut—he picked it up and turned his attention back to the girl in the chair. "I guess you made your decision," she said, her voice trembling.

"Well, darling, I guess I have. Poor Paul took a hell of a beating just now."

"Is he dead?" She knew he wasn't.

The man walked over to the window and peered down to the street below. Paul was lying motionless on the road, there was blood surrounding him. "Yeah, I'd say there's a pretty good chance he's dead."

Marie Antoinette closed her eyes. "I spent this life doing charity work."

He spun around, so confused he was actually *angry* he was confused. "Post about that on your MySpace, did ya?"

She ignored him; "I've been all over the world, never having more than two thousand dollars in my bank account at any time. I gave away whatever I could."

The man with the knives backhanded her, but she kept on describing her life, never opening her eyes. "Please, dear, do have a point."

Her words became whimpered and shaky. "It doesn't come down to nature versus nurture; not for us. Our new lives are a reflection of our first lives. If this life was only an opportunity to make peace with our sins, then it was more than worth it."

The man rolled his eyes. "I liked you better when you acted like a Kardashian."

She opened her eyes and looked deeply back into her kidnapper's, completely at peace with the moment at hand. "You chose Paul, didn't you?"

"I did."

"Changed your mind?"

"*I did.*"

He slid the knife into her chest and slowly through the tissue of her heart. Her head fell onto his shoulder and he held her for a moment, kissing her softly on the head. It was excruciating, but she managed to speak one final whisper into his ear as she began slipping away.

"I know who you really are."

And not a moment further, Marie Antoinette died on his shoulder.

CHAPTER FOURTEEN
The Motel Pool is for Lovers

The Middle of the Night
Motel Estándar, outside of
Lawrence, Kansas

Alex dropped his phone on the counter and flipped on the air circulation in the bathroom to cover up the cigarette he was about to smoke. "Why did I send that text? Alex, you *idiot,*" he scolded himself quietly as he lit the cherry of a Marlboro light. His breath seemed to freeze in his throat as he waited for the phone sitting on the counter to vibrate twice. "Maybe it didn't actually send," he absent-mindedly mouthed as he checked the timestamp on the text message for the fifth time in the last hour.

He grabbed the phone and started typing out a second message before slamming the phone back onto the counter and scolding the idea.

Cigarette ash swept across the air as it fell to the toilet.

Alex's hand stopped shaking long enough to notice how much blood was caked onto it. It felt as if his heart was skipping a hundred beats every time he closed his eyes and saw Paul Revere plummeting to the ground across the street from the hotel. If not for his forceful removal from the scene by Janey, the police would have arrested him on sight for any number of felonies he had or had not committed. The scenario played out over and over, with wildly divergent nightmarish results. In one, Paul died grasping his collar; in another, an officer thought he was the murderer—trying to finish Revere off—and shot him dead.

Even though none of those scenarios had come to pass, the human mind is rewarded no consolation in discovering and repeating new ways in which it could have been in a disaster.

Alex had been unable to get an update from the hospital, but knew that Revere was still breathing. The group had watched him be loaded into the back of an ambulance that was flanked with an army of squad cars. A man being stabbed and thrown from an abandoned department store is a news-making affair, so the four of them found themselves glued to the television screen throughout the night, hoping to get an update on the well-being of Paul (who was identified on the news as one Blake Albateek). If not for a hasty phone call from Stack, he would not have learned the victims' identities in the brutal attack across the street.

Marie had somehow been *less* lucky than the thrice-stabbed revolutionary thrown two stories, shattering most of his bones on contact with the pavement.

He jumped at the sudden knock at the door on the bathroom door.

"Are you okay in there, Lex? Do you need anything?" Janey whispered through the door, careful not to wake the boys passed out on different ends of the bed in various states of sock. "I think there's a magazine about canoe restoration out here somewhere," she trailed off in jest.

Alex looked toward the door and then back toward his phone, which buzzed twice loudly on the counter. His hands fumbled across the marble-like finish of the plastic counter and tried to quiet the loud buzzing before Janey wondered why he was in the bathroom smoking and texting people.

"Why are you in the bathroom smoking and texting people?"

Okay, new plan, he thought for a moment before going off in an unspoken tirade about the usability of a "silent" function in modern handsets that was anything *but* silent. "Out in a minute," he exclaimed as he checked the text on his phone, which contained a single word.

Pool.

His hand waved around the air in that way all smokers wave their hands around to hide odors. Surprisingly, it did little to mask the nicotine-soaked stench in the tiny plastic bathroom. He hopped to his feet and jerked open the door, startling Janey who was browsing through hotel literature to slide under the door.

"Did you want this one on proper check-out procedures? I was skeptical at first, but the section on taking the bathrobe home with you was a real pamphlet-turner," she deadpanned with a smile. "Speaking of, you just blew smoke all over it didn't you? Pretty sure you just bought it."

Alex looked nervously to his phone and back to Janey. "Are you going to bed soon?" he asked nervously.

"If by soon, you mean forty-five minutes ago, then yes."

"I'm probably heading out in a minute," the phone slid back into his pocket.

Janey motioned to two couch pillows and a comforter from her bed, "but I made you this deluxe queen-sized carpet bed!"

He stepped closer and grabbed her arm. "Where's your pistol?"

She gave him a sideways glance at the clear urgency in his voice. The gun slid out from her bathrobe pocket and she checked the slide for a round before holding it up for Alex to see. "I always have this on me."

"Move the boys to the bed away from the door."

"Alex, what did you do?" she scolded, no longer in a jovial mood.

He checked through the curtains for any sign of movement outside. "I sent a text message."

Janey plopped down on her bed and buried her face in her hands. "Jesus, Lex—you didn't?"

"I needed to know."

She threw a pillow at him in disgust.

He threw one of the couch pillows from his makeshift bed back in trade. "That will be far more comfortable, thank you."

"Curb the macho 'needing to know' bullcrap, do you have any idea how much danger you just put these children in? What the hell is wrong with you? I thought you were supposed to be this brilliant strategist." She was beginning to raise her voice.

Alex put up a hand and motioned to 'bring it down,' before turning to the door. "She has a lot to answer for."

Janey hopped off the bed and slammed the door back with her arm, cutting him off. "We have to get out of here *right now*."

He lifted her arm in the palm of his hand, calmly, which scared her even more. "She's already here."

She stood in stunned silence.

"Move the boys to the other bed and put the gun on the door. I'll slide a room service menu under the door so you know to open it. Anything else happens outside that door, you friggin' put 'em down. You copy?"

Janey grabbed the desk chair and used it to rest her elbow as she kept the gun trained at the center mass of any would-be target on the other side of the door. "Copy that. Just go get it done so we can sleep."

He turned back to the door but stopped short, knowing she had one more thing to add.

"Lex," she began softly, "just one more thing."

He knew her all too well.

"If anything happens to these kids, I'll put you down," she spoke in a startlingly low whisper.

He did not know her as well as he thought he did.

Alex grabbed the handle and swung it open, his other hand already pointing his pistol out into the exterior catwalk of the motel. The door shut behind him as he slowly moved down the third story of the outdoor motel that charged for trips to the ice machine. The pool was visible down below and there was a hooded female sitting in one of the deck chairs.

She was staring directly at Alex as he made his way down to the pool area. His phone buzzed twice in his pocket, which caused a quick pause near a custodial hallway to check it without unwanted supervision.

No guns <3

This rule remained a rule for approximately the same amount of time it took Alex to toss the phone back into his pocket and secure his grip on the pistol in the waistband of his pants.

The rest of the trip down to the motel courtyard was mostly quiet if not for the growing lapping of waves in the pool. The grip on his gun tightened as he scanned the fenced area for any unwelcome surprises.

Chloe Freimont was just sitting there, taking in her surroundings and looking as healthy and alive as ever (if ever excludes that time Alex had to identify her corpse at the mortuary).

He lifted the latch on the fence and recoiled at the rusty screech that echoed around the inward facing motel rooms. He mouthed the words "I'm sorry" as made his way into the caustic blue lights of the pool deck. Feigned embarrassment was a believable entrance, or so he thought.

She waved her arm to have a seat at the deck chair to her left; there were two glasses of whiskey on the rocks melting away on the table. Chloe grabbed for hers and took a slow sip; the subtle rise in the corners of her mouth gave Alex pause. The image of her enjoying drinks and food burned the subtle smile she didn't even know about into his mind.

But Chloe hated whiskey.

He pulled the pistol from his pants and had the hammer back before she could put the glass down. His shoes slid across the deck to place his firing distance at least ten paces from where she was sitting. There was much that she was capable of, least of which was—

"I think that text was pretty clear about the no-guns thing. I won't be sending the hearts anymore if we can't follow directions."

—Sarcasm.

"You're dead," Alex felt the words grind up his throat like sandpaper.

Chloe smiled and tossed the empty glass into the overgrown bush behind her. "That's a solid opener, Alex. Though, and not to be a

Debbie Downer Does Dallas here, but I have some pretty compelling evidence to the contrary."

He stepped forward, his face contorting at the reality before him. "No. *No.* I was there, I saw your body, Chloe."

"You saw *a* body."

"Freimont, I saw *your* god damn body," he struggled to steady his gun. "I know every inch of you."

She dramatically waved her hand in front of her face as if to cool off. "Is it getting hot out here? I feel a run of the vapors coming on," Chloe touted in a surprisingly well-executed accent of a Southern belle.

"One more. *One more* and I am putting a bullet through your forehead. Explain to me how you're still alive!"

"Let's start with how *you're* still alive," she spat with a venomous change in tone.

Alex took another step forward, keeping the sights of the gun squarely planted on her center of mass. "Explain to me. Explain to me as you would a child."

Chloe stood up and cocked her head to the side. "Don't shoot me in the face, please, because I'm not pulling the bitch card right now—but did you just quote *Galaxy Quest?*"

His eyes darted to the side as his lips pursed in thought; as they darted back, he realized that he had. "Pretend that didn't happen."

She took a deep breath in preparation of the exposition dump forthcoming. "I have gone out of my way to keep you alive, you psychopathic man-child." Chloe gauged the widening of his eyes and believed she had made the correct impression. "The returners are an anomaly that doesn't mean anything—a blip in the fabric of accidental science."

Alex was disturbed by what he was hearing. "No. That doesn't make sense."

"Of course it doesn't," she replied calmly. "Mr. Heton, do you know what a 'risk matrix' is?"

He refused to answer with anything that wasn't an eyebrow.

She smiled. "As I'm sure you know, it's a simple organization of data to measure the likelihood of an event happening versus the consequences of any action taken to create the event."

"Which has what do with this?"

"I trust you'll forgive me for any data I gloss over with a gun to my head, but we should start with consequences. We can look at it both proactively and reactively."

"Did you go to night school or something, when did you get so smart?"

"Shut up, Alex. Now, in the proactive column, which is where the stupid Buck Rogers bullshit you seem to peddle comes from, the belief is that the returners were brought back for a reason and we must band together to save the world."

Alex sat down in a chair a few feet away, carefully keeping the gun trained on her in a more relaxed position. "And you think we just came back for no reason?"

Chloe turned her chair to sit face-to-face with her former boyfriend. "Stay with me here, Bieber-hair. On the other side of the spectrum, the reactive side of things, it's possible that doing nothing will save the world and that bringing everyone together could destroy it."

He scoffed. "How could that happen?"

She didn't respond and instead turned to the pool as tears welled up in her eyes.

Alex could tell she was actively fighting real emotion. "Chloe…"

Her index finger waved him off as she tried to regain her composure with the help of a few tissues stuffed into her purse. "Okay. Let's continue."

He nodded.

"You were correct," she said, sniffling through tissues and wiping the tears away. "It was my body at the morgue."

Alex could feel the world grow gigantic around him and start to spin.

"That night in the taco place—you heard the gunshot down the street, right?"

He nodded again as he tried to stop his hand from shaking.

"I fired the shot."

No. No. No. No. No. No. His hand wouldn't stop shaking. *Please don't finish that sentence!*

"There were two of me. How weird is that," she asked with the deadpan of a witness to a serious trauma.

Alex stood up so fast the chair spilled backward and rolled across the deck making a terrible racket. Lights around the courtyard began to flip on, including the room Janey and the boys were currently in. He could feel a panic attack coming on and his knees buckled as he fell to the pavement, desperately trying to hold the gun on his target.

She limped over to the crumpled shape that was Alexander the Great just moments before who had become simply Alex Heton, newly traumatized accounting student. Chloe put a hand on his face with a gentle touch, sliding down his cheek the way she used to calm him down. "Two identical particles cannot occupy the same state at the same time. We are like atomic bombs, Alex." She began to sob and struggled to get the words even a few inches out of her mouth. "I saw the look on my own face before I did it." She sniffled and chuckled through the tears. "I was pretty mad at me."

"So you didn't kill those kids?"

Chloe's look was sideways and angry. "In Kansas? Jesus, Alex. I killed Genghis and the other me—and Genghis was to keep *you* alive."

"But you told me—"

"I told you not to go to Kansas because the killer was there! I might think you're an asshole but I don't want you dead."

"So, who?"

She shrugged and inched closer to Alex. "Paul is the only one that got a look, and he's in a coma right now." Chloe put her head on his shoulder, much to the surprise of Alex. "That's not all of it—Janey," she trailed off.

He looked up to his motel room as the shape peeking through the curtains disappeared from his gaze. "Oh god. It doesn't matter which side of the risk you believe, does it?"

"Nope," she said, knowing he finally picked up on it.

"Even if we're meant to be here, if there's," now it was his eyes fighting the incoming emotions. Swallowing became torturous. "It's her, isn't it?"

"I'm so sorry, Alex. I tried playing bad cop, but that is one tough chick, man." She laughed.

"How many?"

There was a long silence at the pool as both of them looked up to the motel room they knew Janey was waiting in. Chloe swallowed hard, stood up from the pool, and said one final thing before walking off into the darkness.

"There's four Janey's."

CHAPTER FIFTEEN
Who Invited That Guy?

Three Days Later
A Condemned Frozen Food Warehouse in Lawrence, Kansas

Detective Stack, correction: *formerly Detective* Stack startled himself as the giant metal door slammed shut to his rear. As his eyes adjusted to the dark entryway decked out in wall-to-wall 1970's wood paneling and nigh-unidentifiably colored shag carpet, it became clear that this space had not been used in a long time. The reception desk featured a day calendar where every day featured a different puzzled looking animal with a speech bubble that read 'Where's the beef?' He picked it up and smiled to himself, muttering "There was a time in my life I was disappointed I never lived to see this future." The calendar flopped back onto the desk with a dusty thud, "toss that in with my VHS copy of The Untouchables. I'm sure every boy dreams of one day being played by Jake from Silverado," he laughed to himself.

"Oh my god, Stack!" A voice yelled from behind him. The former detective spun around in the darkness and into the incoming hug from Alex; he was unable to divert the course of the embrace. "How the hell did you get out of there? I figured the Los Angeles county police department would be making lunchmeat out of you by now."

"Please let go of me," Stack said through labored breaths.

Alex released him and took a step backward into the darkness, embarrassed.

Stack looked around for the overheads. "Is there a light switch in here somewhere?"

"The breaker only works in the warehouse. Come on, there is a lot of people here already." He turned and began to walk down the maze of hallways meandering toward the warehouse, "I don't think there's been any food stored here for fifteen years and the place *still* smells like goddamn fish sticks."

"Wait, are there other returners here?"

Alex smiled. "Quite a few, actually."

"How on Earth did you get in contact with all of them?"

The kid smiled again, reaching into his pocket and pulling out a small stack of crumpled papers. "Stole your list when you were still clinkin' bars in the joint."

Stack's brow advertised his lack of amusement. "Don't try to talk like me."

"You don't have a patent on cool-ass 1920's slang. I'm twenty-four hundred years older than you, you friggin' *chelóna*."

Stack blinked.

"It's Greek for turtle—in my day that was a big insult. If somebody called me that I'd have stabbed them all up in their face-brains—oh, we're here." Alexander put his shoulder into a metal door and stumbled into the large open (and lit) warehouse. "Welcome to home base, man. From here on, you're just Eliot."

Eliot Ness removed his cap and looked around in awe at the size of the warehouse towering all around them. "Are we safe here?"

The two continued talking as they made their way across the distance of a football field to where the others were sitting and talking. "Minimal points of entry. We'll need at least one person awake on a twenty-four hour rotation. You know, after a couple of days, it really hasn't been that bad."

Eliot could see a few familiar faces and a few he could not yet recognize. "I imagine you set up sleeping areas in the warehouse."

Alex laughed. "It's 2012, man."

"No reason to upset common courtesy. I sleep in boxers with an *open* front."

The kid stopped Eliot short of the group. "Eliot. Modesty went out the window when a psychopath, who, by the way, killed Marie Antoinette and put Paul Revere into a coma four days ago, decided to pick us off!" He turned back to the group, mumbling as he rejoined their ranks. "Grow the hell up, man."

Eliot ran after Alex, trying to catch up. "Then I will need two pairs of sweat pants!" He froze. A rush of embarrassment came over him as he realized that he just shouted that in front of a table of six going to town on two massive trays of Bagel Bites.

"Don't eat the cheese ones! I want the cheese ones!" Richie screamed at Albert, trying to protect his undercooked bagel pizzas.

The cacophony of the bagel pizza-apocalypse was difficult for the older gentleman to deal with. Eliot walked around the edge of the table, situating himself in the middle of everyone, and announced loudly to the group, "How many people in this room are currently wanted by the police in any state?"

Five hands shot up, most not resting their ulterior bagel-shoveling hand in the process (John Quincy Adams chose to abstain from the pizza bagels on the grounds that "the food was an abomination, and further, a lack of sausage toppings was an egregious oversight.")

"Richie, put your hand up!" Albert scolded his young friend across the table from him. "You've been kidnapped."

"Oh yeah!" He squealed through his high-pitched East London accent, propping both hands in the air as a cheese bagel drooped from his mouth.

Alex attempted to take a seat next to Janey, but she got up in a huff and left the moment he sat down. She relocated next to Harriet and pretended to be completely unaware he was even in the room with them.

Since the run-in with Chloe at the motel pool, he was in the doghouse when he put them all in danger. Worse still, upon returning to the room, he refused to divulge any of the information he learned out of fear that Janey would go ballistic. It was not his finest hour, as the resulting argument was out of control, and she was not entirely wrong. After he held Paul, bleeding in the street, he became reckless.

Which meant he now had information that no one else in the group possessed. Alex looked across the table to Eliot, watching him suss out an oven-baked pizza bagel as he attempted to eat the thing with a fork and knife. The former police detective had to be the first person he informed of what Chloe revealed.

John piped up. "Excuse me, if we are all present, do you think we could address the issue of a psychopath trying to murder us all?"

Harriet shot a sideways glance to John. "Really? In front of the kids?"

"Due respect, as I have adored your work for two lifetimes now, Ms. Tubman, but Richie and myself have seen more bloodshed than everyone else at this table combined." Albert said with an even tone, careful not to offend. "He killed four armed men with a pair of dulled kitchen knives on my birthday—saved my life."

Richie excitedly extended his fist across the table in cheerful hope that Albert would return his fist bump.

He did not.

"Kid's got a point," John laughed and pretended to pour Coke into his rum and rum. "Probably doesn't hurt that he has the highest IQ in the room."

Albert raised an eyebrow and looked back. "We all retained the memories and education from our previous lives, so you're half right. From an early age we all started to recollect memories of a life we were not currently living. While the information is there, our brains are still far too small to process any of it."

John took a swig, taking a moment to enjoy the burn on the way down, and wondered, "So, what does that mean, kid?"

"It means I'm about five percent as smart as I should be, and my name is *Albert* not 'kid.'"

The rum disappeared into a funnel of trapped ice cubes. He slammed the glass back down onto the table. "Me too, Al."

"This isn't going well," Eliot angrily whispered down into Alex's ear.

"Well, what do you want to do about it?" He whispered back.

Eliot pulled out his service revolver and fired once into the ceiling of the warehouse.

Everyone stopped what they were doing (except Richie who was still piling pizza into his mouth,) and turned their attention immediately to the gunfire.

"Everyone shut up for a second."

They did.

"I've been trying to get a group of returners in the same room for months now. Do you think this was easy? If this is amusing to you in some way, then, by all means, there's the door." Eliot pointed off behind him. "I knew Marie. She was a friend and she was brutally massacred fourteen miles from here, only a few days ago. I didn't come here to babysit a bunch of immature knuckleheads; I came here to help us stay alive long enough to understand why all of us came back for a second round. I gave up my career, a career I love so much I did it twice, to come make a game plan and hopefully work on finding others like us."

"How many of us are there? Do we even know?" Harriet asked politely.

Albert raised his hand and wiggled it around as if this were fifth period English class.

Eliot scratched his forehead. "Yes. Albert."

"As you all know, I've been working on my data-basing software. Well, Eliot doesn't, but I'm sure you can figure it out. Actually, if you wouldn't mind spending some time with me later I bet you could help me refine it." Albert waited from validation from the man who had recently fired a live round into the ceiling to continue. "Okay, in a nutshell, I pulled phrases from the profile my psychologist kept on me. This lead to Richie, whose phrases I added into the database and so on. Harriet and Janey then supplied records from their high schools that I was able to widen the search with. With a wider breadth of phrasing, and a highly illegal database worm, I can pull information from all over the planet and rank it based on how closely it matches us. From there we'll have to investigate by hand." Albert finished.

"You're a *genius*," Eliot said without thinking.

"He's Albert fuggin' Einstein," John slurred from across the table much to the chagrin of Harriet.

"So how many returners do you think there are?" Alex piped up suddenly.

Albert took a deep breath and scribbled a few things onto the reverse side of his paper plate. "Without knowing what percentage were never discovered by the system—"

"Just guess, Albert."

He let out a deep sigh. "Uh, as few as forty—as many as two hundred, probably."

Harriet did a spit take with her water. "Two *hundred?*"

Albert shook his head. "I can only guess with basic percentages based on the data we have collected. It's possible we won't ever know without a better way to spread information to potential returners."

Eliot grinned and stepped back into the conversation. "Doesn't that excite you guys? There are possibly more than a hundred other famous historical figures out there somewhere, waiting to be discovered. Wow, to think they're all different—"

Alex touched his shoulder. "Eliot, that's not exactly correct."

"You bastard!" Janey slammed herself up from the table and yelled across to Alex.

"Can we try to keep it to one conversation at a time? When did this shit turn into a Mamet movie?" John growled as he poured another rum and rum.

Eliot again thought about The Untouchables. "Mamet!" he cursed quietly to himself.

"Now, Janey, just hang on a second. I—I do have information from Chloe."

The whole room got louder at the mention of Chloe Freimont.

"You talked to Chloe and neglected to tell all of us that?" Eliot was yelling at the top of his lungs now. The meeting was quickly spiraling out of control.

"Where are my gummy worms? Dude, did you take 'em?" Richie was yelling at whoever would listen.

Alex looked at the table and realized that everyone was arguing with someone else. Not knowing what to say, he took a deep breath and prepared to come clean about everything. "Okay! Here's what I found out from Chloe!"

The slamming of a door on the other end of the compound stopped him cold. He pulled his pistol out of a thigh-holster he found in the warehouse offices.

Three other guns cocked around him and they all aimed toward the noise looming across the complex.

Footsteps began to echo across the hundred-or-so yards of concrete. A minute passed before a figure emerged that none of them recognized. He was in his early thirties with dark hair and a square jaw with a none-too-accidental five-o-clock shadow plastered across it.

The man recoiled when he realized he was at gunpoint from four people. "Whoa, whoa! I was told to come here," he spoke in a soft French accent.

"Who told you to be here?" Eliot barked as if he were still on the job.

"Paul! Paul Revere! I was his friend and he told me to meet here on this day," the man screamed in terror. His eyes darted around to the pistols drawn in his face.

Alex walked up slowly and patted the man down, keeping his gun trained at center mass. Coming up clean, he turned his attention back to the conversation at hand. "You're clean. So who the hell are you?"

"Did he not tell you? He said he was going to tell you," the man said, suddenly on the verge of tears.

Harriet stepped forward, putting forth a sympathetic smile. "Son, Paul was attacked." She swallowed. "He's in a coma—we don't know if he's gonna make it."

The man took a moment and fell into a squat as he covered his face in his hands. "I talked to him—I talked to him a week ago. Oh my god. *Oh my god.*"

Eliot and Alex exchanged the same uneasy look, gave each other a knowing nod, and squeezed in on the flanks of the man on the ground. They grabbed his arms and lifted him to his feet. "You really need to tell us who you are. Now, please," Eliot spoke calmly, finger lingering on the trigger.

The man looked back into Eliot's eyes with his own swollen tear-filled eyes. "Sorry, I just lost track there. I'm Richard—my name is Richard."

The room maintained its silence, waiting for him to finish that thought.

"Richard the Lionheart?" he looked around puzzled. "Paul told me you would know of me?"

Every mouth in the room, save Richie's, fell agape.

Alex pushed the newly discovered Richard with an incredibly aggressive force and wheeled around to the rest of the group. "Get Richie out of the building now or we're all dead!"

Janey grabbed Richie and ran from the room without needing any further information.

Alex knocked the older Richard to the ground and put his gun firmly against the forehead of the terrified man beneath him.

"Oh please don't! I'll leave—I'll do whatever you want; just don't shoot me. Oh God!" Richard pleaded from the ground.

Alex could feel his finger squeezing down on the trigger.

Was he about to kill this man in cold blood?

The Returners

Season One Part Two

CHAPTER SIXTEEN
Mu-Mu-Mu-My Chelóna

Three Hours Later
Backroom of the Frozen Food Warehouse

Richard did his best to keep the blood dripping from his wrists in check. The handcuffs were applied far too tightly, so after three hours locked in a dank space that smelled of decaying fish guts, he decided that showing up unannounced was probably not the most winning strategy one could exercise. They had removed his shoes, socks, jacket, keys, and wallet before threading the cuffs through the open back of the chair to ensure any escape attempt would be forded with a cheap piece of lawn furniture in close tow. He did his best to get his toes out of whatever cheap aquatic genocide was swathed across the concrete and hastily sprayed into a nearby drain.

He looked up at the ceiling and said, "should have just gone to Cinnabon," under his breath.

The door opened with hesitancy, as if walking on eggshells about an unprovoked three-hour kidnapping, with no explanation, was a topic that could be danced around with intricate kindness. Harriet slowly lumbered across the length of the room, setting her jacket on a nearby crate of descaling tools. She pulled a second crate up close and took a seat right next to Richard.

Eliot followed her in, careful not to imply he had any feelings whatsoever under a gruff retired cop's exterior. He took a stance behind Harriet just out of range of the overhead light.

Richard rolled his eyes and scooted the plastic chair closer to the two people that recently entered the room. "Could one of you kindly explain why I'm handcuffed to a chair like a criminal?"

"Are you?" Harriet asked with more than an unwelcome hint of accusation.

"Am I what?" He replied.

"A criminal?"

"I'm sorry, can we do a felony headcount real quick? Which one of us tied a guy to a chair *after* inviting him?"

Eliot stepped presumptively in between Richard and Harriet. "We didn't invite you. Answer the question."

Richard shook his head in disbelief, favoring an arm that was falling asleep from resting in such an odd position on the chair. He scowled at Eliot. "No. No, I am not a criminal. I am friend's with Paul Revere and he asked me to be here!" he shouted with a growing indignation toward his kidnappers.

Harriet spoke in a low droll. "What did he say?"

"What do you mean?"

She persisted. "What did he say, *exactly*, about us? You obviously knew where to go to find us. It stands to reason he would mention finding another Richard—"

The man in the chair cut her off. "Why am I *another* Richard? Just because you got some snot-snozzed little scrubber bangin' about in between eating an unhealthy amount of Spaghettios?"

The former detective raised a suspicious eyebrow. "And how did you know he liked Spaghettios so much?"

The indignation manifested itself across the face of Richard the Lionheart once more. "Because I like Spaghettios *so much*, you moron. Weren't you a police officer?"

Eliot began scribbling on a pad of paper, pretending to disseminate the fascinating data they were collecting while in actuality attempting to save face through silence. He turned to Harriet and gave her an affirmative nod to continue.

She pulled in her brow and turned her mouth to the side as she made strong eye contact with Richard in the chair. "I can assure you that insulting language will not get you out of that chair any faster."

"What? What will get me out of this chair faster? To recap, you pulled guns on me, clocked me in the face, which, *thanks by the way,* and then you handcuff me to this chair for three hours without telling me a damn thing about it!" He yelled back at his accusers.

Harriet took a moment to keep her emotional state as flat as she could. "I'm sorry you have to be in the chair. Even if you didn't realize it, your arrival put us all in a great deal of danger. So, I'll ask again. What did Paul tell you about us?"

He shot back with a puzzled sigh. "What kind of danger?"

Eliot interjected. "It doesn't matter."

Richard crumpled his face into an annoyed mess and shook his head back at the former detective. "A great deal of danger that doesn't matter? Remember that I am no different from you. I'm a returner too, and with Paul and—," he took a moment. "Marie. With Paul and Marie so viciously attacked, I'd like to know if I am in danger here. Is someone trying to kill us?"

"I think you know that someone is trying to kill us," Eliot replied.

Harriet brought her arm back and socked Richard right across the jaw as hard as she could. He reeled in the direction of the punch and blinked his right eye a couple of times, letting the blood drip from his mouth for a moment. His gaze returned to the woman who had just struck him seemingly out of nowhere. "So, *ow!*"

"I wanted to see how you took a punch," she grinned back.

"I fought in wars my entire life, including the second crusade—"

"Third crusade," Eliot cut him off with a corrective immediacy.

Richard smiled. "So you did do your homework?"

Eliot Ness dropped a manila folder onto the floor with around two hundred pages of printed documentation sticking out of it in all directions. "I have information on every returner we've been able to identify. So, I spent some time on the internet while you were stewing in here." He looked over the man handcuffed before him. "You were one of five sons, well, of five *legitimate* sons of Henry the

Second, and spent most of your life picking fights with whatever trifling idiotic nonsense would make your Daddy accept you for who you were. When that didn't take and he passed on, you, despite being the middle child, somehow rose to become quite a reviled ruler of England, some would say one of the *most* reviled—which is no small feat in that country. You spent almost all of your time in France, even refusing to learn the English language, the language of the country you were supposedly ruling, in favor of continuing the charade as the bastard son of France. If I'm not mistaken, you were once quoted as saying that you would have sold London if you could have." Silence sat awkwardly between the two of them for a moment before Eliot blurted out, "Wikipedia is my jam."

Richard spit a little more blood onto the ground. "What can I say, Viva La France," he replied with a wicked grin. His eyes drifted back to Harriet. "So Harriet, did I pass the punch test?"

She buckled her fist, casually leaned to her rear, and struck him across the jaw once more. Harriet shook her hand as the pain subsided. "Still gathering data."

The blood was falling from his nose to the ground at an alarming rate. Richard took a moment as he stared at the ground, trying to make the pounding in his head go away. He returned to his normal posture in the chair and just let the blood flow down his face and onto his shirt. The look he was giving Harriet was no longer of a jovial nature. "Are you trying to get a rise out of me? Just say what you've been wanting to say this whole time."

Her knees buckled for a brief moment as it sunk in they were really about to have this conversation, right out in the open. "We both think you're the one killing the returners."

Richard laughed, swearing to himself in French for a brief moment. "*Voila!* There it is."

Eliot cleared his throat loudly and purposefully. "It stands to reason that the killer is a returner his or herself. Once I compiled a psych profile on you—"

"A psych profile you compiled using Wikipedia," sneered Richard.

He continued. "Coupled with your random appearance and the numerous, *numerous*, conversations I had with Paul Revere before he was viciously assaulted into a coma, that never made a single mention of you."

Harriet stepped forward, clearly hoping to falter the rising tension. "Richard. Look at it from our perspective. What would you think of your sudden appearance?"

He wiped a generous amount of blood from his nose onto the sleeve on his shoulder. "Here's the rub, and I know you already know this, but you two are trying so desperately to appear on top of the situation that you would rather just rock me in the face than have the conversation where we all agree to leave me handcuffed to a chair." Richard laughed a hearty laugh as his blood dripped down onto his three hundred dollar jeans. "I get that I showed up unannounced and put you guys in quite the pickle. That puts the burden of proof on me does it not? If I can just prove that I know Paul, then there's no question that I didn't make this all up, right?" He paused in wait for the two exceptionally non-committal nods to drive him forward. "Pull out my phone and look through the photos. There's a ton of photos with Paul and I in there—he's my best friend for Christ's sake." He took a deep breath. "Which leads me to the fact that none of you ever met him in person. Paul communicated with Detective Costner over here only through email, and only three times. The bearded guy knocking back his fourth Sam Adams at Hooters is a man you won't even recognize as the outdated photo you saw on the news. So, let's curb the puffed-out chests and malleable recollections of events you didn't witness or comprehend and just get back to punching me in the face."

Eliot paused to allow the information to dance around in his head for a moment. He looked over to Harriet who looked equally taken aback by all the information exchanged before motioning Richard's attention back to her. "She saved your life, you know."

He took a deep breath. "Yes, I remember that emotionally unstable wreck trying to bore a gun through my face."

She took two steps closer to him, her own battle scars now much more visible under the lights of the backroom. "I made a deal with Alex to get that gun out of your face."

"Oh, yeah? And what was that deal?"

She put a toothpick in between her lips and wriggled it to a familiar spot. "That I would hit you three times so you would know this is for real."

Richard squinted as he recounted in his head. "Well, folly for him because you only hit me tw—"

Her fist landed square in his cheek, making a wet-smacking sound as it collided and opened a cut on his face.

CHAPTER SEVENTEEN

The Kitten Yawned in the Doorway

Meanwhile

Abandoned Groovy's Department Store outside of Lawrence, Kansas

My view from the bottom of the bottle is transfixed on the other bottle. The full bottle. The game of liver-killing hopscotch was afoot, bouncing from whiskey to scotch to margarita mix, adrift in a dreary haze of bickering neighbors, truant alimony checks, and losing consciousness on a pizza. The life of a cop. A good life.

(Excerpts are taken from the never-produced screenplay of Ransic Yarbo's cop noir thriller "The Kitten Yawned in the Doorway.")

Detective Ransic polished off what was left of an under-cooked Healthy Choice Lobster Cheese Ravioli and tossed the recyclable tray into a nearby garbage can. He wiped his hands clean on the front of his slacks and headed back into the store for another check around the crime scene

Since the ill-timed departure of Detective Bob Stack from the ranks of the Los Angeles police department, the day-to-day responsibilities of Ransic had increased with overwhelming momentum. Gone were the days of milling around in the background, attempting to find the point on an asymptote well balanced between receiving the maximum amount of credit and placating the brass with a charade of value and reliability. He knew that his calling was to step into big shoes and give everything he had to protect the fine citizens of California.

Today was not that day.

"Rancid! Where's that Grande White Chocolate?" one of *them* half-yawned from the safety of the perfume counter, not looking up from a text that was surely of minimal importance.

I fired back with a smile so manufactured Henry Ford would have stopped and asked me to put on a clinic.

"It's *Ransic,* sir," he replied. "I'm here for the crime scene—I'm Julius Ransic. From Los Angeles." He smiled nervously, held up his badge, and hoped the man behind the counter would elect to point him in the right direction.

If the right direction was a grunt of ill-defined subtext, then he was off to a great start. He tucked his badge back into his jacket pocket and pushed further into the sea of feds, doing his best to get through and across the condemned department store floor.

When the Feds slink down from their ivory tower long enough to choke on the unfamiliar aroma of actual police work, we get a peek up their skirt and instantaneously recoil at their rotting intuition concealed under their unkempt bravados—a lifetime spent unwaking from the childhood dream of cowboys and Indians.

George Armstrong Custer is dead, and the war is long over, but the men in the Reagan-era haircuts bark orders and sling condescension amongst one another in a never-ending battle for anthill supremacy.

"Hey, watch it, man! I'm dusting for prints here," a Fed spun and yelled in a hushed whisper after Ransic collided into the poor man's back.

"Sorry about that. Just looking for the—Looking for someone."

"Ransic!" he heard his name shouted from the other side of the perfume and jewelry counters. He spun round to see his boss Waylan Dwight Jessup III talking to a small group of men in blue track jackets that said "FBI" on the back. "I need a minute of your time, kid."

I follow orders handed down from the brass, but I never polish them. Sure, I had a few drinks for breakfast but when I look around, I grimace, surrounded by knob-polishers and pole-jumpers, drowning in a sea of double entendre.

He walked over to his boss and leaned against a nearby counter, trying to look suave and collected. "What's up, boss?"

Jessup focused on the rest of a soft taco resting on a nearby counter. The man always seemed to chew with his mouth open, something that drove Ransic positively bananas on a daily basis. The detective would often find excuses to duck away from any would-be dining experience with the Chief. "So, did you run through the scene with one of the Federales yet?" he said, mashing his words into a vulgar mess of chicken, cheese, and lettuce.

Ransic recoiled. "No sir, I've been waiting around all morning. Do you know who I should report to?"

Lettuce exploded from the Chief's lips and fell to the floor. "Kid, just stick around for a few hours and go tour the college or something. These blowhards don't want us giving any insight into their crime scene. Do the dog and pony; then sit back and enjoy the trip, man."

It was in that moment that I knew there was no such thing as a real cop. They sprinted in a race to the bottom, each day some black and blue found a new way to crawl up under my skin and die. A real cop will pick up the pieces and assemble a masterpiece. A real cop will compose a glorious symphony on the sides of shell casings. Was I the only real cop who would stand up and do what was right?

"Sir, this is a serial killer who started in L.A shouldn't we do our best to help them find the culprit?"

The Chief laughed. "Sometimes it doesn't work that way. We'll be home solving crimes in no time." As he finished the sentence, and the taco, he turned and began to walk away.

Ransic gave him a quick tap on the shoulder. "Wait, sir, I had a quick question for you if you've got a moment."

Jessup turned back, eyebrow at attention. "What's up?"

"Did you get a chance to read my screenplay? I want a professional eye on it before I run it by a few agencies in town."

"I don't recall you giving me a screenplay, Detective."

"Sure I did. I left it on your desk with an orange sticky note reminding you to read it on the plane if you got a chance."

Jessup pursed his lips and flared his eyes. "That was yours? It had a weird title and the name on it was like Randy Yardstick or something like that."

"Ransic Yarbo, it's my pen name sir."

"That sounds like a Jewish diarrhetic."

The detective frowned in disappointment. "Well, I'd love to hear your thoughts on it when you get a chance. It's neo-noir-hyper-fable with a hard-nosed detective tracking down a serial killer. The twist is that the killer is his own alcoholism and he kills during his black outs. It's a metaphor about the dangers and reality of the disease."

"Don't you think the audience will be upset if the killer is the main character? Isn't that super cheap?"

"It's a metaphor."

"Yes, you've said that."

Ransic smiled. "Besides, there will always be somebody upset when the story reveals who the real killer is. Just look at Scream 2."

Jessup tilted his head. "There was a Scream 2?"

"There was a Scream 4!"

The Chief checked his watched and looked hurriedly back up to his lead detective basking in the myopic glow of a terrible screenplay idea. "I gotta run, kid. Like I said, talk to who you need to talk to and go have some fun." He tossed on a light brown overcoat and headed for the door to get out of the condemned department store.

All trouble can be traced back to the single and unquestionable root of all problems: women. When that dame walks through the door, licking her wounds with cherry red lipstick, you know it's over. Your life is about to flip upside down and there is not a goddamn thing you can do about it.

He heard someone whispering the word "detective" over and over again to his rear. Ransic turned to find himself staring at an attractive young woman, hair done in braided pigtails with small purple bows, calling to him and waving the detective out of the main crime scene area.

She was standing in a doorway, beckoning him closer. As he reached her location, she yawned and extended a friendly hand to introduce herself. "Hi, my name's Chloe and I only have a few minutes."

"You look really familiar, Chloe."

Chloe Freimont rolled her eyes. "Listen to me, Ransic!"

"This is a closed crime scene, who the hell are you?"

She pushed him back against a wall and the two went completely out of view of any of the other cops. "Okay, seriously, shut up. Your boss orchestrated the group of men that attacked the station. That's why he never went in, he wanted Eliot and Alex dead."

He noticed the curious limp in her foot. "That's a serious allegation, one I'm sure you brought evidence to support," he replied without appearing too surprised.

"Jessup isn't who you think he is."

"Who the hell is he, then?"

She paused and whispered into his ear: "Napoleon."

The dame just ruined everything.

CHAPTER EIGHTEEN
Beer Between Conquerors

That Evening
The Frozen Food Warehouse

He looked through the window at the man who had been savagely beaten both mentally and physically over the past few hours; never changing his story; never breaking from the emotional teetering back and forth between annoyance and terrified exhaustion. Alex knew decision-making under the duress of emotion was, without fail, overwhelmingly imperfect. Staring at the poor man no longer handcuffed to the chair, but shackled to the floor, he questioned any decision that could have been made differently. How can one accurately weigh facts, when the threat of being vaporized in a matter of seconds was sitting just a few feet away, eating a pizza bagel.

Richard looked like a hollowed shell, a husk that spit upon the ground whenever his metallic saliva filled with too much blood to disregard. It was time to talk to him man-to-man, face-to-face, and conquering-war-figurehead to conquering-war-figurehead.

Alex walked into the room, heaving the floor-to-ceiling thick metal door as far open as it would go, offering their prisoner a cooling realization that there was still a world out there. He sat down on a stool within breathing distance of Richard and took a fast-food burger from the sack he brought in with him. There was a six-pack of cheap Mexican beers on the ground, dripping with condensation that was drawing Richard's eyes to the floor. His mouth was slightly agape and his breathing deep and wanting. Alex reached down and handed his prisoner a beer.

"Thank you," mumbled Richard in a deflated tone before taking a lingering swig and placing the ice-cold beverage onto a cut on his temple. "That burger for me?"

"It is," Alex smiled and unwrapped the ambrosia he purchased down the road for $1.99 before choosing to add bacon for thirty-nine cents more. He took a breath and began. "We need to talk about—"

Richard held up his index finger to silence the jailer as he ripped off massive chunks of the burger to shovel into his mouth. "Just let me enjoy this for a minute without hating you," he said in the gargled tenor of a mouth filled with half of a burger.

Alex sat in silence, nursing a newly opened beer and daydreaming in the bubbles racing to the top of the bottle. Moments of eerie silence passed in the backroom of the frozen food warehouse. Once upon a time, things were stored there; things that were not reincarnations of crusading Brits.

"My boyfriend must have called every police department from Des Moines to damn Florida by now. I always check in when I'm on business trips." He whispered, brushing his hands and washing down the remaining mustard with a hasty sip of beer. "I need to call him soon."

"I understand."

Richard raised an eyebrow. "You understand like, 'hey, here's your phone, go ahead and call up that six-foot tall glass of frosty awesome,' or 'I understand that you just constructed words in a sentence'?"

"The latter."

"That's cold, bro."

Alex leaned in. "I'm sorry—for what it's worth."

He was greeted with uproarious laughter from a bludgeoned man using a Corona to lessen his numerous points of swelling. "Oh, is that the apology for putting a gun to my forehead?"

"Yes."

"Please don't be alarmed when I refrain from leaping out of this chair to comfort you."

Alexander grimaced. "So why the hard-ass routine?"

"You guys think I'm a serial killer."

"We left the possibility open, yeah."

"Ergo, hard-ass routine." He stopped himself. "You know the thing is, Alex, you and I are more alike than anyone else in your whole outfit. Tables flipped, should I have met Eliot first, and he sent the Freedom Train to go all Guantanamo on your face—this would be the exact same conversation, just flowing in the opposite direction." Richard pounded the rest of the beer and motioned for a second.

Alex acquiesced and popped open a second bottle for his prisoner. There was a nod of appreciation but little more from across the table. He wondered if the conversation would eventually go anywhere.

"So, what happened with Genghis?"

Alex stopped wondering if the conversation would eventually go anywhere. "He's dead."

Richard set his unused napkin aside and returned his attention to Alex. "Well, I know he's dead. A Mongolian gets his head blown off in a Taco Rita—"

"It was a Taco Baron."

"Are you sure?"

Alex smiled. "Yeah, I'm pretty sure," he parlayed through a smug grin.

"I'm just saying: a gunned-down Mongolian on Sunset Boulevard doesn't exactly go unnoticed in Los Angeles. It was all over the news for a week. What the hell happened in there?"

He paused as Richard spoke, carefully considering the events of that evening for the first time since his girlfriend had revealed herself somewhat of a wildcard in this conflict. "My ex-girlfriend, who I did not know was a returner until that night, put a bullet in his head before I could extract exactly which team he was playing for."

Richard raised an eyebrow. "Did she save your life?"

"No." A pause filled the room with its pregnancy. "I saved hers."

"So which side was Genghis on?"

Alex grabbed another beer and popped the top, nursing the Latin brew as he pondered the question. "He came in to kill Chloe—I'm sorry, Joan of Arc. He came in to kill Joan. We fought for a few minutes and I had him talking, and then he was gone."

"When I was King," Richard started with a cold indifference, like the title held no weight or value, "if I was settling a dispute between two people whose allegiances were questionable at best, I'd cut them away like a cancer and wait. I would never mention or act on it; I would just ignore the people and see how they reacted. The one who was earnestly loyal to the kingdom wouldn't notice anything was wrong and would continue going about business as usual. The one who was guilty would notice immediately and spend all their waking energy talking into the ears of my advisors and trying to manipulate the situation."

Alex leaned across the table. "We'll never know what Genghis was up to because he's dead."

"But the other is still alive. Would you say that your ex-girlfriend Chloe has been taking time to talk into your ear, and the ears of those around you?"

He didn't hesitate. "Yes."

Richard smiled and slid a second empty bottle across the table.

"I don't think you're the killer," Alex said abruptly.

"That works out, because I don't think I am either."

"But they do," Alex spoke in a grave manner. "They forget so many things. Since Paul and Marie were attacked, everyone has been focused on this idea of a serial killer trying to pick us off one by one."

"Isn't that happening?" Richard asked with a puzzled look on his face.

"Yes." Alex stood up from the table. "How quickly they forget that Eliot and myself were attacked by ten men, ten of the *same* man, in an LA county lock up. That Harriet was followed and almost murdered at a gas station. There are more than two sides in play here and I want to get behind the curtain."

"Do you believe?" Richard asked softly.

"Do I believe in what?"

"Do you believe that we all came back for a reason?"

Alex slid the second half of his beer over to Richard. "From a high-level perspective, I think there's an odd specificity to the people that returned. It seems too purposeful to be random."

"A mature perspective."

"Having said that," Alex walked to the corner of the table, "with so many of us already dead, I'm having trouble defining that purpose."

"And if we're weighing two sides of the coin like that, then—Oh, I see where you were going with that. It doesn't matter what we think, does it?"

Alex smiled at his prisoner. "Nope."

Richard set his hands flat across the table. "It doesn't matter what we believe if the people trying to kill us believe we all came back for a reason. Does that scare you?"

"That terrifies me." Alex walked to the door, but turned back before crossing the threshold back into the warehouse. "We're at war and we need all the soldiers we can muster. When the time comes, I want you in our corner because you're up against the same danger we are."

"Thank you for believing me."

Alex lowered his head, not wanting to make eye contact. "Richard, if I catch the first hint that you might be working against us, I'll put a bullet through your skull."

"Understood, Alexander."

"I'm not going to leave the room or give you any privacy whatsoever, but I understand you have issues outside of what is happening here. Make no mention of being held against your will or who you really are. Buy yourself some time." Alex slid his cell phone across the metal table and into Richard's hands.

"Call your boyfriend."

CHAPTER NINETEEN
Ink to the Past

That Afternoon
Morrissey Middle School Park

Janey had argued with Alex for going on thirty minutes before Harriet stepped in and offered additional protection. The disagreement stemmed from Alex insisting that Janey take the kids on a well-supervised visit to a nearby park. It was a trip Albert and Richie were both flushed with excitement about; their spirits crushing every time Janey explained it was far too dangerous to spend time outside.

There was a general agreement that the boys needed some time not locked up in an abandoned frozen food warehouse when Albert hooked up Richie to various over –the-counter batteries to see if his young friend could charge an iPad simply by holding it. Richie had also put the community toilet out of commission for two days by flushing an entire roll of paper towels on a dare. In point of fact, it was a "Heisenberg's dare," or the only way that Albert knew how to escalate, in his own words: "scallywagging."

It was only when Harriet stepped forward with a loaded Glock 17 and offered to join in on the babysitting and bodyguarding that Janey agreed to take the boys out for an hour or so.

The two women, sporting a concealed-arsenal fit for a Bourne film, made the boys put on shoes and follow them over to the middle school two short blocks from the warehouse. In the unlikely event that a suspicious looking person got too close to one of the children, it was entirely possible that they would come down with a sudden case of the shot-in-the-faces (from the Latin: "Violentia in Faciem.")

Albert and Richie ran off toward the nearest jungle gym to continue playing out their favorite fictional heroes; Richie chose Batman, naturally, while Albert confused his young pal when he chose to pretend as Beowulf. As fictional crime-fighting team-ups go, one would be hard pressed to find children who put a more diverse duo than Batman and Beowulf.

Richie burst forth from a slide on the periphery of the jungle gym, "Oh no, The Riddler and Gren-nel, Gren—what was it again?"

"Grendel," Albert offered with a helpful smile.

"Oh no, The Riddler and *Grendel* have robbed the supermarket! Come on Bay Wolf! We must stab them together." Richie sped off into a torrent of throwing punches in all directions, imagining quite the fight in the cereal aisle of a supermarket.

Albert followed suit and began speaking, as one would as Beowulf, in alliterative West Saxon quatrain. "Lo! I am the Wielder of Glory. Be wary o' man of Riddles. Grendel's head will be my earned solace. May the All-Father's hand guide us—" he tried his best not to laugh as he finished, "Batman."

The two ran around for a few minutes, trading gruff proclamations to imagined baddies with non-rhyming stanzas of boastful exuberance. Janey was just glad the boys were enjoying themselves and for once not driving everyone crazy back at the warehouse.

She sipped her non-fat mocha and sat down next to Harriet on the bench. "I guess college towns have their advantages."

Harriet continued looking around the park for any suspicious activity. "How so?"

Janey motioned to the vast empty area around the park, "there's no one here for example. Maybe I just worry too much."

"No such thing as worrying too much."

"I suppose in our situation that makes a lot of sense."

Harriet stood up with immediacy, looking out across the playground toward a nearby street.

Janey panicked and popped up as well. "What's the matter? Do you see something?"

"So, what's the deal with you and Alex anyway? You guys ever … " she raised an eyebrow and tilted her head to the side, which somehow implied sex.

"No, we've never whatever-the-hell your head just did. I don't think our relationship is like that. He's like a brother. Did you see something or what? You scared the hell out of me."

Harriet shook her head. "No, I just wanted to scare you into answering the question honestly." Her grin was wry and mischievous. "And Alex is in love with you then I take it?"

Janey took a surprised step back. "In love with *me?* Girl, you trippin'."

"Don't talk like that."

"Yes, ma'am," Janey replied sheepishly.

"In my experience, any time a girl that says some dude is like a brother to them, that means the guy is in love with them. It's like an estrogen-based guilt defense."

The squeals of boyish combat fell a little further into the distance, it sounded like the Riddler was dead.

"He ever come visit you in that small town?" Harriet continued her line of questioning as she looked around and checked to make sure the boys were still within sight lines.

Janey brushed some hair behind her ear. "Yup."

"You guys sleep in the same bed?"

"Yeah, but he's a friend. No big deal."

"When you woke up in the morning, was he already awake but still in bed?"

"Yeah."

"Dude's in love with you."

Janey considered the idea for a moment before surrendering herself back to the coffee at hand. She took a few labored paces away from the inquisition and felt the breeze dance across her face.

The voices of the two boys continued to move further into the distance, battling a rogue's gallery that seemingly had no end.

"You wanna catch up with them?"

Harriet was already in motion, calling out to the boys to come back a little more toward the playground. They crested a hill and couldn't see the boys anywhere, and they were making zero noise, which was something that rarely occurred.

Suddenly, the two women were very worried.

They lashed out in separate directions and began covering as much ground as possible, calling out the names of the two boys who had somehow disappeared in a matter of seconds.

Then they heard it.

Albert let out a scream of terror.

Janey ran as fast as she had in her entire life.

The women ran, guns drawn, to a metal drainage ditch off to the side of one of the hills. Stagnant water dripped on their hair as they made their way into the tube. Inside, they found Albert, standing over a perplexed looking Richie, who did not look harmed or even aware of why Albert screamed in the first place.

"Albert. Why did you scream?" Janey asked in a tone that reminded her far too much of her mother—her *second* mother.

Albert ignored the request, or even the fact that the ladies were there at all, and sat in a comatose stare at Richie's rolled up sleeve.

"Albert … honey." Janey tried again.

"Kid!" Harriet screamed as she checked all the way down into the pipe for a sign that anyone else had been near the kids. She found no such information.

Albert shifted his catatonic gaze back to Janey, his face as white as a laundered sheet. He spoke in a slow, metered pace. "They met in secret. Ignoring heeds and trifling forward." The young boy trailed off.

Janey walked nearer to him, trying not to startle him. "Albert. Okay, Albert I think we're done with the make believe now. I need you to tell me why you screamed."

He ignored her, staring off into nothing and reciting words like they were burned into his memory forever. "The punishment is laid out and the sentence is—" he broke down as Janey wrapped her arms around him. His head resting on her shoulder, he finished what he was saying. "And the sentence is … Beowulf dead." Albert began to cry on her shoulder, he was so terrified he was shaking.

Harriet turned back and fell into a mortified stupor. "Janey."

She ignored her and continued to focus on Albert. "I guess I don't understand. I know we're all scared, but we're all gonna stick together. We'll protect you guys, just stay where we can see you next time, okay? Not everyone has two of the most bad ass chicks on the planet as their personal bodyguards." Janey slowly brushed the back of his hair, whispering everything was going to be okay.

"Janey," Harriet said with more force, having unmoved from where she stopped in the tunnel.

She looked up after the second urging of her friend. "Harry, what? I don't want to alarm them anymore than they already are. What is it?" she finished in an annoyed tone.

Harriet motioned only with her eyes to Richie, standing straight, his face still to the wall of the tunnel and his sleeve partially rolled up.

Janey gently let Albert go and got to her feet, approaching the other side of Richie cautiously. From the look on Harriet's face alone, she could feel shivers of terror ripping through her body.

She rolled Richie's sleeve all the way up and almost vomited in the tunnel. Janey could not believe what she seeing, or how it could possibly have happened since they had been at the park.

Hastily scribbled in permanent marker on Richie's arm, was verbatim what Albert had said aloud to Janey just moments before.

Someone had been there.

Someone had been watching.

And someone just promised to kill Albert as punishment.

CHAPTER TWENTY
This Ain't a Song for the Broken Hearted

Dusk
Backroom of the Frozen Food Warehouse

No silent prayer for the faith departed.

He let the faintest of swears loose into the quiet air as he struggled with the restraints contorting his body into an uncomfortable mess of asymmetry. There wasn't a limb with enough feeling left in it to grasp the pain he was most certainly in.

Yet what bothered Richard, shackled with no evidence, beaten with no trial, was that he couldn't get goddamned Bon Jovi out of his head.

Luck ain't even lucky, gotta make your own breaks.

Eliot was staring at him again. It wasn't the kind of stare where the person doing it had lost him or herself in thought and allowed their eyes to glaze in someone's general direction. No, this was a stare of repulsion and fear—a stare that Richard had seen in the eyes of men before they made grievous errors.

Any of the eight children born from the union between Eleanor of Aquitaine and Henry II were able to spot a look of repulsion or fear in something as simple as passing bread down the dinner table. A family that eats together, Crusades together.

"I appreciate your civil tongue, Eliot, but your eyes betray some scary truths about you. Tell me, would you shoot me in the head if you thought I was the killer?"

Eliot pretended to cough. "I do think you're the killer."

"But then you'd be the killer," he raised a thoughtful eyebrow and turned in response to the muffled arguments leaking through the wall. Janey and Alex had been arguing for some time, interrupted countless time by the sopranic chirps of a scared and confused Richie.

Richard had no doubts that Eliot would not leave the room, nor the door open, nor anyone attempt to enter, lest Richie was protected in a dungeon-like atmosphere in much the same fashion. "What happened to Richie?"

Eliot turned to the side enough to mask the rolling of his eyes. "You don't need to worry about that."

The Lionheart laughed. "Well, I mean, he *is* me, so I should be more concerned about his wellbeing than any of yours. I trust he's getting plenty of fluids and eating enough pizza bagels, yeah?"

"Why do you try this for hours on end? You know I don't really have a sense of humor."

"Gotta say, I noticed that. Did you have one the first time?"

Eliot raised an eyebrow, "what do you think?"

Richard spit upon the ground—his half-hourly ritual of cleaning his mouth of blood and stale saliva. "I think you know now, for fact, that I have nothing to do with this killer you're all going Salem over. What happened at the park?"

The former detective turned his head back to the prisoner, his ears perked forward like Angela Lansbury just before the big reveal. "How did you know they were at the park, Richard?"

A muffled female voice shouted through the wall, "You're the one that told us to go the park in the first place!"

Richard motioned with his head to the wall. "They keep saying the word 'park' and it felt like a clue to me." He waited a moment before finishing with: "how in all God's Hell did you ever catch Al Capone?"

Eliot snickered. "Good police work and due process—and a hell of a lotta luck. I also never turned down the opportunity to be condescended to by a two-bit street thug. Anyone that cocksure will slip up eventually."

"So then you already know what I'm going to say."

"Do I?"

Richard looked up with exhausted eyes and a mouth so dry his words would need a miracle to spill out into the conversation. "Come on, man. I apologize for the Capone comment but I got no leverage in here if you guys don't own up to the obvious."

The man watching him from across the room loosened and removed his tie, placing it gently onto the seat next to him. "If any of the information coming from Albert is to be believed, and your incarceration would appear to make that distinction for us, then, should you be the killer, Richie would make the least likely target."

"Thank you," Richard said with subtle laughter.

"But," the man spoke again, killing the energy in the room. "You accidentally causing a massive atomic explosion withstanding, you are easily the most obvious suspect and will be held until a decision is made."

"But something happened at the park! Just now, while I was here with you!" Richard was screaming with a ferocity he had not felt in generations.

The man acquiesced. "Yes, Richard. Something did happen at the park."

"And I've been in this tiny room, where I couldn't have done anything to Richie at the park. Have you all forgotten that I'm tied to a chair where I've pissed myself numerous times over days and days because you cockbags forget that you're holding a guy here for no reason—I mean, even if I touched the kid, it would apparently cause a massive atomic reaction." Richard choked on the word as he felt his eyes well up. "I'm just a friend of Paul's and my friend is in a coma. I just want to see him." The tears were pouring down his cheeks now, the days of interrogation finally breaking what was left of the second Richard the Lionheart. "I just want to see my friend."

Eliot made no noise and allowed the silence to swim through the room, echoing around the chamber like a silent condemnation.

Richard's eyes arose to see Eliot staring back with the anger of a man about to kill another. "Why are you such an asshole?" He asked with a wounded simmer.

"That was quite the stirring performance, I must say." Eliot dropped his hand down and came back holding a nine-millimeter pistol. He pulled the slide back to chamber a round, his eyes fixed on his target, as the detective had done so many times in his second life. "Should James Cagney find himself a returner, I hope to share stories of the nuance and delivery of this exchange."

Eliot raised the pistol to the forehead of Richard.

"Please," he begged.

"Any final thoughts?" his finger was beginning to squeeze on the trigger.

Richard grimaced. "I'll just leave. Just let me leave and there can't be an accident. I'll go to Mexico. I have a good life and a boyfriend who loves me." He could only yell, "Please!"

Eliot took a deep breath in, his heart pounding in his chest, standing over the man he was about to execute. "No. Because as little as you think of my police work, you'd have to be a moron not to notice I realized you got out of the shackles an hour ago."

He pulled the trigger.

Click.

"And you'd have to be a moron not to realize I removed all the bullets from your gun last night."

Richard lunged from the chair to Eliot, immediately overpowering him and knocking him to the ground. His fist came down into the face of the former detective with ferocity and emotion, each punch making a sound like a slab of brisket carelessly tossed to the counter at a butcher shop.

He stopped the pounding; his murderer subdued.

The blood marched neatly to the drain in the middle of the floor.

Richard stumbled to the shelf next to him, sending a pile of coupons that no one would ever receive spilling to the side. His tears were tracing serpentine ravines down the blood and the grime. "I didn't want to do that, and you know it."

Eliot coughed and rolled over onto his side, facing the man who had fractured the right half of his face. "And why is that?" he managed to grimace; each word as if he was still getting slammed in the face.

"You pulled the trigger, Eliot." He stopped and looked up at the window atop the shelf, near the doorway that he could escape from at any time. "We both know that no one is opening the door to check on us for hours. I wonder if you'll tell them that you volunteered to watch me so you could execute me."

"We both know I won't."

Richard's glance fell from the freedom atop the shelf and back to the wounded detective near the drain. "Then maybe you should have been the one in the chair, Eliot. I grew up with dysfunction, so I know it when I see it. You're all so preoccupied trying to find a killer out there you didn't stop to realize there was one already amongst you."

"I'm not a killer," Eliot spouted off, becoming disoriented from the thunderous pain in his cheek.

A trembling hand reached down into his jeans' pocket and pulled out a single nine-millimeter round. Richard rolled it across the ground to the man struggling to sit up. "Prove it."

The pain was immense, but Eliot grabbed his pistol and pulled the slide back to lock it. The bullet kept slipping from his bloody fingers as he attempted to chamber the round. His head remained lingering toward the floor, but his eyes rose to meet Richard's.

The pistol slid across the ground through the blood and broken tile, stopping at Richard's feet.

He bent down to pick up the peace offering.

"It's *my* life."

Richard fired the round directly into Eliot's chest.

CHAPTER TWENTY-ONE

Sub-Atomic Derivation and First Whiskies

4 Minutes and 38 seconds prior
Warehouse Common Area

It would happen in four minutes and thirty-eight seconds.

Albert Einstein's favorite food in his previous lifetime was handmade pasta utilizing a variety of techniques. His tastes were known to range from spaghetti in a simple tomato sauce to adventurous (for its time) fettuccini drenched in a fresh balsamic. Though the most brilliant physicist of a generation was a German from head to toe, his stomach belonged in Italy.

The thirteen-year-old version was eating off-brand Spaghettios out of a can, unheated, and reading a vintage copy of Nintendo Power from 1989 he found in a drawer in the locker room. Mega Man II was on the cover and he marveled over the eight-bit pixilated graphics as if it were some post-modern take on animating a Mondrian painting.

Janey and Alex were fighting again, trading blows about responsibility in the face of substantial turmoil. Albert was young but still keen on Janey's propensity to agree to something and blaming Alex for "forcing" the decision at the moment of argument impact. Conversely, he noted that Alex would continually make sarcastic remarks while other people were attempting to discuss an issue. This generally proceeded the moment he would casually insist they were being passive-aggressive and unreasonable.

It would happen in four minutes and seventeen seconds.

Albert hoped they would engage in intercourse at their earliest possible convenience so the aggravatingly numerous arguments would subside. In their place, awkward glances bathed in silence would volley about the warehouse and give them a bit of peace and quiet.

John Quincy sat down across the table from Albert and grimaced at the sight of the canned pasta rings. "Dear god, Albert, how can you eat that garbage? Pasta is not supposed to come in the shape of a ring."

The young boy did not look up from his magazine. "Hogwash, lots of pasta comes in ring form. Penne. Rigatoni. Macaroni. Cartwheels. Tortellini. Manicotti—"

"Okay," he laughed. "You've shown me up, but the original point still stands."

Albert smiled, still without looking up. "I'm thirteen. I have under-developed tastes and no energy for an attempt to acquire them. My body wants carbs? I give it some carbs." He continued the conversation without a beat between topics. "Did you know you have to use the Bubble Gun to defeat Dr. Wily in Mega Man II?"

"Is Dr. Wily a returner?"

The young man's eyebrow went up, "I'm inclined to say no on the grounds of being fictional, but he does seem to return in every one of the games…"

Quincy attempted to muffle his confusion, but Albert was aware he knew absolutely nothing about what the boy was talking about. "Hey kid, do you know anything about Whiskey?"

"No, sir."

"Then I think we're at an impasse."

It would happen in three minutes and forty-five seconds.

Albert looked up at Janey and Alex, still arguing, still doing it in front of Richie. "You should take Richie downstairs," Albert said without breaking his gaze.

Quincy grabbed for a bottle of whiskey, nestled precariously close to the bags of cereal that were carelessly rolled up on the table; he poured a double and shot back a stare at the young man. "We can't keep him locked in there forever, you know. Can't keep locking up the wee one every time somebody needs to go in there, either."

"I understand your objections, Mr. Adams." He did not look up and chose to read on about Super Contra.

A large percentage of the whiskey had disappeared before the glass landed back on the table. "I'll imagine a world where you said that politely. Perhaps engendering your comments with an eagerness to educate us *common*-folk with you dynamic science-brains."

Albert tossed the magazine aside with a laugh. "Point taken. I made no effort to be rude, not on purpose. My brain lately—I mean, there's a lifetime of knowledge up there and my mind is too young to grasp it." He took a moment, scraping the bottom of the can for excess pasta. "Feels like a prison not knowing what I already know."

"I remember the feeling. The awkward teenage years."

The young genius smiled again, enjoying a conversation with someone other than a nine-year-old. "So what did you want to know?"

It would happen in three minutes and twenty-two seconds.

The older man finished the glass of whiskey and slid it to the side. "Start with the bit about how duplicate returners touching causes a nuclear explosion."

"It's an atomic explosion."

Quincy gave a slow whiskey-blink and raised an eyebrow. "Is there a difference?"

Albert poured his friend another double. "I understand the confusion. Atomic bombs use nuclear fission to, you know, go boom. The danger in Richie and Richard coming in contact is potentially a million times more unstable."

"Pretty sure you should make that a triple, kid."

He made it a triple. "I'm not sure anyone really understands how dangerous keeping these guys in the building really is."

"Innocent or not, seems like we should just put a bullet in Richard's head. Needs of the many, and such and such."

The boy lowered his voice and leaned closer. "If you believe that than we should put a bullet in both their heads and burn their bodies on opposite sides of the Pacific."

Quincy's eyes widened, knowing what was just said was an abstract solution that also happened to be the most logical. "How does it work?"

"It's all theory, which is why I think no one is really taking me seriously. Imagine being told to drive a car from Ohio to Florida. There's a nuclear bomb in the trunk, and it will go off if you get in a wreck. Now, put the best driver in the whole world behind the wheel of the car and try to predict a result."

"You can't."

"Precisely. There's no accounting for other drivers, drunk drivers, hell, somebody could try to drive into your car on purpose." Albert looked across at the empty glass. "You should slow down."

Quincy poured another triple. "But why does the reaction happen? You know, 'in theory?'"

"It's all unprecedented and a complete mystery. I mean, it could all be nothing, but we should take all necessary precautions. Common table physics tells us that we cannot, one, create matter, and two, occupy the same space."

It would happen in two minutes and three seconds.

"And how is either of those happening?"

Albert took a giant swig of the whiskey and set the glass back before a stunned Quincy. "Because—" the boy started coughing. "Oh god, that's horrible. Point is, we don't know why any of us have returned or why multiple versions of varying ages have returned. In theory, Richard and Richie's matter, not *created* matter, but theoretically *duplicated* matter, would simply pass through itself." The boy made an explosion shape with his hand and puffed out his cheeks."

"You're saying that Eliot is an idiot."

"No, I'm not saying that." He looked back at Quincy with strained eyes. "I'm saying that a murderer on the loose is literally an acceptable side effect provided, whoever it is, is not—" Albert was cut off.

"He's not a duplicate of any of us," finished Quincy.

"Exactly. It's the guy driving into your car on purpose scenario."

Quincy rubbed his forehead, his already drunken eyes scanning the room and inheriting a sobriety of knowledge. "We have to kill Richard."

"From a moral imperative, we don't have any choice in this."

Albert took another sip of the whiskey, trying to take it slow and use it to dull all emotion in the conversation.

It would happen in one minute and twelve seconds.

"What about the four Janeys?"

The boy's eyes turned a slight pink as he looked over at his friend. "Moral imperative is to shoot her—shoot ourselves—shoot anyone we believe to be a returner to wipe them off the face of the planet. There might be another of *any* of us walking around out there. There could be another John Quincy Adams two blocks down the road!"

"You're kinda depressing, you know that?"

Albert wiped a tear and smiled, "funny, that's what they all say about you."

"Well, I guess we've disproven the 'everything happens for a reason' theory. To be fair, I suggested the killing myself scenario to Harry, like, four times already."

"Everything *absolutely* happens for a reason. But only mankind is so arrogant to believe a 'reason' implies some kind of net-positive or divine intervention." Albert said, noticing the warehouse had cleared out of everyone but them.

It would happen in thirty-one seconds.

Quincy decided the best course of action at that point was to begin drinking directly from the bottle. "You don't think it's possible—and I can't believe I'm the one on this side of the argument—but, you don't think it's possible that we were all brought back to save the world or something?"

Albert grabbed the bottle and took a drink before sliding it back into Quincy's drunken palm. "John, I'm saying that it's possible someone brought us back to *destroy* the world!"

It happened.

The two drunken conversationalists spun in reaction to the loud gunshot they heard emanating from the backroom of the storage warehouse. Albert stumbled off the bench first, but got to his footing before Quincy could even stand up from the table. The boy ran with a shaky stride across the long concrete expanse of the warehouse.

Upon reaching the door to the backroom, he took a long pause; suddenly clear headed enough to know that opening the door was the least intelligent move.

Quincy appeared behind, out of breath and grasping for the door handle.

"Don't," Albert ordered.

"What?"

Albert looked up at his older but equally drunken companion. "I moved the watch order around."

Quincy's eyes narrowed. "Why?" he asked with a deliberate slowness.

"Because I knew Eliot would kill Richard."

"I'll admit that answer would have surprised me twenty minutes ago."

Quincy ushered Albert out of the way and pulled back the door, a rush of air hitting them in the face immediately.

The window above one of the shelves was open, providing the surprising flow of air, as the two glanced down in horror at the sight of Eliot lying motionless against a cabinet, surrounded by blood flowing quietly into the drain.

The leg shackles were collected and spiraled neatly in the metal chair.

CHAPTER TWENTY-TWO
Missed Calls

During the Previous Five Minutes
Streets of Kansas City

Her fingers fumbled through the litany of pseudonyms scattered across her phone directory—none of which listed actual names or even key descriptors. What had she listed Alex's new phone under?

Chloe looked over her shoulder, the familiar three gentlemen in various states of beard making no ruse of their pursuit. There was a phoned in attempt to hide that they were identical human beings, dying and trimming their makeshift facial hair and assembling beach hats into a trio of hipster assassins.

She joked quietly to herself, changing voices with each aspect of the conversation. "Oh, what do you do for a living?"

Chloe replied to herself in a deeper tone, "oh, I'm a clone of myself and I kill people for a living," she paused. "You probably haven't heard of it."

"Archimedes!" she screamed out having remembered what she was searching for.

She had listed Alex Heton under the name Archimedes at a time she believed him to be of great intellect. Lately: not so much. She put the phone call in motion and checked once more over her shoulder at the three men who appeared to have stolen their look from late-80's era Steve Guttenberg.

It rang.

One of the men ducked into a nearby alley, his eyes fixed firmly on her location.

It rang again.

The one with the five-o-clock shadow adjusted his sunglasses and whispered something into a cufflink before reaching into his jacket pocket. "People actually whisper into cufflinks?" she said softly to herself.

It rang again.

The third sharply dressed assassin was nursing a smoothie and taking a casual stroll straight toward her. Was he whistling?

It rang once more and a click was heard on the other end of the line.

"Alex—Jesus! Alex, it's me and I got a small army of guys on my tra—"

She stopped in silence as she was greeted with: "you have reached Alex Heton and I either can't get to my phone at the moment or I probably just sent you straight to voicemail when I saw who was calling." The familiar voicemail played in her ear as she ran in fear for her life. "But for real, drop some knowledge on me."

Chloe always hated that message when they were dating—or *fake* dating—it was fuzzy what state of dating they went through. There was some amount of non-fictional dating but certain information was concealed for personal gain. Given that neither had revealed their true identity to the other, Chloe pretended to be a different personality-type entirely while Alex treated her like a piece of property, it was a rocky foundation to build a relationship on.

She waited for the beep as she ducked into a Vietnamese Laundromat. The tone played in her sweaty ear through matted hair. "Alex, it's Chloe. I'm in trouble." Her eyes darted to the entrance where two had just entered and divided up to different sides of the room. "I screwed up bad. Dude, I need your help and I need it right now. Call me back as fast as you can." Chloe ducked behind a row of washers and pulled out her Glock-17—the slide was cobalt blue and made a strange long indigo reflection across the floor.

There was no way to get a good look at where the men were without sticking her head up. She hung up the phone and continued moving down the row to the corner of the shop. Her eyes were fixed toward the storefront but her index finger felt down the side of her cell phone to find the switch from vibrate to ringtone. It snapped over and Chloe slid it across the ground two rows over.

She wiped the sweat from her brow and leaned against a washing machine. "Alex, dude, you gotta call, man," she whispered to herself in quiet prayer. "Come on, Heton, come on."

Chloe could hear the sockless-feet tapping across the tile in boat shoes. She chambered a bullet and closed her eyes in an attempt to control the volume of her breathing.

Across the room, a Nina Simone song burst forth from a phone vibrating on the tile. *Alex had gotten the message.* She began to count the number of cautious steps it would take to reach the phone.

One.

Two.

Three.

Four.

Five.

Chloe popped up and fired two rounds in the direction of the phone, striking the first man in the cheek and sending him spiraling to the ground, blood splaying out onto confused laundry patrons.

Everyone else in the shop began to scream and run for the door.

The second man in the shop was audibly charging across the Laundromat to her location.

Chloe pushed down into the prone position along the ground, getting a solid vantage on the row of washers that lined the ceiling on the path the man was taking to her location.

The entire row of washers was in use, spinning untold gallons of water, soap, and socks around and around.

The gun steadied in her grip, lining up the first shot. A sound chimed in the background, signaling that she had just received a text message.

She held her breath and fired seven times in rapid succession, each bullet striking the round glass that contained the chaos of spinning laundry. Water and soap exploded out into the aisle and the man took a load in the face while his feet struggled to keep their grip amongst the soapy confusion.

Chloe extended her arm, holding the pistol out, and took a moment. The second gunman slid across the soapy floor and into view. She fired twice into his skull.

Two down.

Struggling to stand up on the floor, she scanned for the third assailant.

The phone alerted her once more to the awaiting text message, which she ignored as she tried to get a bead on the last man following her.

A knife slid across Chloe's throat, cutting a millimeter deep so there would be no confusion as to who controlled the situation.

"There's a service entrance—for future reference," a deep voice mumbled from behind her, his beard itching the skin behind her ear.

"Good to know," she replied. Chloe slammed her feet onto the side of the closest washing machine and kicked back as hard as she could.

The two slid backward across the soap and tumbled apart upon hitting the ground. The cut across her neck was dripping blood down the front of her shirt and down into the soap and water. Her eyes rose to see the third man lunging at her, knife in hand.

Chloe swung open the nearest washer-door, putting it squarely into the man's face, and shattering on impact. She smiled and grabbed for his cobalt-plated Glock.

The last man felt across his face at the numerous deep cuts sustained from the glass. His eyes rose to find Chloe pointing a gun at his chest with one hand and holding her throat with the other.

"I won't tell you a damn thing," he scolded with menace.

"Well, we both know I'm going to shoot you either way." She smiled in a way that would make a thousand men seek refuge.

His tune changed. "But I have information you need."

"But you just told me you wouldn't give it to me. Torture is *slow* and the police are already on their way. Plus, you cut my throat so I'm just going to shoot you in the head, okay?"

The man's eyebrows shot for the sky. "No! No, not okay!"

"Answer two questions, *to my liking*, and I'll let you live."

He nodded, "deal."

"That was the first thing."

"There's a second thing?" the third gunman asked with exasperation.

"There's a second thing."

"What is it?"

The gun kept perfectly trained on his center mass as she knelt down to her would-be attacker. "You have to get these bodies out of here and disposed of where no police will ever find them."

"They don't have fingerprints and neither one of them has a single dental record." He blurted, as if some kind of peace offering.

"Good to know, but you still have to do it."

He nodded as she waited patiently for confirmation.

"Why are you trying to kill the returners?"

The man shook his head and faked a laugh. "We aren't trying to kill the returners."

Chloe scoffed, "I think lying at this point—"

He cut her off. "We are trying to kill *you*, Joan of Arc. There were, of course, two of you mucking about, but you saw to eliminating half of the problem."

She could feel herself losing restraint and housing remarkable anger toward the man bleeding into the soapy water. "Bullshit! Why did you attack Eliot and Alex in the prison?" she yelled back, keeping an eye out for any sign of the police.

"Is that your second question?"

"No."

The man rubbed his cuts and tried to dab some of the blood away with his soaked shirt. "I would hurry then."

A lumbered pause filled the air.

"Are you a returner?"

"No."

"Then what are you?"

The third gunman rolled onto his side, grabbed the first body, and began to drag it to the back room. "Something entirely different, ma'am. And that was three questions"

Chloe ran over to her phone and scooped it from the strange mixture of fluids swirling together on the faded tile of the Laundromat. She ran for the back door and out into the fresh Kansas air.

The phone had one missed called from Alex Heton and two text messages: also from Alex Heton.

She read them as she sped down the street.

If I am going to trust you, you will have to answer one question.

Chloe read the second text message and froze in place. Without thinking, she ran back into the Laundromat and to the second yet unmoved body.

She looked over and saw the third gunman freeze in place when he re-entered the room and saw Chloe taking a photograph of the first dead gunman. Once she had a solid and clear photo, she ran back out of the shop and into a maze of alleys.

Once there was a safe distance between Chloe and the crime scene, she pulled the phone back out and again read the second text message.

Why did you shoot the manager at the taco place?

Chloe attached the photo to a new message and typed out:

Look familiar? <3

CHAPTER TWENTY-THREE
The Moral Imperative

Right After

Backroom of the Frozen Food Warehouse

Alex burst through the door first. Despite his reservations to literally every single one of them, Janey, John, Harriet, an inebriated Albert, and Richie followed him in shortly. They froze in a harmony of disbelief as they stared across the room at the broken and bloody mess that Richard had made of Eliot—an Eliot who was very much alive and in need of medical attention, but curiously not from a gunshot wound.

"It wassa 'lank," the injured detective pushed through the pain in a clever avoidance of hard consonants that would move his jaw. "'Ee's gone. Outh the winnow," he trailed off and did his stalwart damndest not to pass out.

Alex ran over to his friend and turned with immediacy to Janey when he saw how badly the former detective's face was bludgeoned. "Grab the medical kit and do what you can."

"He needs a hospital," she objected.

Eliot hobbled to his feet, a meek shell of the hardnosed detective that had all seen hours previous. "No 'ospi'alls. Too risky."

"Eliot," Janie clamored.

He raised a hand to stall her objections, "is schust my cheekbone. Sew me up."

Albert stepped into group in a far more aggressive demeanor than they were used to seeing from him (though, they were probably also not used to seeing him holding a half-empty bottle of whisky.) "Uh, can we go back to how Richard escaped after firing a blank?"

"Are you drunk?" Harriet yelled with exasperation as she ran to the thirteen-year-old teetering in the center of the conversation.

The young genius nodded enthusiastically through squinted eyes. "In John's defense—" he began to explain, but Harriet already had John Quincy Adams in a headlock muttering an eclectic assortment of injuries she would inflict upon the man. "I was gonna say in John's defense we were discussing that we're all probably gonna die anyway, so, drink up—uh, for science!"

He threw up on the floor.

Alex put his arm under Eliot's shoulder, much to the lawman's dismay, and began walking him out of the room. "We are going into lockdown."

Janey stepped forward, defiantly blocking his path. "Slow down, Alex. We held a man against his will, for days—beat him for answers he didn't have. And I'm not sure if you've noticed but there's not a lot more locked down we can go here," she trailed off.

"I know," he backed off. "No one leaves, is that understood?"

The room maintained an uneasy silence, pins heard dropping the world over.

"I'm going after him. Anyone that isn't thirteen or under is welcome to come with," Harriet spoke, pulling the rounds out of her pistol to count them. "That man is too dangerous to—"

"Too dangerous?" Janey was mystified at the conversation before her. "Is anyone going to take a second to realize we're the dangerous ones?"

John Quincy smiled, "the thought had occurred to," he hiccupped, "me."

"I think your say went out the window when you decided to get drunk with a child in the middle of the afternoon."

Albert smashed the bottle of whiskey on the ground in the middle of the bickering circle. "Okay! Yes, I am drunk and I understand the follies of alcohol quite wonderfully. Now everyone shut the hell up for a moment so I may speak." He leaned over on a nearby work sink and filled up a Styrofoam cup with water. "After I drink water though, hang on."

"Albert, this is an adult situation, why don't you take Richie into the other room?" Alex spoke more softly than usual.

The inebriated young man choked on laughter. "Okay, that's it, Alex. While I appreciate that your arrogant condescension is oftentimes a source of much laughter among the group, your understanding of this situation is not as strong as my own."

Alex shut up.

The boy continued. "The reason I am drunk is because I had a realization while sitting with John about what is happening to all of us. I switched the watch schedule because I knew that Eliot would try to kill Richard if given the right opportunity—which I provided him."

All eyes shot to Eliot and his eyes lowered to the floor.

"But before we all start arguing about that, he was doing the right thing. Keeping two Richard's in the same building was just about the dumbest move possible considering the risks, however remote, by keeping him locked up here."

"Given the events in the park, can't we safely assume he isn't the killer?" Janey asked.

"Logically, sure. And despite the death threat against me, hence more drinking, I'm not sure it's the most relevant question to be asking."

She steadied him, setting both arms on the boy's shoulders. "What is the question then?"

Albert looked longingly at the floor, "I really shouldn't have smashed the whisky. You're all going to want it in a moment." He made sure everyone was paying crystalline attention. "Okay, it's obvious that the most important question is why did we all return? Narcissism would have us believe that we all came back for some higher purpose."

Janey squeezed on his shoulders in a joking fashion, "I might call it empathy."

"Sure, call it empathy. The crux of the issue is we are scientifically impossible to exist. If multiple versions cross paths, the results are catastrophic, in theory anyway."

Harriet piped back up, "Right, so I should hunt him down." Again, she turned for the door.

"That's an option, but given the stakes the most logical move is to shoot both Janey and Richie right here and now, given we know there's multiple version of both."

The room fell silent.

"Don't shoot me. You're my friend." Richie mumbled, his feelings obviously hurt.

"I don't intend to, Richie. You're my Batman, forever and ever," Albert smiled back at the younger boy.

"This is most preposterous conversation I've ever seen," Alex finally spoke up, sounding rightly irritated.

"I agree. Even with the power of minds in this room, we simply don't have the capacity to consider the correct moral imperative. Killer on the loose not withstanding, as I'm sure we can all agree that at some point we should find out who that is and kill them." Albert leaned on Janey; she tugged on the back of his hair to let him know she was there. "I'm going to put this in a different way, in this lifetime it was my first experience with an impossible moral imperative, but I apologize in advance for the obtuse nature of the story."

John smiled, "You're just about the most interesting drunk I've ever seen."

Albert ignored the strange compliment and continued, "So, when I was younger, probably around eight or nine in this lifetime, my parents took me to a Southern Baptist Sunday School where the pastor of the congregation was teaching. I think his intent was to be comforting to us, but he was teaching about why bad things happen and that, sometimes children die." He gave Richie a reassuring nod that he was not talking about his friend. "In his teachings he was explaining that if a baby dies, it automatically goes to heaven because it never had a chance to sin."

Harriet holstered her gun and turned back to Albert, now giving him her full attention.

"My first reaction, even as a younger boy, was to ask him what the age limit was before a sin counted. He danced around the issue for a few moments before I flat out asked him, in full view of numerous parents and children, if he *truly* believed what he was saying."

"What did 'e say?" Eliot whispered through his closed jaw.

"He doubled down in front of everyone that what he was saying was the truth, that God's love was so vast that an innocent child would be welcomed into the arms of the Lord." Albert let out a sigh, "So I stood up and told him to go murder every baby in every hospital he could."

The room filled with audible gasps.

Albert chuckled, "Yeah, the reaction in the Sunday School room sounded kinda like that too. A human being simply does not have the cognitive depth to pretend to understand issues of universal magnitude. Inarguably, any duplicate people should be taken out of the equation—and yet everyone in this room knows we can't."

"I need to sit down," Alex said. "So, what do you think we should do, kid?"

He turned to Harriet and smiled, "Go with your gut."

Eliot stood up off Alex's shoulder and hobbled across the room to where Harriet was standing. "I'm going with her."

"Do you think he's the one trying to kill us?"

The detective stared coolly back into Alexander's eyes. "I don' think we 'ave any evidence to sugges' that any lawn'er, no?"

"So what happens when you catch up with him?"

Eliot paused for a moment. "If ih's down to Rishie or him—I dunno."

Albert smiled. "The smartest possible answer right now is 'I don't know'."

Alex crossed the room to where Janey was propping Albert up near the sink and dropped to one knee. He gave him a big hug around the shoulders. "I know you've been through a lot—sometimes I forget that you're the smartest person in the room and not just a kid."

"Sometimes I forget that too. He killed my parents, Alex. When I lay down at night, I see their faces," he sniffled. "I said all the stuff that needed to be said but the only thing I care about is finding the person who killed all those people at my party and putting them down." He pulled out of the embrace and looked Alex square in the eyes. "He killed everyone I loved in this lifetime."

Alex looked around the room. Harriet was checking ammo with Eliot on a nearby shelf. Richie was sitting next to John and having a thumb war. Janey was forcing a smile just above the two of them.

He turned back to Albert, a boy of remarkable intellect.

"We'll get him. I promise you that."

CHAPTER TWENTY-FOUR
Edgewater

Three Days Later
Downtown Seattle, Washington

Harriet looked up at the Space Needle in wonder. It was a monument she had not seen up close in this lifetime and which did not exist in her first journey through the United States.

"Kinda thought it would be smaller," she laughed, her head cocked slightly to the side.

Eliot handed her a paper cup filled with fresh roasted coffee and smiled as far as his jaw would allow. "You're the first woman in the history of the world to have ever said that."

"Sounds like your cheek is healing pretty nicely in such a short time. I can understand what you're saying again!"

He rubbed the bandage covering the wound on his cheek, "still hurts like hell, though."

She put her arm under his, cowering a bit in the slightly chilly overcast of Seattle in the autumn. "Are you thinking what I'm thinking, Eliot?"

Her arm so alarmingly entering his personal space took the former detective aback, but he played it quiet and led her down closer to the peer. "I was thinking how unsurprising it is that Richard chose to live in Seattle, the vegan capital of my patience."

"Two jokes in as many minutes! Ladies and gentlemen, Eliot's stick-from-ass removal procedure was all we could have hoped for! The surgeons," she feigned a moment where she held back tears. "The surgeons just did God's work on this one."

"Yuck it up, Missy." He glared. "I know where you live."

"In a building that used to ship two hundred thousand boxes of fish sticks a day? It's not hard to find, it says 'Fish Sticks' on the front of it. If you Google the words 'fish sticks,' it's the fifteenth result."

He laughed for a moment before grabbing his cheek from the pain. "I suppose it's not the grandest hideout in the world."

"Far from it, Eliot Ness." Harriet took in the fresh Washington air and slid her arm further under his elbow.

They walked down a hilly street toward pier sixty-seven and looked out onto the bay, a maze of joggers, and joggers pushing children in tiny vehicular teepees, surrounded them on all sides.

"So, where are we meeting this cop friend of yours?"

Eliot grimaced at the notion. "I wouldn't exactly call him a friend. We worked together, but we didn't get along so well."

"You made him look incompetent every chance you got didn't you?"

His cheeks flushed a bright pink. "I would say that sums up my relationship with Detective Ransic, yes."

"Can I ask you the real question?" Harriet said in a lower tone, looking across to the children playing in front of the aquarium on the waterfront.

"You may."

"Ignoring the *how* for a moment, *why* did he have a blank? Why would he go out of his way to prove that he had time to write on Richie in the park?"

"I knew you were going to ask me about that."

"How could I not? We just took a red eye from Kansas to Washington to track him down."

Eliot took a long and knowing sip of coffee. "Because he knew the way to prove to me that he's not who we think he is."

She raised an eyebrow. "Which was?"

"I pulled the trigger, Harriet. I looked him right in the eyes and pulled the trigger—and he knew I was going to."

"I don't—"

"A guilty man will always run. A guiltless man will go to incredible lengths to prove his innocence. He could have run away at any time. He probably could have killed any one of us, and if Albert's come-to-Jesus moment three days ago is to be believed, writing on Richie would have blown Kansas sky high."

They continued walking down the damp Seattle sidewalk, past parked cars and tiny restaurants. The conversation continued to decipher what information they had and if the chaos that surrounded them would ever amount to any sense.

"Is this the place?" Harriet asked as she stared up at the hotel on the bay called *The Edgewater.*

Eliot smiled at the familiar landmark, taking in the surrounding salty air. "Indeed, it is. This is my favorite hotel in the United States—there's a Beatles suite if you reserve far enough ahead of time. The band actually stayed in there!"

"Do you need a moment?"

"No, thank you, I'm quite alright. Ransic is inside and we shouldn't keep him waiting."

He opened the door for her, like a gentleman, and followed her into the lodge-like lobby, complete with the head of a buck adorning the wall behind the check-in counter.

Detective Julius Ransic was sitting in a high-back chair and patiently flipping through an issue of *Esquire.* He looked up and saw the two approaching from across the way. As Harriet came within earshot, he jumped to his feet to introduce himself. "The name is Julius, madam. Pleased to make your acquaintance."

She extended her hand, expecting a simple handshake, but Ransic took a knee and gave her a lingering kiss on the back of her wrist. "So, how are you enjoying Seattle?" Harriet asked with a tiny of confusion.

"I would move to this part of the world if I could—I mean, I wish we were here under different circumstances." Ransic had not stopped smiling at Harriet since she came into the room.

Eliot took a step forward into the conversation. "Did you get what I asked for?"

Ransic rolled his eyes and turned to the man he used to work with. "For starters, I hate you and die. Secondly, yes, I found out who Richard is dating and have a name and an address."

"Can we have it, please?"

The response was an eye roll. "Can we just take a minute to answer some of my questions please?"

The eye roll reciprocated with a sigh. "What questions, Ransic?"

"I got dragged to Kansas to aid the FBI in a murder case that matched up with the open cases we have in Los Angeles, cases you helped us investigate."

"So?"

Ransic poked Eliot in the sternum in a show of misplaced authority. "Don't play stupid, Stack. I know you were in Lawrence when those two people were attacked in the department store."

"There was a stack of what now?" Harriet asked, confused.

"I went by Bob Stack when I was a police," he leaned over and whispered into her arm.

Her eyes swelled. "You told people your name was Robert Stack?" Harriet scoffed and shook her head in disgust. "No one ever figured that out?"

Ransic looked back and forth between them. "Are you talking about the guy from *Unsolved Mysteries?* Wait, your name's not actually Bob?"

Eliot shared a long glance with Harriet for blurting out the information in such a reckless manner. He turned back to Ransic and did his best to feign a smile. "No, my name is actually Eliot—it's a long story. That address?"

Detective Ransic took a step back and stared at the floor for a prolonged moment. "Okay, this is all getting just a bit too weird."

"Which part?"

His gaze came back up. "Chloe, at least she said her name was Chloe—"

"It's Joan," Harriet cut him off.

Eliot punched her in the arm in a playful manner. "Would you stop helping now, please?" He walked Ransic away to a corner. "What did Chloe tell you exactly? Anything weird?"

"Like what? She mentioned an Eliot being in the police station with that Alex kid and I didn't even think about the fact she was talking about you. You, Chloe, Jessup—all using fake names at murder scenes, it's kinda suspicious."

"What did you say about Jessup?" Eliot asked, suddenly alarmed.

Ransic leaned against the canvas of a painting in the lobby. "That Chloe chick said that he was lying about who he was too. He's been acting really weird since you left."

Eliot grabbed the detective around the shoulders and secured his undivided eye contact. "Julius. Who did she say that Jessup was?"

"You've never called me Julius before."

"I swear to god, I will punch you through this wall."

"Holy shit, Bob, er, Eliot, whoever the hell you are—calm down, man. She said he was "Napoleon," which I think means he's like him or something."

Eliot looked over to where they had left Harriet, his eyes wide with surprise, and turned back to Ransic. "I need that address now."

The detective pushed Eliot with considerable force into the opposite wall of the hallway. "I have half a mind to arrest you on any number of suspicious charges right here and now. How do I know you're not a murderer? You lied about everything else."

He straightened his coat and pulled his body off the wall. "I can prove to you right now, beyond a shadow of a doubt, that I am not a murderer."

Ransic backed off a few paces. "And how are you going to do that?"

"Because if I were a cold-blooded murderer, I would have killed you already you feckless child."

The detective dwelled on that for a moment before nodding. "Yeah, that makes sense."

"Name and address, *please*, Julius."

Ransic reached into his jacket pocket and pulled out a piece of notebook paper. "The boyfriend of your suspect is named Francis Martel, he lives in a loft ten blocks away near that pinball bar on Second Avenue. I think it's called Shorty's." He handed over the piece of paper with some hesitancy.

Eliot grabbed it and extended his hand for a shake. "Thank you."

"You're welcome."

"Stay away from Jessup, request a transfer—do whatever you can to get away from him." Eliot said with a sudden gravitas.

He turned and walked sharply away from Detective Ransic and put his arm under Harriet's and led her toward the door.

"What happened? Did you get the address?"

"Yes, but we have a much larger problem, Harriet."

She returned the sentiment with a puzzled look. "How large of a problem?"

Eliot took a moment, realizing what he had just said. "Actually, our new problem is very short."

CHAPTER TWENTY-FIVE
Francis Martel

17 Minutes and 8 Blocks Later
Downtown Seattle, Washington

"Are you married, Eliot?"

He straightened his tie and zipped up his dark leather jacket, buying time with menial activity. "I am not, married, no."

"Divorced?" Harriet asked with wide eyes.

"Is this your idea of small talk?"

"We still got a couple more blocks to go. I wanted to know if there was a Missus Eliot Ness, once upon a time."

The former detective stopped and turned to her with a sudden flare of anger, clearly a touchy subject. "There were three former Missus Eliot Ness's if you must know, but to clarify, there were also two former Missus Bob Stack's—I've been married five times in two lifetimes and I've decided to get off the train before I'm the new Larry King."

Harriet touched his arm with a friendly rub. "I meant no offense."

"Well," he started and turned to walk away, "you made offense."

The two walked the rest of the way in silence, making vague grunted affirmations whenever they needed to agree on the direction to go in.

Eliot and Harriet were winded after walking the ten blocks from the hotel to an older building that had seen many renovations in the last few years. They stared up at the fourth floor, the boyfriend's place.

"If he's there," she started, swallowing hard before knowing how to finish that sentence. "Eliot, are you going to shoot him?"

"I'm sorry I was short with you, earlier."

She pulled her hood up over her head and looked back at Eliot with a blistering candor. "Over that. Are you going to shoot him is what I asked you."

He stared up at the window. "Do we have a choice?"

"There's always a choice."

"Spare me the hippie-free-love." He grasped behind to the gun tucked into his belt, reassuring it was always within a moment's reach. "Any double is a danger."

"What isn't a danger?" She began in a heated frustration. "Crossing the street is dangerous!"

"Yeah, but when you cross the street, if you get hit by a car, it doesn't cause a thermonuclear explosion!"

"A *catastrophic-fission* reaction," Harriet corrected.

"I don't know if you heard, I was never good with science in school."

She checked for her firearm as well, gripping the handle as she stared back at Eliot. "I don't know if you heard, but I wasn't allowed to go to school my first time."

"Then I commend you on being a fast learner."

"You, ass. Let's head inside." She led the way, walking up the steps and opening the door to the large foyer. It was quiet in the lobby: a room decorated with a mixed smattering of rustic furniture and modern art pieces. "Yup. Gay men definitely live here," she whispered so low that only she could hear and then laughed.

"Let's take the stairs, okay?"

"After you," she motioned to a door to the stairway off to one side of the lobby.

They moved up the stairs in silence, checking every floor for any suspicious activity. The two arrived on the fourth floor landing and slowly crept through the doorway. Harriet began walking down the hallway past all matter of strange welcome mats adorning the area in front of numerous doors. They whispered back and forth about the insanity of some of the phrasing on the mats.

"That last one said, 'A bear in the bush, is worth ten in the back.' I'm at a loss for what that even means," Harriet whispered with a scattered giggle.

Eliot eyes were wide at some of the subject matter on display in the hallway. "What's a twink?"

"I'll tell you when you're older. What did you he say the number was again?"

"Uh, four twenty two," he whispered as he removed his weapon from the back of his pants.

Harriet and Eliot took both sides of the door marked '422' and listened ear-to-door for any sign of movement.

"I don't hear anything," he said.

She shook her head back at him, affirming that there was nothing happening on the other side of the door. "You can kick in a door, right?"

Eliot tilted his head and scrunched his face with annoyance. "Can I kick in a door? Lady, please." He took a step back and held for a moment. His leg came forward with incredible force and shattered the wood around the deadbolt on impact. Like a gentleman, he motioned for the lady to enter first (not thinking about the situation, clearly.)

Harriet pushed in through the front door and immediately sensed that something was amiss within the apartment. "Do you smell that?"

He sniffed for only a moment before responding. "Gun powder."

She chambered a round into her pistol and kicked off her shoes, leaving her barefoot to walk silently through the apartment. The living room was a clutter of magazines and takeout boxes half-eaten or discarded without care; the type of haphazard construction of garbage that gave the world the term 'roach motel.' Harriet motioned with her head for Eliot to observe the congregation of refuse.

"Somebody living here was worried," he whispered back; his own shoes neatly kicked onto the carpet.

"A missing boyfriend, perhaps?"

He began to nod in agreement but stopped himself as he looked over the substandard living area once more. "No, actually. This isn't fear, this is depression."

Harriet puzzled over the statement as she moved into the kitchen; the mess on the counter giving the living room a run for its money. The stench was anything but breathable. She coughed and pushed past Eliot into the breakfast nook.

There was a body on the table, shot twice through the back of the head. She recoiled at the awful display of a man with his skull collapsed on the breakfast table.

Eliot got to his knees and began examining the scene without hesitation. There were two broken bottles of beer: Mexican brand, both full before they crashed into the ground, and two rotting lime wedges sitting on the reclaimed wood floor. "He's about fifteen feet from the door, and he dropped the beers after the shots to the head, not before."

She was careful not to look at the body on the table. "What does that mean?"

He grabbed for the man's wallet and began rifling through it for identification. "It means, he offered the person who was here with him a beer." He took a long breath in and slowly out, "he probably knew him."

"Do you think Richard was here?"

Eliot held up the license, concerned. "This is definitely Francis Martel, I'd say there's a good shot he was here, yeah."

Harriet wandered from the room and into an adjacent bathroom, leaving Eliot alone in the kitchen examining each aspect repeatedly in an effort to put this together.

She called from the room over. "Eliot, I think we have a problem."

"Not right now, Harriet. I'm having trouble finding the second shell casing—that might give us a clue." He hollered back to the bathroom.

For a moment, Harriet did not respond and he continued sweeping his hand across the underside of the table. "Eliot Ness, if you don't stand up and walk in here right now I will drag you by the chest hair you wear v-necks to show off—as if there's anyone in their right mind that finds that attractive anymore."

Eliot hopped to his feet, hurried into the next room over, and stopped dead in his tracks.

The blood was everywhere.

In the middle of the bathtub, fully clothed, was Richard, shot an indeterminate amount of times in the chest because the *blood was everywhere*. He turned to Harriet, "go get some air."

"Is he dead?" She was gasping on the words as they came out.

He put his arms around her, trying to calm her down. "He—he looks pretty dead, yeah."

"We tortured him," Harriet could barely speak. "We tortured an innocent man, and now he's dead."

"Go get some air, Harriet. Now, please."

She could feel his arms ushering her out of the apartment and into the hallway. Harriet turned to dispute the plan just as the door closed in her face. For minutes, she paced up and down the hallway trying to figure out a next move. Without thinking about it, she dialed a familiar number on one of the throwaway phones they bought on a gas station.

It rang three times.

John answered, slurring his salutation. He continued, "Harry, what is it? Is something wrong?"

She swallowed. "Richard's dead. So is his boyfriend—there is blood everywhere."

"Harriet, did you guys check every room in the whole apartment?"

"I walked out before we checked the bedroom. John, I'm pretty sure they've been dead for days."

He began to yell. "You left Eliot alone in there?"

Harriet looked up and down the hallway for anyone in earshot. "John, we will be on our way back in twenty minutes, I'm sure of—"

She dropped her phone on the ground, still on the line with John Quincy, as the plastic bag wrapped tightly around her head and dragged her back into the apartment.

As she struggled on the carpet to get a good look at her assailant through the bag, Harriet felt a strong blow to the head as the inside of the bag began to fill with blood; *her blood.*

"Eliot!" she screamed as loud as she could across the living room. "Eliot, help me!"

There was no response from Eliot. She had no time to wonder what had happened to him as she saw the arm rear back for a second blow.

The first one had not knocked her out as intended.

As the arm came down a second time, everything went dark.

Harriet woke up, hours later, in a dark room she was unable to make out. She was tied to a chair and the bag was still on her head, covered in dried blood that made it impossible to see where she was or who was there.

A series of quiet footsteps began walking her direction.

A knife came down with force into her leg and she screamed with everything her lungs could muster.

The voice, muffled by the disgusting bag, whispered into her ear far too quietly to identify. He spoke a single word that shut her up immediately.

"Don't."

CHAPTER TWENTY-SIX
The House Divides By Itself

A Sobering Hour Later
Abandoned Fish Stick Factory

The sound of John Quincy's boots stomping up and down the aisles of the factory, from his bunk to the table a hundred feet away, could be heard by everyone inside. "I need a gun."

Alex Heton attempted to slow the proceedings, offering a calm arm on his shoulder, "I don't have a gun to give you—"

"I need *your* gun," Quincy cut him off.

"John, we need to calm down and think about this before we do anything rash."

"Rash? Rash like moving a group of people across the country and into a fish stick factory that is no safer than a donut shop?"

They had not realized Richie was sitting at the other end of the table drinking orange juice and looking through issues of Mad Magazine from 1973. "Donut shops are really safe. That's where the Police are—usually."

Alex smiled back at the nine-year-old and turned his attention back to Quincy. "They left on their own volition. I warned them—you know I warned them."

The conversation was not slowing John Quincy from packing a rucksack full of knives, turkey jerky, and socks. "Do you have any idea how confusing all of this is, Alex? You act so on top of it all, so one-step ahead of everyone else. But you aren't—" He took a moment to rip off a piece of jerky in his mouth, "You're the guy that lived with a girl for months and had no idea she was Joan of Arc. So *stop* acting like the leader we all asked for—or need."

Alex took two immense strides to close the gap between the two of them. He picked John forcefully from the ground and slammed him down into a chair. "If you really want to start pointing fingers," he began in a whispered growl. "I would suggest pointing one at the man who his entire time here getting drunk and finding every excuse not to help us survive. We aim to survive, John. Nothin' else."

"I suppose next I'll get a speech about getting a thirteen-year-old drunk again."

The hands holding John in the chair let go slowly. Alex took a step back and composed himself once more. "Actually, I don't care about that. It might be a thirteen-year-old, but it's Albert Einstein, and I think he can make decisions on his own."

John's eyebrows came together in the middle of his forehead. "So you guys aren't mad at me for that anymore?" He asked sheepishly.

"Are you even listening, John? We are being kidnapped and murdered out there faster than we can even find each other. Marie is dead, Paul is in a coma; we lost Genghis, Voltaire, and Tycho!" He stopped himself.

"And Harry."

"Harriet *and Eliot*," Alex corrected with a sideways glance. "They could already be dead, John." He reached out to put a hand on his friend's shoulder, but John recoiled.

"No. I refuse to believe they're dead."

"Do we have any reason to believe that they aren't?"

John stood up from the chair. "Yes, we do. When Paul and Marie were attacked, there were so many wounds in so many places: bruises, cuts, burns—and that was all before he started stabbing them. Whoever we're dealing with takes his time." He took a moment to look through what was in his rucksack before extending his hand once more to Alex. "Your gun, please."

"John, we have to make a plan here."

John Quincy looked back with a disdainful annoyance. "Just give me the gun, Alex. You're safe here."

"Yes, *we're* safe here. The more we split up and go all cock-diesel action hero, the faster we all die."

"You put live ammunition in a deep fryer because you thought it was cool!" John shouted back with force.

"It *was* cool!" Alex shouted back with equal veracity not realizing neither of them knew what they were shouting about. He calmed himself, took a breath, and spoke softly once more. "You can't go back out there alone, John."

"He won't be going alone," a female voice yelled from across the warehouse.

Alex turned away from the voice, over to the kitchen table some fifty feet on the other end of the compound. Janey was folding laundry for the group and looked back at Alex with a tilted head and a deep sigh. She mouthed the word, "no," back in his direction.

He spun back around the other direction, greeted with the site of Chloe walking up nonchalantly with two bags of tacos. "You brought tacos," he feigned excitement. "I'm sure, ironically."

Chloe spun both bags around and revealed that the name of the taco place had been crossed out, in its place was a new name written with a Sharpie: Taco Serf. "This place is hard as shit to find, dude!" She yelled into the community space.

"That was the idea," Alex called back, clearly annoyed by her unexpected presence.

"I think you'll note that I still found it, though."

"That was *not* the idea."

Chloe gave Alex a two-bag taco hug, one he did not return, and plopped down in the chair John had recently vacated. "Thanks for the help the other day, Alex." She grabbed for a bag and started pouring tacos onto the table. "Who wants a taco?"

Janey had been listening from afar and slowly made her way to where Alex was standing. "What does she mean, 'Thanks for the help?'"

"I'd prefer you didn't talk about me like I wasn't sitting right here," Chloe spoke with a mouth full of taco.

"I'm pretending you're not," Janey replied with smug resolution.

"Both of you quit it, god dammit! Look, I get the tough-chick angle but give it a friggin' rest already." Alex yelled between them. "Now, give me a taco, I'm starving."

"Hey, I'm cool, man. *She* shot *me*." Chloe announced.

"You put a gun in my face and threatened to murder me," Janey said back.

"Water under the bridge, my Indian princess?"

"Why are you here?"

Chloe stood up from the chair and walked over to John. "I heard what was going on and almost got killed the other night—so consider me part of the team."

John watched intently as she draped her arm over his shoulder. He brushed it off within moments before dryly replying, "no."

"Good. Teams are stupid," she yawned.

"Alex! Why is she here?" Janey yelled loud enough that Albert looked up from the stack of 1980's Mad Magazine issues from across the entire warehouse.

He looked around the room at all the inquisitive faces staring back at him and waiting for an answer. "Because I told her where we were," Alex said quietly, his eyes wincing as they braced for impact.

Janey smiled and cleared her throat. "You told a murderer where we were hiding when we were hiding from a murderer?"

"Hey, I think we covered that it was you who shot me," Chloe returned fire.

"Chloe. *You* shot you, remember?"

"Whoa, that's meta."

Janey raised her arms and made fists, shaking at the spectacle before them. "Alex, get her the hell out of here before I shoot her in the other leg!"

John Quincy Adams put his arms up in an attempt to slow the fight. The room fell silent as they waited for him to speak. Instead, he turned and whispered into Chloe's ear, "do you have a gun?"

She turned back to his ear and whispered back, "I have four."

He turned back to the group and announced, "I'm going with Chloe to Seattle."

Janey threw her arms up in disgust and walked slowly away from the group and over to where Albert was sitting quietly.

Alex took a step forward, dizzy from the speed at which decisions were being made. "Do you even know where to look?"

John held up his phone, a text message glowing on the screen. "She texted me the address of Francis Martel before they went inside. Harriet wanted the information backed up somewhere."

"And Francis Martel is…" Alex trailed off, waiting for an answer.

Chloe spoke up, "that's Richard's boyfriend."

"How do you know that?" Alex asked.

"Eliot's contact at the Los Angeles Police Department is Detective Julius Ransic. I've been following him ever since the taco place," she responded.

"The guy working for Jessup?"

John jumped in. "I got a text from Harry that said he was actually Napoleon."

Alex grabbed his hair and pulled as hard as he could "And you thought *now* was an appropriate time to bring this up?"

"I forgot until now, Alex."

Chloe smiled back at Alex. "To be fair, I'm the one that told Ransic that."

Alex Heton screamed at the top of his lungs and threw himself into a nearby chair. "We are going to start having returners staff meetings where all information will be logged on record. Okay, Chloe, you go first. Why the hell are you telling people, *civilians mind you,* that someone is actually Napoleon?"

"Muggles."

Alex's eyes shot open. "What?"

Chloe shot back with a mischievous grin. "I like to call civilians 'muggles.' Makes me feel awesome."

"Please answer the Napoleon thing, Hermione." He rubbed the sides of his temples and rested his chin on the table.

"I knew you read those books, you liar," she spoke under her breath. "Okay, dude, so check this out. Who do you think Genghis Khan was working for?"

Alex nodded. "That explains how the police got there so fast after you shot him."

"After I *saved your life*, yes."

John put his arms on both of their shoulders. "Alex. Harriet and Eliot are in serious danger and we are leaving right now."

"No, yeah. Go—get out of here. Keep your phone on and tell me anything that happens."

John grabbed his rucksack and turned for the other end of the warehouse. Chloe took a lingering moment standing with Alex. She leaned in and gave him a soft, and fleeting, kiss on the lips before turning and running to catch up with John.

He stood there in stunned, overwhelmed silence for twenty seconds, watching them walk together and trade firearms on the way to exit. Finally, he managed to scream out "be safe!" after they had already gone out of the side door.

Alex turned back to the table; Richie was still sitting there reading his magazines. He looked up and offered a confused look.

"Only four to go, huh?"

CHAPTER TWENTY-SEVEN
What's Love Got To

Seconds After

Abandoned Fish Stick Factory

Alex watched Chloe walk away with John Quincy; pining and confused, he pretended to check his phone for emails on an account he didn't have or any business setting up in the first place.

"Pretending to check for emails that don't exist?" A voice said from behind him. Janey had been pretending not to watch the sordid affair from afar. "I'm just playin', Greek boy. You got a second to talk?"

He looked up from the mobile inbox that didn't exist. "I'm sorry, what were you saying?"

"I was gently mocking the fact that you look like a lost puppy dog in the rain."

Alex looked out a nearby window. "Oh, is it raining?"

She crooked her neck forward, eyes widening. "Let's talk later when the soundtrack to your life isn't the Vince Guaraldi Trio."

"Sorry, I was just—what did you want to talk about?"

Janey sighed and pulled up a chair at the nearby table. She brushed aside a plate of half-eaten pizza bagels and took a moment to collect herself. "So, we're all going to die—well, I mean, we're all going to die, *again*."

Alex took her lead and sat down across from her. After staring at them for a moment, he made a move and started devouring the lukewarm remnants of bagels gone by. "Should I go get what's left of John's whisky stash?"

"No, I'd like to have this talk sober."

"The talk about how we're all going to get murdered?"

She bit her lip. "Kinda, but no. I want to talk about," Janey paused, staring out the window for rain that wasn't falling. "Us."

His eyebrows rose.

"I've watched you my entire life, bouncing from woman to woman like disposable playthings."

Alex put down what was left of the cold food and gave his full attention. "I'm not sure I follow. I mean … I'm not going to deny that I've spent the better part of this life being a womanizer."

"There's an informative Encarta CD in the back office that points out you were into boys as well—in a life gone by."

He laughed. "Yes, once upon a time I was—is 'boymanizer' a word?"

They laughed for a moment and fell back into awkward silence. The only sounds heard in the warehouse were of Albert and Richie jumping back and forth across the makeshift bedding area in the common space.

She spoke first. "Alex, why do you always fight with me?"

"I could ask you the same question."

"No you can't, I asked you first." Janey punctuated the sentiment by sticking her tongue out at Alex.

"Very mature."

"Answer the question, dammit!"

He twisted his lips around as he collected his thoughts. "Eliot and Harriet were kidnapped—and is this really the best time to be talking about stuff—"

She cut him off. "Yes, doofus. We're all going to die."

"You're trying to get me to say I like you, aren't you?"

"This would be your cue to do so."

A pizza bagel rolled back and forth between his hands. "Yup."

Janey scooted her chair around the edge of the table, not breaking eye contact with Alex's evasive gaze. "Good. I like you too. Now stop being a jackass all the time."

He smiled back, something he had not done for quite some time. "But."

A hand slid across the table and into his. "Before you say what you're about to say, allow me to just do it for you." Janey gently massaged the back of his hand. "The woman you lived with and were pretty into turned out to be somebody else, somebody you find yourself secretly texting when you think all of us aren't looking. You are not as secretive and suave as you think you are."

"Hey," he feigned anger. "I am *totally* as suave as I think I am!"

"I'm just saying I get it. You're surrounded by a fantastic array of badass chicks that could dismantle you like a wet garbage bag. I'm sure that's intimidating."

Alex laughed loud enough that the kids looked up and thought something was wrong at the table. He turned back to Janey. "I'm worried about Eliot and Harriet. Should we have gone too? We're just sitting at this table, eating pizza bagels that I'm pretty sure Richie ate for breakfast yesterday—if anything happens to them," he trailed off and came crashing back to the reality of the situation they were in.

She grabbed his other hand and pulled him closer. "We need a break—and you didn't hear this from me, because on the record I hope the bitch chokes on a staircase of waffles, but I think Chloe is going to get them back."

"That description defies all reason and yet makes perfect sense to me."

"I know my audience."

Alex craned his neck. "Thanks for the pep talk, Janey." He stood up and leaned over, resting his chin atop her head and holding her in a strong embrace. A kiss landed on the top of her hair, right where the hair parted as it had since they were tiny children. "I think you could have gotten them back too."

Janey pretended to brush her nose to conceal the wiping of a rogue tear that got away. She sniffled, "somebody's gotta stay here and protect your goofball-ass."

"I beat up Genghis Khan that one time," he smiled, noticing her charade.

"I shot Chloe in the foot."

"And Chloe shot Genghis in the head. You win this round," he paused a moment before finishing, "you." Alex rubbed his chin softly on the top of her head, her arms tightening around his. "Remember that time you kept saying we are all gonna die?"

"I remember it like it was five minutes ago."

"You were right, by the way. We're all gonna die."

Janey placed her cheek on the top of his arm and breathed softly across his skin. "Here's a question, and you must answer it honestly."

"Scout's honor," he said, holding up three fingers in front of her face.

"Okay, here goes," Janey began with a grave tone. "Lewis, or Clark?"

Alex laughed so hard there was a significant chance he had spit saliva into her hair. "I hate you. Also, Clark."

"Me too, man. Me too." She closed her eyes and allowed the moment to swallow them whole. Two friends in a situation that defied all logic or reason in a loaded embrace that would decay once they broke away from each other.

Alex's phone on the table began to vibrate in pulses on the table; a number few people had and a nightmare scenario should anyone find the need to call it. Janey broke free of the embrace and shot over to the other end of the table. She picked it up and stared in some confusion at the caller-ID glowing in the middle of the factory. "It's a hospital," she said.

Alex took a moment trying to decipher what that meant before motioning for Janey to answer it.

"Hello?" she greeted, listening intently as a litany of information Alex couldn't hear was rifled off on the other end of the line. "I—"

began her attempt to interject but whoever was speaking from the hospital was doing so as a one-sided conversation.

Several minutes went by as Alex watched Janey attempt to get a word in edge-wise, eventually giving up before beginning to nod as if that was something they could see *over a cell phone.*

She hung up and set the phone down on the table, the color from her skin having escaped to some far away land where happiness settled down to die of old age.

Janey mouth was moving but words were not coming out.

"What happened?" Alex tried to get her to speak.

She looked back at him, in total shock. "Paul's awake."

CHAPTER TWENTY-EIGHT

Deliver Us

Late That Night
Streets of Seattle, Washington

Detective Julius Ransic took a slow drag of his menthol cigarette as he scanned the street in the rental car—a car where smoking was clearly labeled as forbidden.

He leaned his head against the window and sighed with the knowledge that something was terribly and irreparably wrong.

There was a voice recorder on the seat next to him. He grabbed it and began to record a monologue to use later in his screenplay. "The night air mingles with the swirling nicotine and danced as if sugarplum fairies were engaged in their familiar ballet. The masses twiddled about, their stenches mixed into the musk of life—"

There was a loud knock at the window that startled the detective something terrible.

"Mother f—" he swore, rolling down the window for Chloe. "Oh, it's *you* again. Here to tell me that one of the other cops I work with is Sherlock Holmes, are ya?"

Chloe shook her head and checked to make sure John was still within shouting distance. "Sherlock Holmes wasn't a real person."

"What do you need?" He said back with a clear lack of patience. "I've been sitting in this car for an hour and a half."

She whistled to John to come over. "We got stuck on the runway when we landed. Ransic, we don't have a lot of time."

"And why is that?"

Chloe put her hand on the car window. "Eliot and Harriet got taken by the killer. We are already out of time."

That can't be," Ransic paused. The detective turned to the dusty windshield and stared off into the fresh rain turning the street into a refracted collection of mirrored images. "Eliot's an asshole, but he's a fantastic cop."

The rear door swung open and John Quincy jumped into the backseat, shaking off the fresh rain as it tracked down the side of his jacket and onto the cloth seats below. "Take us to the boyfriend's house."

Ransic's eyes rose to meet John's in the rearview mirror. "Who the hell are you?"

"I'm the gentleman that's going to slam your head into the steering wheel if you don't start driving."

"I am a detective with the Los Angeles Police Department!"

Chloe leapt across the hood of the car, sliding along the wet surface in a way that looked entirely accidental but alarmingly cool, before grabbing for the door to the passenger side of the car. Her wet coat slammed down onto the rental seat and her attention turned once again to the man driving it. "You're not a cop anymore. You haven't been since Kansas." She took a moment to catch her breath. "What happened?"

"I met *you*, Chloe." He murmured as he spread his mouth, revealing a crooked bottom row of teeth nervously biting back over the top lip. "I got kicked off the force when I didn't show up for an entire week."

She put a wet hand kindly onto his shoulder. "At least you're alive, Ransic."

His smile was as wry as it was fictional. "I'm pretty sure Jessup is following me. He didn't see me, but I know it was him—was traveling with a group of oddly dressed triplets."

Chloe stifled her laughter in such a way that she began to cough as the air fought in her throat for which way to go.

"I'll take that to mean something really scary is going on here."

"You take that correctly," she said and returned his manufactured smile. "Please, take us to the boyfriend's house."

Ransic fired up the engine and threw the vehicle into drive. The old rental lurched forward and began its three-mile journey across the downtown area. "I need information."

John Quincy leaned in from the backseat, coming alive at the request. "What kind of information?"

The fired detective ignored John and accelerated above the speed limit as the car moved up the hill. His eyes slid across the interior and fall directly onto Chloe's. "Who are you?"

"Chloe," spilled forth from her lips lacking any of the trademark gusto.

"I'd much prefer it if you could answer me for real, my dear Chloe," he murmured as the rental car continued to gain in speed as it traveled up and down the hilly downtown Seattle area. "You told me Jessup was *Napoleon*. Surely the subtext of such a thing was lost on me."

"Would you mind slowing down?" she sheepishly spoke before throwing a nervous glance back to John in the backseat.

"I lost my job for you lot!" said Julius Ransic with explosive and unexpected rage. "The least you could do is let me in on it!" he screamed as his foot mashed further down on the accelerator pedal.

John Quincy sat forward in his chair, readying his old hands to subdue the driver. With one glance into the rearview mirror, he slammed the brakes and put John's head squarely into the headrest—sending him back onto the seat in a thick haze.

"I'm not going to hurt you, but I'm afraid I do need answers," Ransic spoke as a collected person again. His voice was smooth in timbre, controlling, assessing. That is, until he felt the cold plastic of Chloe's Glock press against his temple.

"Slow down."

Ransic swallowed hard. "What? So you can murder a cop in broad daylight?"

Chloe could see his nervous sweat begin to collect on the end of the barrel. "Firstly, you're not a cop anymore. Secondly, we both know the sunlight in Seattle is anything but broad."

"Touché."

John came to in the backseat and sat up. He took off his seat belt and turned back to the front seat only to be greeted by Chloe's free hand warning him away from any sudden movements.

"My name is Joan," Chloe spoke to the man driving the car like a maniac through downtown.

Ransic slowed down to make a right turn and headed up the hill away from the bay. "Yeah, I already picked up on all the fake names you guys were using."

"Joan *of Arc*, you clod."

The vehicle turned, but he did not attempt to bring it back up to speed, choosing instead to idle up the incline. "I don't understand."

"We're the returners and that means exactly what it sounds like. We haven't found everyone, but someone is certainly trying to kill us—and succeeding."

Ransic looked up once more into the rearview mirror. "Then who are you?"

"John Quincy Adams—and about four hours late on a double of Macallan to boot," the man in the backseat hastily mentioned.

The car slowed to a stop in front of gas station that was no longer in use. "And Eliot?"

"Eliot Ness," the two passengers said in unison.

Ransic's eyes lowered and shame fell across his face. "Figures I would constantly shit on one of the greatest police officers of all time."

Chloe smiled and tussled his hair. "Don't beat yourself up about it."

"Why?" He replied with cold insistence.

"No good reason. Just—don't and maybe you'll be of some use yet."

"I have not been entirely honest with you two. This isn't the boyfriend's apartment." Ransic's head arose from the steering wheel and focused on the section of town not up to the standards of the neighborhoods and buildings around it. This was a section of downtown Seattle that had not risen to prominence over the years but instead had fallen into disrepair from abandonment. "I'm quite afraid I've put us all in substantial danger."

Her eyes darted over as the door locks slammed down in the car. "Ransic—" she trailed off. "Where are we?"

The man's voice began to drop and break as it wallowed in the substance of regret. "There was a van outside of Francis Martel's apartment. It was there for days and days—it didn't move over the four days I monitored the building."

Chloe's fingers curled back around the firearm she had lowered earlier. "Ransic, where the hell are we?"

He ignored her question for the second time. "The van was simple. White—with the name of the company painted onto the side in black letters." Ransic let a modest laugh escape his lips. "It said, 'Grey Area Deliveries' and at first I just figured that it went out of business and that's why the owner never moved it."

John tried to pull the handle in the backseat but found it had been detached from the child safety locks. He looked up to Chloe who had a similar concern growing on her face.

Ransic leaned back in his chair, hands on the wheel of a car that wasn't moving, and began to slow down his breathing. "I figured that Eliot and Harriet went into Francis Martel's apartment and found nothing. The police were not notified so I just figured they hadn't found anything and went home." His eyes were glassy, like he was forgetting to blink—his throat was hoarse, like he was forgetting to swallow. "I—I don't know why I went back that night. That last nagging shred of the detective you write stories in your mind about because you wish you were that person. That hero." His head turned to Chloe. "That legend."

There was a shuffling in the backseat as John tried to open the door on the other side of the vehicle.

"That same van was parked backward in the alleyway—back doors ajar as if attempting to make a delivery."

Chloe put her arm on Julius's shoulder, giving it a tender rub to bring him back to reality. "Ransic. You gotta let us out of this car."

He again ignored the words that were coming from his passenger. "The van that had refused to move for four business days, suddenly has an emergency delivery to cross town at four in the morning?"

She grabbed his chin and forced Ransic's glassed over eyes to stare back into hers. "What were they loading into the van?"

"I followed the van across town—doing my best to stay a few blocks behind and even guessing where to take turns early to arouse no suspicion."

Chloe squeezed on his face harder, eliciting no change in tone or subject.

"We ended up down here. He parked it a few blocks down in a deserted fashion boutique. There were mannequins crowding up the front window so I didn't get a good look inside. I didn't even know something was wrong. No one told me something was wrong."

She handed the gun back to John and motioned with her head toward the nearest window. "What did they load into the van, Ransic?" She yelled over the sounds of shattering glass in the background.

"I just wanted to be a cop again. The good cop," he held back a sob.

"Ransic!"

He swallowed. "It was trash bags! He was loading trash bags into the van!"

CHAPTER TWENTY-NINE
Guess Who's Bringing Burritos to Dinner

Eleven Minutes Prior
An Old Boutique

Eliot attempted to slow down his breathing as the stench of his own saliva permeated the interior of the bag. Murmuring could be heard as he accosted himself in a series of mumbles for eating chili-cheese burritos force fed to him under the bag. The bag fell limply onto his shoulder and he spoke. "Hey, Harry. How many of your ribs are broken?"

The crinkling of another bag was faintly heard; the grunts of pain informing Eliot of the answer before she replied. "Only three—no, wait." He heard Harriet move in the chair. "I think I got a hairline in there. So, four."

"Sounds like you put up a better fight than me. I got seven just on the left. Every time I breathe or move in the chair—" He growled in pain. "Yeah, I can feel the bottom two separate and pinch the inside of my skin when I exhale."

"That's disgusting, Eliot," the other bag replied.

He grumbled exhaustion before shaking his head back and forth, unable to send the plastic off and onto the floor. "Harry," he spoke softly.

"Yeah?"

"Did you get the bag off your head yet?"

The sound of Harriet shaking her head was heard in kind. "No, sir. I think he super-glued it to my hair."

Eliot looked down through the opening at the bottom of the bag at his bare feet nailed to the creaky wooden floor. "Yeah, mine too."

They sat together in silence, as they would at the end of each tiny conversation throughout the day, and slowed their breathing inside of the bags that would soon become horticulture experiments.

Harriet spoke again after three minutes. "Have you tried inhaling the bag and trying to eat it?"

"*Have I what?*" Eliot asked with exasperation.

She laughed. "Have you tried inhaling the bag into your mouth—"

"And then what?"

"Then bite down, and pull it away from the top of your head. Hopefully, it will tear a hole in the bag."

One bloody plastic bag turned to the other. "No. I have not tried that, Harry. Have you?"

"Yes, but my hair's too long. I can't rip it."

Eliot's bag returned to front and sat in stunned contemplation. "Okay."

"Okay, what?" she said.

"Okay, I'm going to inhale the bag and bite a hole in it."

Her bag turned to his as well. "Don't forget to pull away from your hair."

He grunted a sound of approval and inhaled as much of the bag into his mouth as he could. Alternating top to bottom, he slowly pulled in more of the bag by grinding his teeth across the thin plastic. Eliot wretched as the hair near his bald spot began to tear from his scalp in numbers.

"Did you get it?" A clueless voice called from other side of his plastic prison.

There was a pause in the muffled squawks of pain for the amount of time it took Eliot to roll his eyes. With one final thrust, he pushed his bottom jaw out as he tore at his left shoulder. A semi-circle tore out of the bag and fell forward, leaving a generous hole to see out of into the world around them. It took a moment for his eyes to adjust in the dark. When they had, he turned to check on Harriet.

Her arms had twenty-or-so burns up and down both of her arms. "A fire-poker," he quietly exclaimed to himself at the grizzly site.

Harriet's bag turned to him. "What did you say, Eli? Wait. Can you see now?"

He smiled back, even though there was no way she could see it. "The burns on your arms, he used a fire poker."

"How do you know? It felt like he was rolling it all around—the bastard."

"It looks like twenty Fleur-de-lis, Harry. He was rolling it, all right. He was rolling it on purpose. I guess our killer has a thing for—" Eliot screamed at the top of his lungs.

The killer was leaning over him; a black ski mask concealed the man's face. Eliot could feel the breath coming through the fabric just three inches from his face. The mask slowly looked down at the fresh blood pouring out of Eliot's feet as the fright reopened the wounds.

"What the f—" His heart was beating at a thousand miles an hour.

The killer held up a white paper bag that said 'Taco Baron' across the side. "I have burritos," he spoke. It would be clear to anyone listening that he was disguising his voice in a jilted tenor.

Harriet's bag snapped to where the killer was standing, she was not aware of his presence until he spoke of showcased burritos.

"Eat fast, we only have four minutes," the killer wolfed as he threw a burrito into each of their laps.

Eliot accidentally knocked his burrito from his lap to the ground. The paper surrounding the Mexican meal began to soak up the blood on the floor. The man in the mask hurriedly reached to the ground and placed it gently back into the lap in front of him.

"Why do we only have four minutes?" Eliot asked of the man.

The ski mask tilted as if confused before grabbing another burrito from the greasy bag resting on the bloody floor. "Because that is all the time we have together, Eliot."

Harriet swallowed. "Are—are you going to kill us?"

The ski mask was lifted *just* enough to eat the burrito and remind all invested parties why it's not polite to chew with one's mouth open. He ignored the question, instead choosing to dig sour cream out of the burrito with his finger in a disgusted manner.

Eliot piped up. "If you're going to do it, why wait another four minutes?"

The man in the ski mask jumped to his feet and threw the remaining half of his burrito into Harriet's bagged face. She recoiled, looking around in total confusion as to what just happened; sour cream dripped from the bag to the floor. The man walked back to a table set up in front of the two prisoners and unrolled a blanket outfitted with all matter of knives. Eliot watched as the hand of the man ran meticulously across the surface of every blade.

"Change your mind?" Eliot spoke.

"Sometimes," the mask fired back, still scouring the array of cutlery. "You haven't touched your dinners," the man with the knives yelled as if imitating someone else entirely.

Harriet adjusted the bag on her shoulder. "We—*friend*, you tied our hands to the chairs."

The man looked up from his weapons and then down to their arms, tied with wire so tightly they were caked in blood. "So I did."

The man with the knives went back to what he was doing.

Harriet tried again. "So maybe you could untie one of my hands."

"Or maybe just let us go one at a time," Eliot piped up following her lead.

A knife blade slammed half an inch into the table and wobbled back and forth from the force. "If you don't finish your dinner tonight, you'll be eating it cold for breakfast in the morning!" The man with the knives screamed at full blast through the quiet boutique before taking a moment to collect himself once more. His gaze shifted from Harriet to Eliot and back to Harriet again.

The man collected three knives and walked across the creaky wooden floor.

"Kill me first," Harriet sputtered through the bag, exhausted.

Eliot watched the man stop in his tracks before turning and taking a long look at the glass door with mannequins piled up in front of it. He turned back to the woman in the chair. "Did you think you were here to die?"

Through the hole in the bag, Eliot looked over to the other chair. "Harry."

Her bag looked back at him. "Yes?"

"Shut up, please."

The man with the knives took two steps closer, securely tucking the blades into his belt. "Two minutes now," he paused. "It's not time."

Eliot straightened his back against the chair, each nudge putting his smashed ribs through nearly unbearable pain. "It's not time for what?"

"Time for you two."

It was faint, but a window shattered somewhere off in the distance.

The man with the knives rushed over to Harriet and rolled the bag up and over her hair, leaving it as a crumpled mass atop her head. "You will die when you are selected."

Harriet took a startled breath, her eyes widening at the proximity of the man and the sudden rush of cold air brushing against her face. "Who was selected?"

The mask appeared to smile. "That would be telling."

Her intensity increased. *"Who was selected?"*

The man rushed a hand into her hair and pulled back with force, enjoying the fear the rushed across her. "Oh sweetie," he began with a ruthless whisper. "I'm going to take my time with you."

He let go and Harriet's head came rocking back into place. She struggled to catch her breath as he ran between the chairs and off into the back of the shop.

Fifteen seconds passed in silence.

A Government Issue blue mailbox came crashing through the front window, shattering glass in many directions and making a pathway through the mannequins.

Eliot watched through the hole in the bag as Chloe climbed briskly through the wreckage at the door. She jumped down and ran into the room, gun drawn and checking the corners and behind numerous headless mannequins in sparkling cocktail dresses.

She stopped short when she saw the battered husks Eliot and Harriet tied to the chairs before her. Her eyes widened and three words escaped her mouth.

"Oh my god."

CHAPTER THIRTY

This is the Last of Earth! I am Content!

Five Seconds Previous
The Old Boutique

John Quincy Adams stared in wonder as Julius Ransic hurtled the massive blue mailbox through the front of the boutique.

Chloe pushed between the two men and climbed down the pile of headless mannequins decked to the nines in Guatemalan Versace knock-offs (the mannequins, not Chloe—she was adorned in after-work sweatpants). Gun drawn, she closed the distance between the window and the two prisoners tied with bloody wiring to the chairs.

Her eyes rose and fixed on the lady in the chair: pain emanating from Harriet's eyes like a stone dropped into a still pond.

"Oh my god."

John Quincy was soaking this in as he slid down the plastic genocide of fallen mannequins lining the smashed window. His arm went up to Chloe's shoulder and attempted to provide a reassuring hand, which she brushed off with immediacy. "Just get them out of the chairs," she murmured, still stunned at the amount of blood dripping from their fingers and onto the cement floor.

Both of the men she came with dropped to their knees and began uncoiling the slippery crimson wires. They paused for every wince of the cool evening air entering the cavernous raw skin where the metal wires were uncoiled. John was slowly taking the wire off Eliot, trying to reassure him that he was going to be just fine. A reassurance Eliot did not seem to reciprocate or agree with.

Harriet wrenched her left hand free of the restraint that Ransic was carefully cutting through—wasting no effort to yank the right hand free in a most painful way. She rubbed her wrists to regain feeling and stood up. "His feet are nailed to the floor, John."

The words echoed around the room and fell on ears that could not comprehend what had just been said.

John Quincy's eyes dropped and his body recoiled in horror at the sight of Eliot's bare feet driven into the floor by five-inch nails. "Oh my god," he spoke softly.

"I already said that." Chloe replied, sounding more rattled than usual.

Harriet bent over and lifted Ransic from the ground. "The circumstances lend themselves to saying it twice." She turned to Chloe, held out her hand, and nodded.

It took Chloe a moment to process what Harriet was asking for. After a few seconds, she put the barrel of the pistol into her hand and outstretched the handle of the gun to Harriet, who snatched it up without hesitation and chambered a round.

"We go now. He's not far," Harriet spoke quietly enough that her broken ribs would not scream out in agony.

"Aren't you in pain?" Chloe said.

"Of course I'm in pain."

"Then let us get you guys out of here. The killer booked it, Harry."

Harriet scanned around the room, her eyes stopping and examining each discarded mannequin with more fervor than the last. "No, I'm quite sure he hasn't gone far."

John was searching loudly through a desk drawer nearby. He carefully pulled out a claw hammer and looked back at Eliot with regret. "I'm sorry, we gotta do this."

Eliot motioned to his feet. "Just do it and get us the hell out of here."

A shaking hand lowered the claw hammer to the floor, carefully sliding the prongs under the head of the nail. The blunt of the hammer slid between the two largest toes and tilted back, applying pressure to the nail. John could feel the man nailed to the floor begin to tremble.

They all jumped as the air conditioner rumbled to life, vibrating the floorboards under Eliot's feet and shaking the nails from side-to-side.

Harriet hobbled across the room and slowly made her way up the pile of clothed plastic. She turned back, "Chloe, get Eliot to the car. Ransic, you're with me."

Doing as he was told, Ransic slipped in the blood on his way to help Harriet up and out into the street.

Staring down at the hammer perched between his colorless toes, Eliot called out into the room. "Don't hesitate."

Ransic chambered a round. "I won't." He smiled and turned away with Harriet into the night.

Eliot laughed and reached for the side of his abdomen. "I was talking to you, John—and please don't make me laugh, it hurts like you cannot believe."

John Quincy wrapped his free hand around the ankle, applying pressure to keep the foot on the ground. "I'm gonna count to three, okay?"

Eliot shielded his eyes with lacerated arms and took a deep breath.

"One…"

Chloe slammed her foot onto the wooden handle in John's hand. The prongs flew up and the nail came ripping out of the foot.

The scream was inhuman.

John jumped to his feet and pushed Chloe back in a fit of rage. "What in the hell are you doing?"

She slid out from beneath his grasp and headed back to the whimpering shell of Eliot slouched down in the chair. She turned over her shoulder as she bent to pick up the hammer. "Trust me."

"Not the most believable thing to say when you rip a five-inch piece of metal out of someone's foot, girlie." John announced with exasperation.

Chloe set the hammer around the second nail. "Ever call me 'girlie' again and I'll puree your tongue in a garbage disposal." Her grip loosened around the handle and turned back to John, still standing in awe against the wall. "Have you ever been burned alive at the stake?"

He pushed off the wall and began a few careful steps back toward Eliot and the chair. "No. Chloe…" John trailed off, his voice cracking.

She sniffled and put a reassuring hand on Eliot's knee. "They don't much like it when you try and run away. Ropes burn, John."

The hammer shot back with another burst of force and Eliot let loose a pathetic squeal before passing out.

Without hesitation, John pulled his shirt over his head and tossed it to Chloe.

She ripped the yellow golf shirt in half and began wrapping the feet to prevent any further blood loss. "I need to get him to the car."

"Do you need help with that?"

She put her arm under Eliot's shoulder and motioned to the other side. "Help me get him up."

John rushed over to the chair and helped Chloe lift a dying Eliot from the chair. He murmured something about wanting a stiff drink and fell onto her shoulder.

They walked together across the floor, the blood sliding the three of them around and glimmering like oil in the moonlight.

It took a number of minutes to scale the mess they had made in front of the window, careful to keep Eliot's already mutilated feet from scraping against any of the shattered glass that littered almost the entire surface of the shop.

As the three of them made solid contact with the sidewalk, Chloe looked around for any sign of Harriet or Ransic, but none were seen or heard.

Eliot stirred on her shoulder, exhaling some attempt at a word.

"Sit tight, dude. We're getting you out of here. Don't try to say anything."

"No." His head lifted up and he put a bloody hand onto John's chest. "Wait. He said—" Eliot trailed off and dropped his head once more from the blood loss.

"He's trying to tell us something," John said with alarm.

"No shit, Quincy-cheeks. We are getting the hell out of—"

The other blood-drenched hand grabbed her squarely by the chin and cut her off. "No!" Eliot managed to half-shout in the quiet street. He steadied his other arm on John's shoulder and said three breathy words in measured succession.

"Harry.

Me.

Nh-chosen."

Eliot's head fell once again, blood dripping from his mouth onto the sidewalk.

Chloe tried to pull away to the car. "He's fading, John!"

"Wait!" John hollered back and made his way around to Eliot's front, crouching in the moonlight. His hand gently lifted Eliot's bleeding chin and gave it a gentle awakening shake. "Eliot. Eliot! What do you mean chosen? Who was chosen?"

"John! Find out later!" Chloe's eyes burned with aggravation.

"Wait!" He shook Eliot's face once more, whispering the man's name like a prayer over and over.

"No." Eliot said.

"No, what?"

His eyes dimmed, but he was determined to say it again. He spoke once more, the same dream-like stupor encompassed every word.

"Not.

Chosen.

Me and Har-Harry.

Not chosen."

The sound of plastic hitting the floor made John brush past Chloe, now holding Eliot up by herself in the street.

He stammered.

A headless mannequin in a blue-sequined dress was closing the distance from the back of the shop to the shattered window. A black mask popped out of the dress and scaled the rubble near the entrance with startling efficiency.

The masked man leapt wildly into the air, a knife's glint pulsed in the light of the moon.

Chloe recoiled in horror as the blade slammed into John's sternum, the cracking of bone sounded like a popping firecracker.

A vicious kick sent Chloe and Eliot toppling on top of each other and into the street, her head slammed into a parking meter on the way down.

Still holding the knife, the man in the mask looked deep into John's eyes—just long enough for a connection to be made.

John was trembling, seconds from death; he leaned in closer to his murderer. "I fuggin' knew it was you."

The killer tore downward with the knife, cutting all the way through to the stomach lining. He kicked the lifeless body from the buried knife and bolted off into the darkness.

John Quincy Adams was dead, discarded in the street like a piece of garbage.

Silence.

It would be sixteen minutes before Julius Ransic would come upon the corpse, unsure of who lay dead in the pile of unconscious bodies. He ignored John, who was clearly dead, and did his best to prop the other two up and apply pressure to any wounds he could find.

"Harriet!" Ransic called out into the night, having seen dead bodies before, but never like this.

Never like this.

"Harriet!"

But she did not answer.

CHAPTER THIRTY-ONE
Aren't We All Killers?

The Next Morning
Rouen General Hospital Waiting Room
Lawrence, Kansas

Richie muttered various nonsensical phrases in his sleep before yelling something about "Pokemon Gangsters" and stirring Alex awake. He jumped up from the chair and looked down as Richie fell back asleep.

"… time is it?" Alex Heton mumbled back to Janey, waking her up as well.

She yawned and looked down at the digital calculator watch Alex had given her when she was seven-years old. "It's the morning," she took a moment to yawn. "One of the numbers is a six."

He turned to her and rolled his eyes. "That was very informative, thank you."

Janey rose to her feet, carefully leaning the unconscious Albert from her drooled-upon shoulder and onto Richie. Her hand searched the waistband of her pants before coming to rest on the pistol tucked away there. Like a hung over ballerina, she spun back to Alex, already rummaging through the magazines he had read many times over. "We can't all rifle off ill-timed diatribes as to how inaccurately someone named their taco restaurant."

"How did you hear about that?"

"Girls talk," she shrugged.

His hands came together like a monk preparing for a prayer circle. "I use my gifts for the good of man."

Janey rested her chin on Alex's shoulder, yawning slowly into his ear before whispering, "When Alexander looked upon the breadth of his domain—he wept, for there were no more worlds to conquer."

His head fell onto hers, his eyes closing with comfort. "I love it when you speak Die Hard to me."

"I thought I was quoting Plutarch."

He laughed. "No you didn't."

"No. I didn't." Janey spun around to the Alex's front and gave him a big hug.

The hug was returned, but he cut it short with a nervous smile. "What was that for?"

She did not respond with words.

Janey grabbed Alex's face and pulled his mouth to hers. They kissed with closed eyes, like the first kisses of so many campers behind a nearby cabin. They embraced the other's lips for as long as the unstable world surrounding them would allow.

"About friggin' time, you two," Albert yawned at them as he stretched to his feet and began the search for his sneakers. "Thought you guys would wait around forever to do that."

Alex brushed back dark strands of hair out of her face. "I guess you could say it's all relative," he said with a huge smile.

Albert Einstein chunked a copy of *Good Toddler Weekly* across the waiting room at them. "Yeah, no, please feel free to cheapen my entire life's work as your personal flirt-a-day calendar," he harped back at them.

A voice cleared her throat from the other side of the room.

The dysfunctional trio turned to find a nurse holding a chart. She had been waiting patiently in the doorway for someone to notice her, with no choice but to witness the strange interactions between them. "Are you guys…" she stopped herself.

Albert froze in place, trading looks of horror with Alex that communicated, "did we just tell a random person we were returners?" without uttering a word.

The nurse spoke up again. "Are you guys rehearsing a play?"

Janey stepped in front of Alex. "Yes. It's a play. It's by David Mamet and it's just talking from start to finish. Have to work in rehearsals when we can, you know?"

The nurse blinked a few times before extending her hand out. "That was very informative, thank you…" she trailed off into a question.

"My name is Janey."

"Nice to meet you, Janey. I'm Liz Schiefer, and I'm the Charge Nurse in the Intense Trauma Recovery Unit." She took a brief glimpse down onto her clipboard. "Which one of you is Alex Kincaid?"

Janey mouthed the words "Alex Kincaid" as a question from behind the nurse. It had slipped her mind that he was still wanted in connection with a series of murders in California. The very murders they were hoping Paul could help them solve.

He stepped forward and extended his hand as well. "Nice to meet you, I'm Alex."

The nurse glanced down once more, "and how do you know Blake Albateek, Mr. Kincaid?"

Alex took a moment to remember Paul's fake name was Blake Albateek, a fact they learned on the news after the attacks on Paul and Marie. "We have a mutual friend named Richard." He looked down at the ground, his demeanor changing for the somber. "I'm afraid we come bearing the news that our friend Richard has passed on."

Liz the nurse cupped her hands over her mouth in shock. "Oh my god, that's terrible. I'm so sorry for your loss. How did he pass, if you don't mind me asking?"

Alex nodded, "skiing accident in Taos—we were at the hospital in New Mexico when we heard the news that Paul—sorry, when we heard the news *Blake* had woken up. We call him Paul."

"Mr. Albateek has put up a hell-of-a fight over the last couple weeks. He's been in and out of consciousness for a few days now." She looked out over all four of them sitting around the room. "Did you all want to see Mr. Albateek? I'm afraid we can't accommodate all of you at the same time. Perhaps your wife," she began to say while motioning to Janey.

Alex jumped in before Janey could protest. "Yes, I'll leave my wife with the kids. They sure love their *stepmom*."

Her eyes narrowed.

Albert threw his arms around Janey and closed his eyes. "Yes, Janey, tell us that story about your reservation bingo hall again. I'm *tired* of rehearsing that boring play over and over." He buried his face in her side, trying not to burst in laughter, ruining the whole charade. Janey tugged on his ear with force.

Liz stepped back into the hallway and motioned for Alex to follow her back into the unit.

He stepped over, gave Janey a kiss on the forehead, and rubbed Albert's hair. "Be back soon, *honey*."

She leaned in close to his ear. "Next time you get to be the stepparent."

Alex saluted as if Janey were a Captain in the Navy and made his way out of the waiting room. Liz and Alex walked side-by-side through the various maze-like hallways of a hospital, each stretch of rooms and equipment even more the same than the previous.

"I'm sorry to ask this, but it would be better for Blake if you didn't mention the passing of his friend. His body has undergone such trauma, any shock to his system could have lasting and detrimental effects," she began.

"If you think that will help, then I won't speak about Richard at all."

"Good. Thank you, Alex." Liz motioned down another side hallway into a darker corner of the hospital. "This is where all ICU patients go for recovery. You will be the first visitor he has been able to receive. He's been such a fighter to come back after such a vicious attack." Just outside the doorway to Paul's room, she stopped Alex and pulled him aside. She began to speak in a low whisper. "Do you know if they're any closer to finding out who attacked him and the woman?"

He shook his head. "Nothing yet. Have the police been by to talk to him about it?"

"They came by twice, but were only allowed to talk to Blake once. He says he doesn't remember anything from the attack." She brushed a hand through her hair and let out an audible sigh. "I mean, who could blame him?"

Alex turned to walk into the room and gave the nurse a nod.

"Hit the call button if you two need anything," Liz called back as she walked away.

The massive door creaked as it opened. Alex proceeded into the room, stepping loudly enough that Paul would hear. He knew that appearing silently at the foot of his bed could possibly send someone into the shock Alex was instructed to avoid. He rounded the edge of the curtain; there was Paul, beaten and broken, but curious of the stranger whom had just appeared in the room.

Paul reached immediately for the box with the nurse call button.

"Wait." Alex blurted immediately. "*Paul.* Wait."

The finger cautiously pulled away from the big red button. He struggled to speak. "The last person that called me by that name stabbed me a few times and threw me out of a window," Paul answered back in a gravely hush.

"My name is Alexander."

"The Great?"

"The Great." Alex answered back in a reassuring voice.

Paul struggled to sit up better in his bed, still visibly skeptical toward the unannounced visitor standing in his room. "Is he still killing?"

Alex bit his lip and looked out the window at the sunny morning sky. "He is. Paul, we need to know anything you saw or heard. Had you ever met the guy before?"

"Is Marie alive?" the bedridden man ignored the previous question.

"I'm supposed to refrain from giving you any news you would find upsetting."

Paul brushed aside the cords protruding from his arm. "Don't be an asshole, Alexander."

He swallowed. "She died."

"Anyone else?"

Alex sat down on the end of the bed with tired eyes. "Two of ours were kidnapped, Harriet Tubman and Eliot Ness, Joan of Arc and John Quincy Adams went after them in Seattle." He paused. "I haven't heard back from them yet."

Paul managed to push himself up onto his side. "I had no idea there were so many that came back. Was there anyone else?"

"The nurse—what was her name?"

"Liz."

Alex snapped his finger in the air, "Yes, that was it. Liz said I can't give you any information that might put you in danger."

Paul shot back a look of annoyance and rage. "*Who?*"

Alex placed his hand on Paul's knee and leaned in, knowing this information was going to absolutely crush him upon hearing it. "I'm sorry to be the one to say this, but Richard and his boyfriend were both killed in their apartment in Seattle."

Unexpectedly, there was no reaction at all upon saying the name. Paul looked as if he was ready to hear the second half of the information. "And then what happened?"

"What do you mean, and then what happened? Paul, I'm telling you Richard was killed in Seattle by the same guy that attacked you."

"Richard who?" his voice was beginning to give out completely.

"Richard *the Lionheart*. Paul, how much do you remember before the attack? Richard was one of your best friends."

Paul shook his head and shrugged. "Who was the boyfriend?"

The room was beginning to feel stuffy and cramped. Alex looked back at Paul, a broken portrait of another man in another time. "The boyfriend was a civilian. He wasn't a returner."

"So, what was his name? You said he was from Seattle."

Alex took a moment to try and remember the information. "Uh, his name was Francis I think." He looked down and Paul was squeezing his hand with immense force.

"Last name?" He questioned as his eyes welled with tears.

Alex cocked his head to the side and finished the question without thinking through what was about to happen. "His name was Francis Martel."

The normal rhythm of the electronic beeps began to accelerate. New alarms blared into the space and increased in frequency.

Paul dropped back onto the pillow and began to breath faster and more out of control. His eyes widened as tears traced sideways down his cheek and onto the flattened headrest.

The alarms made it difficult for Alex to hear what Paul said next. He had to say it three times before Alex understood what he was mouthing.

"That's my brother."

Liz the Charge Nurse ran into the room panting as if she had run from the other side of the hospital. "What did you do?" she screamed at Alex as she pushed him out of the way. Liz slammed a button on the wall for a Code Blue. She screamed again at Alex to try and get him out of the room.

More nurses and emergency personnel entered the room as Paul began to seize on the bed, but the tears had not stopped flowing.

Alex pulled out his phone and dialed as fast as he could for Janey. It rang twice as the largest of the orderlies grabbed him by the arms and began escorting him backward from the room.

She answered and sounded like she was in tears. "Alex, Chloe just called me—"

"Janey, I need you to put us on video chat!"

"There's been another attack. In Seattle."

"Put me on goddamn video chat!" he yelled back, ignoring what she was saying.

Within a moment, Janey's face appeared on his phone, looking confused as ever. She was about to speak when Alex cut her off once more.

"Give the phone to Richie."

He could see her getting annoyed with all of the yelling. "Alex—he's not even awake. Listen to me!"

"Wake him up, then!" He said as he looked back around the corner into the room, making sure that Paul was still awake. They would knock him out any second. His gaze dropped back to the phone and there was Richie, poor tired Richie rubbing his eyes.

"Hi Alex!" He said with a big smile.

Alex ran back into the room and pushed one of the orderlies out of the way.

Liz pressed the call button down and screamed that she needed security to the room immediately.

Paul looked up as a phone appeared in his face, he could barely focus, but he could make out a confused little boy walking around the room with the phone.

"Is that the person that tried to kill you?" Alex screamed over the noise and continued to fight with the orderly. "Paul, add twenty years to that face! Is that the man that tried to kill you?"

"Yes," he answered back and turned away from the phone.

Alex turned and ran out of the room at full speed. He was making his way down the maze of hallways when he heard Janey's voice coming from the phone again.

"Alex? Alex, are you there?"

"I know who it is!"

"John is dead. They killed John," she broke down as she tried to complete the sentence.

He stopped running down the hallway and leaned against a wall, exhausted. "What did you say?"

Janey could not stop herself from crying. "The killer, he got John. He's dead, Alex!"

For many moments, Alex did not move or make any attempt at sound. His back slowly moved up against the wall and to a standing position. He put the phone back up to his face so he could see Janey.

He finally spoke.

"They got it wrong. He wasn't dead."

There was a sniffle on the other end of the line. "What?"

"The killer is Richard the goddamn Lionheart!"

The Returners
Season One Part Three

CHAPTER THIRTY-TWO
Nabulio Complex

Three Days Later
Taco Baron Parking Lot:
Novato, California

There are many consequences to living through life a second time; full of memories; full of regrets, and on rare occasion, the uncovering of forgotten letters a historian dug up to make one appear, more or less, like a dickhead.

To JOSEPHINE, AT MILAN.

Modena y October 17, 1796

The day before yesterday I was out the whole day. Yesterday I kept my bed. Fever and a racking headache both prevented me writing to my beloved; but I got your letters. I have pressed them to my heart and lips, and the grief of a hundred miles of separation has disappeared. At the present moment I can see you by my side, not capricious and out of humour, but gentle, affectionate, with that mellifluent kindness of which my Josephine is the sole proprietor.

It was a dream, judge if it has cured my fever. Your letters are as cold as if you were fifty; we might have been married fifteen years. One finds in them the friendship and feelings of that winter of life.

Fie!

Josephine. It is very naughty, very unkind, very undutiful of you. What more can you do to make me indeed an object for compassion? Love me no longer? Eh, that is already accomplished!

Bitching out his wife with a passive aggressive letter: Napoleon Bonaparte, 1796, just before conquering Corsica.

"Oh, bullocks!" Waylan Dwight Jessup III exclaimed aloud as hot taco grease fell from his dinner and onto the first of multiple chins.

Waylan Jessup had been born into the world once before. Like Alexander the Great before him, Napoleon Bonaparte was a widely feared emperor and a brilliant tactician. Conquering Europe was his drug of choice and the addiction was flatly insatiable.

For his second foray into the world, his sights were set far lower and his addiction was to food and a purposeful dearth of exercise. Obesity gave him little pause, save for the need to purchase a second plane ticket should the need arise for him to fly anywhere; and lately, the necessity was constant.

A San Francisco Police Department squad car pulled up like a silent assassin: lights off and idling into position as if to strike. The female officer on the other side of the windshield sat quietly for a moment; Waylan returned the immobile truce, unmoving with a cold stare in her direction. The woman drew in and released a lengthy sigh before opening the door and stepping out into the lights of the restaurant parking lot.

"This isn't my precinct. *You know* this isn't my precinct, Jessup!" Officer Stephani Turner called out across the vacated cement parking lot as she checked her watch (which read: 4:37 AM.)

"Yes, we're here because *I know* this isn't your precinct." Jessup called back. "I don't like it when people can see us shitting where we eat."

Stephani moved across the lot and sat down on the hood of his matte-black Crown Victoria. "I can't think of anyone would want to watch people shit on their food before eating it."

"You know what I mean."

She smiled. "I never know what you mean you fat old bastard."

"What did I tell you about calling me *old?*" He replied as he crumbled up what was left of the taco and wrapper. His view dropped to the ground, staring for a moment at his well-polished shoes, before taking in a beleaguered breath of salty San Francisco air. "You heard about John?"

"Yes, sir." She said softly. "Was it Richard?"

Jessup nodded back.

Stephani pushed off the hood of the car, taking a few steps away from the conversation. "That wasn't the plan."

"He's off-message. I'll get him back on." He replied.

The sound of worn-down leather boots scraped aloud as she spun back toward the Chief's squad car. "He's a *psychopath!*"

"I'd go as far as *sociopath.*"

"Jessup. Those are practically the same thing." She yelled back.

Taking a moment to unwrap another cold taco, Jessup made Officer Turner wait impatiently before he replied with a mouth full of food. "Both have a tenuous relationship with social norms. If he were a psychopath he would have abnormally violent tendencies," he took a slow sip from what was left of his Diet Pepsi.

"He murders people with a palette of knives he has painstakingly collected from around the world! Which aspect—"

"Lower your voice, Corporal." Jessup cut her off.

"Yes, sir. Sorry, sir."

"What were you saying?"

Stephani spoke again in hushed tones. "Which aspect of him doesn't strike you as psychotic?"

Waylan Jessup smiled.

She swept her fingers through her dark hair, thoroughly exhausted after working a double shift, feeling the weight of her eyelids a good seven hours since her last cup of coffee. "I hate when you put on that condescending smile. Just say it, Chief."

The straw was gurgling against the ice at the bottom of Jessup's Diet Pepsi. "Who killed Tycho Brahe?"

Her face melted, wounded by the comment. "You told me to do that."

"I certainly did." Jessup said quietly, walking from the hood of the car to where she was standing. "You know why you did it, too." He swept his fingers gently across her ear and brushed her hair over one shoulder.

Stephani Turner brushed aside the unwanted intimacy. "Do they know who I am?"

"I'm not sure they know who *I* am yet," he laughed. "Couldn't have billboarded it any more clearly to Eliot. For a detective, he can be awfully obtuse sometimes," Jessup let go of her hair, trailing off.

"What about Chloe?"

"Do you know where else I can get some more tacos at five in the morning?" He said with a yawn.

The officer rolled her eyes. "Yes. Learn to cook," she yawned back. "What does Chloe know about me? Don't dodge me on this, I don't work for you." Stephani followed up with grit.

"No, you work *with* me."

Sirens could be heard in the distance. The radios in both of their cars were spouting all matter of code names and numbers. Neither turned to check on what was going down somewhere else in town.

Stephani grabbed the Chief by the lapel and put him down onto the hood of his car with force. "What does she know?"

"Chloe knows who you are and I don't know what she could possibly know beyond that." He pushed her arms off his pressed shirt and struggled to get back up off the car.

She extended a hand to help the struggling whale de-beach itself from the hood of the Crown Vic. "And?"

Jessup brushed down his shirt once back on his feet. "And what? She stopped playing for our team a long time ago."

The sirens drew closer.

"That's my cue." Stephani murmured.

"Oh, come off it. There's a liquor store shooting somewhere within miles of here and you're afraid some car is going to drive by and realize everything we have been planning?"

She scoffed. "No. I'm afraid some car is going to drive by and think you just banged me in the parking lot of a taco joint at four-thirty in the morning."

"That's an understandable fear then," he said.

Officer Stephani Turner grabbed for the handle of her squad car's door. "I'm leaving."

Waylan Jessup took a purposeful step away from the cars and the officer, searching his jacket pocket for what was left of his cigarettes. A steady pair of fingers reached into the packet and pulled out two filtered menthols. By instinct, he held the second one out of the side, knowing there would be a hand to grab it and a mouth to smoke it within moments.

She ripped the cigarette out of his hands and motioned for the lighter. "Whatever you have left to say," the dialog paused as she lit her smoke. "Whatever you have left to say, make it quick, sir."

He took another step away from her. "Do you know what my parents—I mean, my original parents; the first time—do you know what they used to call me as a child?"

The smoke from the menthols danced in the air between them.

"Your name wasn't originally Napoleon? Is that not your real name?"

Jessup stifled a laugh. "No, it was my real name—but they had a pet name, one of those names you call your kids to force a giggle yet somehow still appropriate when you're screaming at them."

Officer Turner pecked away some ash and watched the cherry burn down to the filter line. "This set of parents always called me Stephie when I was a kid." The sweetness of the nicotine made her rise like a wave when she took in a breath without the cigarette. "Why? What did they call you?"

"Nabulio," Jessup trailed off. "I was a rotten stubborn little runt—always focused on being in charge and what that meant; as if it meant anything. There goes little Nabulio, demanding that the bread maker down the road make his crusted loaf over and over again." He flicked what was left of his cigarette off into the darkness of the parking lot. "As if being seen eating a loaf of bread that was slightly burned on one side would be a sign of weakness to anyone."

"But you're the Chief of Police."

"Indeed I am, Officer Turner."

Stephani stood shoulder-to-shoulder. "So, why did you tell me all of that?"

"Because even if we don't care about something as we once did," he began. "There is no escaping who we are and what we were meant to do. I am meant to lead an army into battle until I can no longer."

"And then what?"

Jessup butted her in the arm with his elbow, cracking a smile. "Well last time, I was exiled for a few years onto a tiny island and then unceremoniously poisoned." He took a moment before turning back to his car. "Though, at that point it was nothing I hadn't already tried on myself. A tip if you're interested, friend. Replace your cyanide capsule every few months, as it will grow weaker with age."

The sound of Stephani's steps followed Jessup's back to his car. He grabbed for the door and held it open for a moment.

"I will see this through to the end, Chief. I just need to know what to do." She said.

Wayland Jessup took a brief moment to consider what the woman before him was asking.

"Win the battle; win the war. Everything."

CHAPTER THIRTY-THREE
Group Therapy

Four Days Later
Seattle General Hospital's Lawn

The sun was beginning to set just beyond the western lawn of the hospital. The fiery colors glistened in the recently dropped rain; it formed a radiant canopy over the grass. Harriet's feet were frigid as she slid barefoot through the surreal inferno, paying no heed to the mixture of pain and numbness in her toes. A twice-puffed cigarette slid from her fingers and extinguished itself upon contact with the wet ground.

This beauty was simply of no use to her at the moment.

Not with John gone; not with Richard still alive; not with this heartache, like collapse, like a wound, like cowering in a foxhole where there is no war to fight though a battle rages forward; pulling; needing; pointless.

Harriet reached for a second cigarette and one of the five lighters stuffed into her sweater pocket. The flint struggled twice before lighting the end; there was a passing mumble about getting her hands on another lighter. It had not come to her attention that the cigarette she just lit was backward and the filter was almost completely on fire. She catatonically groped for the middle before recoiling when the flame scalded her index finger.

It fell to the mud in similar kind.

"I'm pretty sure hospitals have a few opinions about tossing cigarettes on their lawn," said a voice to the rear.

She knew it was Ransic, but he sounded different somehow. Or perhaps he sounded exactly the same, and she now listened differently. It was muffled, as if there were water in her ears. Harriet continued to dwell on the acoustics of the situation and not the content of whatever oratory was spilling forth into the air.

"Are you even listening to what I'm saying?" He asked a third time.

"No." She responded.

Ransic's eyes lowered to the ground and noticed her feet losing color in the stirring winds and post-rain air. "Aren't you freezing, Harry?"

"Don't call me Harry."

"Harriet!" He spoke with gravity. "Your feet."

"I don't care."

His fingers wrapped around her arm and offered up a gentle tug back toward the building. "I care."

She took two steps further down the hill in retreat. "Your concern has been noted."

A condor flew overhead, circled once, and continued on route before disappearing in the glow of the setting sun. Harriet tracked it out of sight before turning back to the former detective. "Are you here to try and make me feel needed again? I think I'm still fresh out of candor, so trot on."

John would be proud of that last bit, she thought.

Harriet spun away again; careful to ignore the relentless speechifying Ransic was doing as she moved further and further down the hill. A rabbit ran by in the grass and ran into a bag from a seafood place called *Pirate Mike's*. She called out over her shoulder, never breaking visual with the bunny and the bag. "Wait. You told Chloe that Richard had been loading trash bags into the van outside Francis Martel's apartment."

It took him a moment to realize what had just been yelled at him into the wind.

Ransic narrowed his eyes. "He *was* loading trash bags outside of Francis Martel's apartment."

"Right."

"*Right?*"

"I think that's right." She said.

"*What* is right? Which part of that was wrong before?" Ransic stammered.

Harriet was pointing and spinning on the grass, piecing everything back together on the lawn of the hospital. "I found Richard in the bathtub pretending to be dead. Francis was in the kitchen, *actually* dead—how many trash bags was he carrying?"

"It was three or four. Tough to tell in the dark."

"That's too many bags."

He grabbed her by the arms and kicked his shoes off, feeling the intensely cold rain begin to soak through his socks. "Harriet, put those on, dammit." Ransic waited for her to slip the Chuck Taylor's over her bare feet. "Okay, what do you mean there were too many bags?"

She continued laying it out, her voice becoming more gravely by the word. "Richard planted the information about Francis Martel where he knew *you* would find it. That's game step one. Follow the fake boyfriend."

Ransic began to shake his head with caution. "The information was protected. Got a ping on a single arrest record for Martel from a female officer in San Francisco a few months back. Under additional notes, it said that his boyfriend *Richard Matterhorn* bailed him out."

"So either Richard actually picked him up or they have a cop on the payroll to plant his name."

He rolled his eyes. "Now you sound like television. You can't just pay someone to magically change data. Every change would be logged and tracked through its revision history—and the arrest report was filed after he was bailed out, so it was just the single entry." He said.

"The cop's your suspect then."

"We'll pretend that's true for the time being. Game step two?"

"He knew you would pass on the information and we would go right in. Richard was set up all pretend-dead in the bathtub well before we got there. Game step two."

"Next?"

Harriet peeled the sides of her mouth back in condolence and offered up a stoic nod to keep going.

Ransic nodded. "The trash bags."

She waited for him to put it all together.

"There was nothing in them." Ransic slowly rubbed the bridge of his nose and took a heavy breath. "If it appeared that you and Eliot had already been killed—John and Chloe would become emotionally reckless and come right to him. Game step three."

Harriet rubbed the fleur-de-le-like burns across her arms. "And then the torture. He likes to hurt people, but he knew that we would split up and search the area. Game step four."

"Leaving John in front of the shop."

She dropped her head. "I shouldn't have left." Tears formed in the corners of her eyes, she did not bother to wipe them away as more would surely take their place.

"I left too, Harriet."

"I told you to come with me because you were a wreck that day."

Ransic lowered his head. "Sorry."

She shook her head in confusion. "It means you're human. You thought I was chopped up in a trash bag when you drove them over." There was a moment of silence between them before she spoke up again. "It means Richard played the game better than we did."

Without warning, Harriet stopped what she was saying and walked back inside of the hospital, leaving Ransic running to catch up from behind her.

He followed her through the massive entrance area—more like a Las Vegas hotel than a hospital. Sculptures composed of hanging glass spun around on wires casting a rainbow of colors on the area they were walking through. Harriet swiftly moved past couch after couch, trying to get to the elevators in the back.

Ransic caught up to her at the elevators. "What was that about?"

"I don't want to go any further without talking to Eliot. He used to be a detective."

"I used to be a detective!" He yelled back loudly, echoing around the vacated entrance area. The area contained exactly forty-two couches but over the days they had visited the hospital, only one or two were ever used at a time.

The elevator dinged. Harriet laughed. "I'm messing with you. I thought telling a joke would make me seem more together."

"Are you more together?"

Her eyes darted over to him as she pressed the button for the eleventh floor. "Heavens no, child."

The elevator beeped with each passing level, every floor containing some collection of broken people and families with no idea what kind of world existed around them. Ransic always said the same thing when they passed floor seven. "Cancer has a way of making everything else in the world seem like it doesn't exist."

Harriet had not thought about why he always said that as they went up and down the elevator. This time she did. "Did you know someone with cancer, Ransic?"

He swallowed. "Yeah, my dad had it. Lung cancer. It came and went."

"Did he beat it?"

Julius Ransic widened a smile with unmoved eyes. "No, he uh—he died a year back. Never had to see me kicked off the force."

They arrived on the eleventh floor and the doors opened up revealing the reception desk. As always, one of the nurses greeted the pair of them as they began the zigzag walk back toward room 1128.

They had taken this walk together many times before. Generally, they would take their breaks together, especially if Eliot needed some type of care that was clearly embarrassing for him to partake in with witnesses nearby.

Since the boutique, neither Ransic nor Harriet knew anything about where Chloe went after the attack.

Until the moment they walked back into Eliot's room. Chloe was standing at the foot of his bed, engaged in a heated exchange when the pair of them walked across the slick floor with wet feet.

Harriet piped up first. "What's going on? Why is she here?"

"I asked her here," said Eliot.

"No," Chloe corrected in a condescending tone, "you asked Alex to ask me here."

Harriet raised an eyebrow. "Is there a difference?"

"Of course there's a difference, dude." Chloe scoffed, "If Alex asks me to go somewhere, there's a damn good reason. If Eliot asks you to a hospital, it's to see your arm."

"Let's not get ahead of ourselves and openly believe calling me dude is a thing you can do." Harriet stepped forward. "Now. What are you saying about your arm?"

"There's our girl," Ransic whispered so only Harriet could hear him.

"Eliot wants to see the tattoo on my arm." Chloe pointed to her forearm.

Harriet shook her head and lifted her bottom lift with confusion.

"The body of the other Chloe—sorry, the other *Joan of Arc* in the morgue. She had a tattoo of Saint Barbara on the inside of her arm. Eliot here, has just a little too much time to stare at the ceiling and piece things together," said Chloe to a captive room, all putting it together at the same.

Eliot smiled. "I can't believe none of us thought of it sooner. Alex is going to lose his mind when he finds out."

Chloe's eyes widened. Her anger rose. "You wouldn't dare tell him."

Ransic put up his hands and stepped into the conversation. "I'm gonna go ahead and try to catch up here. When Alex and Eliot were in the morgue, Alex was able to identify his girlfriend's body based on the tattoo on her arm—Oh, I just got there." His gaze darted accusingly back to Chloe. "Pull up your sleeve, please."

She looked up at the ceiling in disgust as she rolled her sleeve up, revealing an identical tattoo of Saint Barbara, the same tattoo that Alex used to identify the other Joan of Arc that Chloe had murdered.

Eliot smiled as Ransic continued.

"When did you switch places with her?"

Chloe took two steps toward the open window, curtains blowing softly in the breeze of the eleventh floor. "You don't understand."

Harriet piped up. "Alex was dating the *other* one, you managed to sneak in, and he never figured it out."

Chloe sat upon the window ledge, leaving an uneasy energy in the room. "That night—that night I shot her. That was the night she was going to kill Alex and myself—he was running away because he knew someone was coming after him. When *that* Joan was down, they sent in Genghis to kill me."

"Who sent in Genghis? Was it Richard?" Harriet asked.

"It's really dangerous for you guys to know this stuff," Chloe trailed off and leaned her head out the window and into the breeze.

Ransic leaned against a nearby wall. "Well, you're shit-deep in it now."

The woman who was once Joan of Arc took a deep breath of the outside air and came back into the room. "There's another group of returners. Jessup, Genghis, Richard, other-Joan." She paused. "There's a lot more than that—and I know all about them."

Eliot sat up in his bed. "How, Joan? How do you know all about them?"

"When they had found out what I had done, Jessup sent the groupers after me."

Harriet raised an eyebrow. "What's a grouper?"

"The attack on the police station. The cashier at the taco joint. The guys in the Laundromat. The man following you in the minivan at the gas station, Harriet." Chloe paused to make sure Harriet was offering her full attention. "Those were all groupers."

Eliot interjected once more. "But what did they find out, Chloe? What did you do?"

"Dude." She sighed. "I killed one of 'em and pretended to be her."

CHAPTER THIRTY-FOUR
Adagio for Helio 31

Five Days Earlier
Location [REDACTED]

He blinked awake, dumbly transfixed on the stucco with the knowledge that the alarms would wake everyone up in moments. There was no use closing his eyes again. The breathing all around his cot felt shallow and aware, he thought they might be staring at the same stucco with the same trepidation.

They were all the same man after all, all one hundred and eighty two of them.

Helio 31 matched the pattern of his breaths with the chorus around him. *Don't be different. Be the same just enough,* he stared at the ceiling and wondered. There wasn't a time he could remember not sleeping in the same warehouse like this, with all of the Helios, Bakers, Polars, and Shades. *Shade 11 could be so unique, why was he so different? Why does he get to sleep in five extra minutes in a corner bunk? It's not fair!*

Under the looming finality of an alarm clock, all thoughts become unfocused whining. It was *The Pit and the Pendulum* ad infinitum, only without such a blatant disregard for facts about the Spanish Inquisition.

BWAAAAAARRR.

The alarm clock in question was a fire alarm from the seventies. The wail was outrageous, bouncing around the entire warehouse. Somehow, Shade 11 could sleep through it for an additional few more minutes before his phone woke him up. *He probably just faked being asleep so everyone would be jealous.*

Helio 31 sat up, much as the rest of the men on the lined cots did. He arose and rubbed his eyes, staring down at a pillow there was not an excuse on Earth he could use to return to. Six hours sleep: no exceptions, no changes.

His feet lumbered forward at one of the several lines branching off into different directions. They all knew this routine by heart. For Helio 31, it went: breakfast, bathroom, treadmill, inspection, and finally, email.

The day's breakfast was pasty egg gruel laced with protein crust and that, which appeared to be, bell peppers of an unknown color/phylum/birthright. Vegetables of questionable origin oftentimes appeared toward the middle of the week, but this was a Monday, and the start of the week meant protein shakes on a liquid diet.

Helio 31 knew that when email rolled around, there would be missions—the type of missions where Helio 17 did not come back alive from the laundromat. Though all groupers were discouraged from redundant fraternization—insofar that groupers should not show favoritism toward any one grouper over another—Helio 31 and 17 enjoyed spending time together. Despite appearances to the contrary, the groupers were encouraged to develop personalities different from one another. This would allow them to make decisions in the field that were less predictable (especially after they all heard about the police station in Los Angeles where Helios 1, 16, 22, 48, Polar 3, 4, and Shades 1 through 4 were killed by walking through the same door in the same way.)

This push for personality among the groupers was most evident in the bathroom.

As he walked barefoot past the mirror, Helio 31 pushed his fingers along the part of his hair to check how discolored the roots had become. After checking them for twenty seconds, he sighed and turned to the dye cabinet.

There was always trepidation among the men about a trip to the dye cabinet. It was packed to the hilt with over a hundred variations in color, to further differentiate the men from each other. Once a color was chosen, it was checked against a master list of all hair colors from other groupers. At that moment, Helio 31 had decided to reapply "#8.4 Medium Coppery Blonder" to his roots and beard. With a casual swipe across the counter, his wrist tracker logged that his day would now be off by roughly thirty-seven minutes—enough time to apply the dye and trim his facial hair back to the design logged in his file.

There were signs next to the counter styled after propaganda posters from the Second World War. They said things like: "Compare your facial hair to the man next to you. On a subway, would you two look too similar?" and "Tattoos and piercings are always encouraged. Check with your sub-lead before applying to get one!"

Thirty-eight minutes later, he finished wiping down the counter and carefully put away all grooming tools he checked out from the grooming cabinet.

Helio 31 decided to skip the treadmill that morning. The hair upkeep alone was obnoxious and threw off his entire day, but he knew that his weight was 1.2 pounds heavier than the average. This anomaly was a result of running on the treadmill at a slightly accelerated rate and a non-standard weight distribution on the barbells. This was frowned upon in the organization, but the differences were so slight, it was never possible to track by a sub-lead or a conditioner. He enjoyed getting away with doing it differently.

Today was not a day to draw attention to diversions.

When he was nervous, Helio 31 would whistle Smoke on the Water as he moved around and did his daily chores. He whistled it on the way to inspection, knowing something was already amiss as people got pulled aside in the hallways. That was how they all knew missions were being doled out. If any grouper was pulled aside by a sub-lead before reaching inspection, that meant a dangerous mission—the kind of mission where the success rate since going after the targets had become zero percent.

His sub-lead, Baker 13, was standing in the hallway holding a clipboard against his chest and scanning hair color as groupers walked by. There was little doubt in his head that with the reapplication of dye, Helio 31 would be picked out with little effort.

"Foxtrot Heirloom thirty-one," he heard his sub-lead call out his radio call sign from across the hall, a strange practice considering that all other sub-leads always used given names and not call signs when communicating with their subordinates. Helio 31 also despised his tone. Despite being two men with identical vocal chords, he believed that Baker 13 would call everything out in a shrill manifesto.

His hair stood on end. *This is the beginning of the end for you, thirty-one,* he thought to himself before replying. "Yes sir, I serve at your pleasure. Do you have orders for me?"

"You know the protocol, Foxtrot Heirloom thirty-one," Baker 13 barked back, shrilly.

Why does he insist on saying all of that? I'm standing right here. "Yes, I am aware of the protocol, sir. Call and response circumvents the delivery of orders. Ready on your mark."

Baker 13 stood taller and spoke a seemingly unrelated series of words. "Catatonic. Blue Velvet. Mittens. Ostentatious."

Helio 31 quietly giggled in the back of his throat at the idea that mittens could ever possibly be construed as 'ostentatious' and replied. "Firefly. Diego. Many Trumpeters. The tea in China."

The call and response protocol was simple, both the sub-lead and the grouper memorized a series of words that mirrored a different series of words. The lists were extremely difficult to memorize, and made even more difficult by having to know the correlation between words—which was an entirely different person's list of responses to the same calls. It was the simplest way to ensure no participant forged their way into a mission not explicitly assigned to them. Helio 31 knew this was dumb—no one would attempt to go on a mission where death was the only likely outcome.

"Protocol has passed." Baker 13 said after a look over the call and response clipboard. "Are you ready to know your mission, Foxtrot Heirloom thirty-one?"

Helio 31 was not ready to know his mission. "Of course, sir. I serve at your pleasure. What will you have me do?"

"Target suspension. Are you aware of what that means?"

That means I have to murder someone. "Yes, sir. I am quite aware what that means. Target suspension is a necessary step in world-loss."

Baker 13 pulled a pale manila envelope from his jacket and handed it over. It read 'eyes only' on the front. "Study this and then raze it. The plane ticket is for you, forty-one hours from this moment. When the target has been suspended, notify me and you will be sent a return ticket."

Helio 31 flipped the brad on the back of the envelope and pulled out a series of photographs.

"Do you understand everything in your mission, Foxtrot Heirloom thirty-one?" Baker 13 put an uncaring hand on his shoulder.

But he did not respond. The target in his envelope was someone he had heard much about, but not in a lifetime did he expect that anyone, let alone himself, would be the one to go after him.

Helio 31 had been sent to kill Alex Heton.

Two Days Later
Westfield Air Flight 0416

He sat down in his seat—a first class seat—and looked around the cabin with an antsy stupor. Helio 31 had never flown in anything but a middle chair toward the back of coach, so to be flying in first class was a culture shock. The stewardess had just been by to pour champagne to the passengers up front. He declined politely and said that he didn't want to spend any money on the flight. The stewardess gave him a confused look and tried to stifle two businessmen that were clearly having a laugh at his expense. Once he understood that the champagne was free, he mixed it together with a complimentary orange juice and discovered what a mimosa was.

After he had done away with two pre-flight flutes of this mystery beverage, Helio excitedly turned to the woman next to him and asked if she had ever had something like that.

The woman sharing the drink tray in the seat next to him was a tennis instructor for trophy wives at a country club. As it says in the bible, "Again I tell you, it is easier for a camel to go through the eye of a needle than for a 41-year-old divorcee tennis instructor at a country club to have never heard of a mimosa."

Helio was making all manner of missteps on the flight that were drawing unwanted attention in his direction. He recalled a propaganda sign in the bathroom that read: "If you encounter suspicious people, pretend you work on a political campaign." At first glance, it seems oddly specific, but he knew that the majority of all people have never seen the inside of one and it's the simplest way to bore people away from asking any further questions.

His yawn was loud and theatrical, drawing attention. Helio turned back to the tennis instructor; "It's been a rough six months working on this campaign. I feel like I haven't slept more than four hours in ages. I'm sure everything out of my mouth is just rubbish at this point."

The tennis divorcee smiled back, making no charade that he appeared to have money now, so he was worth talking to. "Perfectly fine. So, do you work in advertising or what?"

"Oh, let me tell you. Sometimes I wish that were true—but no, I work on a Congressional campaign. Re-elect Tina Yothers for Nebraska!" He watched as she began to flip through a magazine before pretending she had never asked the question. As a child growing up, he would watch syndicated reruns of The Facts of Life whenever he could. Despite being an actress on the show, and never having been near a congressional seat, Tina Yothers drew no suspicion, and in fact provided quite the opposite.

The plane began to tilt back as the landing gear parted with the runway. He leaned his head back against the seat in an effort to appear asleep, his mind racing with trepidation about his mission.

Was he ready to kill a returner?

Could he point a gun at Alex Heton and pull the trigger?

His eyelids were no longer pretending to be heavy.

I wonder where the hell I can get another one of those mimosa things.

The Next Morning
Lawrence, Kansas

There were always stories around their compound—rumblings of a man named Jessup, who was Napoleon in a former life—rumblings of a man who would stop at nothing to rid the world of what he, himself, was; a walking oxymoron; a gasping contradiction; an adverb coupled with an ironic noun.

The gun drop had not gone exactly as planned. Helio expected that a grouper in the area would smuggle a firearm with the serial number filed off into the area. The last thing he could have expected was being face-to-face with a returner, an idea he swore to rid the world of on a daily basis—so why was he expected to work with one? Nothing that night had gone according to plan.

He stared at the gun sitting in the seat of his car, a gun he would be using to evacuate a man's brain cavity onto the sidewalk in a number of minutes. *How in the hell did that just happen?*

Like a child going to college and questioning their religion out of view from their parents, a grouper will begin to question their reality the moment they step away from the compound.

Helio thought back on the exchange between the woman that dropped off the gun and himself about an hour before that moment.

He had awoken in his shadily parked rental car to a rapping on the window; cheap press-on nails hammered away on the glass to get him awake faster. The conversation had not lasted long. Once the window was rolled down, they exchanged a few sentences back and forth. He opened the conversation with a puzzled yawn. "You're not a grouper."

He remembered her eyes swelling. "This is the not the place to have a conversation."

"I just want to know who you are," Helio responded to the mystery woman.

A paper bag was placed in the window and landed with a metallic clink. "I don't care what you want. I deliver this and we never see each other again."

Thinking back on it, there was no reason that Helio would ask the question he did. "Wait. Are you one of them? One of the returners?"

She dumped the bag into the car and began to walk away. "You have the piece, do what you are made to do." She paused briefly, and added "To you, I'm no one."

As if not in control of any of his own actions, he remembered swinging the driver's side door open before walking after the woman. "I just want to know." He began to increase his walking speed down the sidewalk after the woman. "Please, I *need* to know the truth."

The woman then ducked into an alley. He certainly understood that she had been running away from him. Perhaps scared, or perhaps that's what she was trained to do if a grouper went off-book.

He turned in after her and noticed that she had broken a heel while trying to get over some old garbage. "Do you need some help?" he had asked.

"No, please do your job." She called back; tossing the busted heel into the garbage that had claimed it.

"Yes, but first, are you a returner?"

There was no question that this was the point in the conversation where the woman had grown angry at the belligerence of inquiries. "You aren't like the other ones. Why the hell are you asking so many god damn questions," she replied back in a hushed anger.

Helio 31 did not move or speak.

In the process of removing the other heel, she relented. "Fine. Yes! The orders come down from Jessup and we do what we're told. Just like you. So yes, I am a returne—"

The gunshot entered her throat and sent her gurgling backward onto the pile of rotting garbage.

He remembered feeling outside of his body as the smoke from the shell casing drifted past his face—a face identical to so many, but only he experienced the moment—the sensation.

Helio 31 looked down at the gun again. It had already taken one life today. Was it about to take another?

Alex Heton was sitting on a park bench half a block away with two young boys and more than enough ice cream between them. They were smiling and laughing, and more importantly, paying no attention to what was happening behind them.

He took a moment in the car to remember all of his training—all of the mentoring the sub-leads had given him to prepare for a situation like this. The life of a grouper was never supposed to be fair, he thought. They existed to fix a bug in the world's programming.

The Returners.

Before he had thought through any of it much further, Helio found himself walking down an alleyway with his fingers wrapped around the pistol in his pocket. Smoke billowed from the windows of nearby restaurants and busboys slogged the previous evening's trash out to the dumpsters.

He peered around another alley, and out into the street. The three of them were still on the bench and none the wiser to his advances. Helio 31 chambered a round and looked up at the sky.

It was a sunny day in Kansas.

The birds were flying silently amongst the cloudless blue.

This was a world worth saving.

A thunderous pain shot through his body, emanating from his throat. Instinctually, he attempted to breath in as he slid backward down the wall. But he could not—he could not take a breath. It was if the wind had been knocked out of him.

He looked up and saw a woman standing there. She was teeming with fury, clearly directed at him.

Helio guessed she was mid-twenties, of American-Indian descent, and before he had the opportunity to guess any further, she ripped two inches of a box cutter out of his throat. He knew now why he couldn't breath. She had sliced his esophagus completely in two.

The Indian woman mentioned something, but Helio was unable to make out what she was asking—on account of dying. He motioned for her to say it again with the hand that was not applying pressure to his gushing neck wound.

"Are all of you returners too?" She said much more clearly that time.

His brow furrowed, upset at the sentiment. "No," he mouthed, but no sound came out. He could feel the world begin to dim around him; it had been almost two minutes since he had been able to breath in or out.

She knelt down and tossed the box cutter aside on the concrete. "What can you tell me that I can use?"

There was no response. Helio's eyes were starting to lose their ability to focus and there was a pleasant chill washing over him.

The Indian woman grabbed his face and screamed once more. "Tell me something I can use!"

As the last bits of life ebbed from Helio 31's body, he looked back at her and mouthed one final word.

"Mimosa."

CHAPTER THIRTY-FIVE

First Dates and Extraneous Corpses

His Final Moments
Lawrence, Kansas

The dying man on the ground attempted speech but vomited instead. With swollen eyes, desperately blinking away the blood he kept coughing onto his face, he looked over the pile of trash bags that would be his deathbed.

Alex could see the frustration on his bloody face: the man would die atop week-old rotting lasagna and whatever-the-hell a Lean Pocket was.

Janey knelt into the garbage and grabbed their attacker's hand in her own. At first, he recoiled, choosing to perish on his own terms, but after another attempt, he relented. She held his hand firmly, controlling the shakes of a body shutting down for good. "It's okay to go, friend." She whispered and mopped the blood from his eyes with her shirt. "We don't win 'em all. Sorry it had to end like this, but it's okay to go."

"You're a good person, Janey." Alex said, smiling at the way her hair spun behind her head as she turned.

"Everyone deserves a pleasant death." She turned back to the dying man. "Go with the wind, friend."

"Stop calling him friend."

"Don't tell me what to call him. You're the one that brought me to a murder scene on our first date!"

Alex stamped his foot. "The murder scene came to us—and hang on a second, let's just remember who boxcuttered whom here!"

"Wait. Where are the boys?" She looked around the deserted alleyway.

"I put them in a cab with Ransic a few minutes ago. Glad he came back into town last night."

The man's eyes widened at the mundane conversation happening in front of him.

"Where the hell did you get the box cutter anyway?" She spoke as she picked up the orange tool with her free hand (as the other was softly stroking the man's hair) and held it up. "Look at it—it's all rusty and shit. That's a good way to get an infection."

"Janey! You just killed the guy! I don't think he's exactly worried about getting an infection."

"Well, he's not dead yet, now is he?" She said, motioning behind her.

The man's head slid onto his shoulder and he took his final breath.

"Oh, well okay—yeah, *now* he's dead."

Alex knelt down and gave Janey a kiss on top of her head. "We gotta go, sweetie."

She stood up and took a few steps away from the fresh corpse. "How many is that this week?"

"Baby makes three," he pointed in the direction of the dead grouper. "Really getting tired of watching that guy die. Wonder who he really is, you know?"

Janey began to pull the dead grouper by the hands; she walked him to a nearby dumpster and set the lifeless bulk against it. "They're not returners."

"What?"

She let out a huge breath. "These guys, they're not returners. That's what Harriet said on the phone to me."

"Did Chloe say anything about them?"

Her brow inched closer to her eyes. "Can we not have a conversation about your ex-girlfriend on *what-was-supposed-to-be* our first date?"

He helped her lift the body up and into the dumpster. It landed with a flattened thump. "I'm not talking about her vaginal history or anything; I just want to know if she said anything about the groupers."

"Dear Christ, *yes!*" Janey yelled, slamming the lid of the dumpster down hard. "Chloe is the one who gave us the information about these guys; she called them 'groupers.' She told Harriet, and I'm telling you—and this last bit's important, *can we please* not have a discussion about Chloe's naughty parts?"

Alex scooped the box cutter from the ground and walked across the alleyway to a nearby gutter. He used the excess water draining out of it to give the tool a quick wash. "So, if they're not returners, what are they clones or something? I mean, they can touch, right?"

"They travel in groups, Alex. Didn't you fight a whole bunch of them at the Police Department?"

He continued to scrub the box cutter, thinking to himself for a moment. "Yes. I guess there was, like, ten of them in the precinct?"

Janey looked down at her watch.

"How much time we got?" Alex said.

"Truck is two minutes out."

"Throw some bags on top. Pad the landing."

Janey walked back across the alleyway and grabbed some trash bags from the ground. As quickly as she could, she threw a multitude of bags on top of the dead grouper, trying to cover up the body somewhat.

The screeching of heavy brakes could be heard down the street, catching both of their attention.

"Right on time," Alex huffed under his breath. As he stood up, he reached back and grabbed the pistol from his trousers with a smooth motion. He walked with Janey into a roomy doorframe nearby.

"You really gonna use that?" She said softly, motioning with her head toward the firearm.

He shook his head 'no' before pulling the hammer back on the pistol. Alex shrugged.

The garbage truck's heavy engine rumbled into the alleyway on the other side of the wall. The brakes screamed as the massive vehicle slowed to a stop by the dumpster. The mechanical arm whirred about, bending over to pick up the only bin in the alleyway.

This was not what one would consider normal behavior.

Alex Heton and Janey Baptiste were dating.

They were also exceptionally good at disposing of numerous bodies in inconspicuous ways. The two had memorized the trash route and knew that this specific alleyway, and this specific garbage dumpster, was the third to last stop on the route. The dumpster was only used by a donut shop nearby that was always closed before they arrived; there would rarely be anything resembling an interruption. Being so late on the route, they knew that Jonathon Vasquez and Dietr Maronne were tired and less attentive this late in their shift. Alex and Janey knew that Jonathon's real name was Juan and his favorite beer was Newcastle—whereas Dietr's favorite beer was Miller High Life. This was in addition to knowing their shoe sizes, waist sizes, and inseam.

Alex and Janey knew that this was the best place to hide a body. Practicality was king and they had done this twice already.

"So where did you want to go for dinner?" Janey asked. "Got something hot and steamy planned—like a Texas Double Whopper," she dropped into sexy voice. "*Extra* bacon?"

Alex heard the garbage fall into the back of the truck. He waited a moment for the truck to drive off before answering. "Listen, Misses Burger-King-sexy-voice, you can't just say bacon in a sexy voice and make a guy melt."

"It's actually *Miss* Burger-King-sexy-voice, and have you met guys?"

He poked her in the stomach. "I actually do have something pretty romantic planned—I mean, once you wash the blood off your hands and everything."

"I've been with you all day, Alex. You don't have to pretend you had time to plan something."

"No faith, Sacagawea. You have no faith in me."

Janey gave Alex a quick peck on the lips. "Your ex-girlfriend was burned alive for her *faith,* if I do recall."

"What happened to not talking about Chloe?"

"She was burned alive for being a crazy person. This is a topic we can talk about all you want to. Hey," she paused for a moment. "Hey, do you remember that time Chloe was burned alive at the stake for being a crazy person?"

Alex rolled his eyes and motioned to the door beside them. "Your dinner awaits, madam."

Janey had to yank on the rusted metal door a few times before it opened. She took a few steps and allowed her eyes to adjust to the room before her mouth fell open in awe. "You said you put them in a cab with Ransic!"

A man emerged from the darkness to her right. "We'll all be in a cab soon enough—tonight, we go together." Ransic smiled in the candlelight, holding five plane tickets in one hand, and for security, a Glock-17 in the other.

"Thanks for coming back, Ransic." Hand on her chest, Janey tried to slow down her breathing. Her gaze returned to the two young boys, dressed in matching suits, standing over a single table dressed with flowers and a tall candle. "You look very nice, boys."

Albert and Richie smiled at each other and tried to stifle laughter.

"Right this way, my lady," Albert said with a gentle bow. The young man walked Janey to the table by her hand as he had carefully practiced with Ransic. After he had pushed in her chair, he returned to the front of the table. "Can I get you something to drink? Perhaps a sparkling water? On special tonight, we have a wonderful Arctic Rush Gatorade that pairs well with most store-bought cheeses."

Janey did a spit take with her glass of water, laughing at the menu selection.

Alex sat down on the other side of the table and smiled in the candlelight. "Did I do alright?"

She smiled back at his unshaven face; his vaguely orange beard looked nice in the light, even if he hadn't shaved in a week. "You did good, Alex." Her hand fell atop his, she stroked the back of his wrist with her middle finger. "I am possibly a little concerned about our proximity to a murder scene, though."

There was a broken static crackling behind her. Janey spun to see Ransic hold up a police scanner and give a reassuring nod. "It was still in my car," he mouthed back.

"We're fine," Alex said with a reassuring tone. "Enjoy *our* date tonight. This is the last night we'll spend in this city."

Janey leaned across the table and gave Alex a kiss on the lips. "You better be this cute in Seattle as well."

"You aren't mad we're going to Seattle?" He spoke sheepishly.

She looked around the empty warehouse. "I'll miss Lawrence as much as the next college student, but we need to get our team back together. We still have a crazed mad man out there trying to kill us."

Richie ran over to the table. "I thought the bad guy was gone?" the boy said with a surprised yell.

"Way to go, Jay."

She shrugged and leaned down to Richie's puzzled face. "The bad man is still trying to get us. Are you going to be brave for me? You're the only one that can beat him. You know that?"

Richie stared back in amazement. "Why am I the one that can beat him?"

Albert put his arm around his smaller friend. "Because you know what he's thinking." He took a seat on a nearby sleeping bag and unwrapped a couple of foot-long sandwiches.

For the first time, in a long time, all of them got to sit down and share a nice dinner; exchanging stories about the journey up to that moment and ignoring, at least for a single night, that one or all of them would probably be dead within the week.

Alex knew it was about to get incredibly bad.

CHAPTER THIRTY-SIX

Ringtones or The Third Guy, *We Couldn't Decide*

Sunset Boulevard
Hollywood, California

Relying on the belief that horrendous acts of violence are not only fun but also therapeutic will cement the label of 'psychopath' firmly onto one's person. In such times, the common reactions from the victims were to scream, run like hell, or let fly the occasional terror-belch.

We already did this.

There was certainly someone trailing behind him as he made passage through the hilly offshoots of Sunset Boulevard. *A delusional madness,* he thought of his pursuer. It would most certainly end in the man chasing him screaming, running, or releasing a frightened eructation.

Who is trying to kill us this time?

Richard Matterhorn brushed the hair out of his eyes and examined the inebriated mass of bodies in his way. Pushing through the crowd of drunken smokers in the various hotel driveways, he checked again to his rear to make sure the pursuer in dark clothing had not given up his pursuit.

Where would the fun in that be? One of his personalities continued to narrate the action in his head.

The phone in his pocket buzzed twice, alerting him to an incoming text message. He never turned on the ringer. Richard much hated the idea of a ringtone; an antiquated approximation of a function that a mobile telephone device no longer needed. A cellular only needs to notify the person, the *owner*, of a communication. There was never any reason to notify surrounding people because phones are no longer a shared item. He had killed because of ringtones. In point of fact, he killed a six-foot-five father of two for referring to his as a "baller ringtone" in a crowded movie theater.

Bastard deserved it.

He slipped the mobile out of his pocket and took a quick look at his phone. The text read: "stop running."

Richard started running.

He shook his head in disbelief as he turned past a local bookstore. *There is no way that Jessup could have gotten this number.* Jessup's reach was a mystery; his connections were seemingly limitless for a police captain's pay-grade.

The message: I will get to you. I will hurt you. Always stay on message.

Richard had his own message, a message he was carving into the bodies of dispatched groupers. Of the four groupers trying to kill him, he used a steak knife to slice it into the flesh of three. It was a simple message, easily carved into abdominal areas of identical men.

These men are not currency.

And you are not a bank.

The man following at seventy paces had not turned the corner at the bookstore in pursuit. Something was off. Richard scanned the area for the most likely angle of attack. It would be from a flank toward a hardly defensible position. He backed against the wall and ducked behind some boxes for a moment, looking around carefully.

"The parking lot," he softly said aloud, looking across to a ten-dollar all-day parking lot that ran between a historic hotel and a drive-through steak restaurant.

The parking lot is too obvious. Don't be a dummy. Also, what is a drive-through steak restaurant? That shouldn't exist in the corporeal realm.

He closed the distance to the parking lot in a matter of seconds, ignoring whatever argument was occurring in his head. There was a couple making out against a Beamer, sunglasses holding their hair back.

They look clean. We know it's not them.

The man chasing him wasn't a grouper; that much was obvious. It was a returner and certainly one that he, every one of him, wasn't aware of. It's difficult to recognize someone that could literally be any single person from the whole of history

"Balls." Richard exclaimed aloud, startling the couple into a brief disruption from the kissing. "No, not you guys. Just pretend I'm not here," he offered up. They did not carry on, electing instead to walk hand-in-hand to the drive-through steak diner.

The lot became quiet, tense and dangerous. This is where it was going to go down. Somebody was about to die and somebody else was going to spend their night running away from the cops. Richard pulled a sawed-off shotgun out of a laptop bag he had strung over his shoulder and spun to face the rest of the lot.

We like to keep this handy for close encounters.

There was a man standing on the other end of the lot, dressed in black, standing perfectly still; his face obscured in the street lights.

Richard called out. "Who are you? If you've come kill me, I'm afraid I might be in the market to disappoint you."

The man did not respond. Richard walked closer, gun trained on the target.

Put him down. Do not do the clever banter thing.

"Answer my question so I can take you from this place. If you don't tell me, it will keep me up all night." He pulled the hammers back on the shotgun.

"W-wha-what are you talking about?" The man called out with a stammer. "I-I was just w-w-walking by and you—you pointed a gun at me!"

It's not him. Get out of here.

"It is him," he said softly as he emerged under the same streetlight as the man dressed in black.

"I'm sorry?" The man asked, puzzled.

"I know it's you." He pressed the gun into the man's ribcage. "Who are you? I will not ask again."

You shouldn't be asking at all.

Richard's nostrils flared at the sudden stench of urine.

"My name is Stephen," said the man who had just pissed himself. "My name is Stephen—Stephen James Toulouse."

"Yes, I don't care about that name. I want to know your true name. Your old name."

"That's the only name I have." The man continued to tremble.

"No. It isn't."

"Yes it is!"

Dispose and fly.

Both barrels emptied into Mr. Toulouse's chest cavity, spreading pieces of his lungs all over that end of the parking lot. The gunshot was not followed with screams or terror, as no one had seen it firsthand. The people partying in the hotels nearby reassured each other that it was probably just a car backfiring.

He tossed the shotgun into a nearby storm drain and took a moment to drag the body out of where people walking by could stumble upon it. There was a super-duty truck parked in the middle of the lot. It took twenty seconds to get the body shoved under the car—there wasn't much he could do about the lungs.

Richard ran downhill through an alleyway—going three streets over from Sunset Boulevard and coming to a roundabout where he stopped to catch his breath. The phone in his pocket buzzed a couple times.

His demeanor quickly changed as he read the text aloud. "His name really was Stephen."

Stephen F. Austin. Steve McQueen. Stephen Crane. Stephen Douglas. Saint Stephen. Wasn't there a Pope named Stephen?

The phone buzzed again.

"Stephen was not a returner."

Oh.

A pistol cocked behind his head. Richard put his hands up in surrender. "Do it fast."

"No," said a defiant voice from behind him. It was distinctly high-pitched and gravely, but it was not a voice Richard had ever heard before.

"Please?"

"I'm not going to kill you," the voice spoke again.

Richard turned slowly and looked straight into the eyes of a man with a gun to his forehead. "Who are you?"

"I don't say much."

"Not what I asked you."

The man lowered the gun slowly, took two paces back, and crossed his hands in front of him.

Richard relaxed and took a deep breath. "I want to know who caught me."

The man thought it over for a moment. "I've nothing to gain from revealing that. I'm to take you back to Jessup, so come with me."

Richard crossed his hands defiantly in front of his body.

The man rolled his eyes and acquiesced. "Fine. If your read Dante's Inferno, you'll remember in the last circle of hell, the Devil has three heads and is chewing on history's most reviled men."

"Judas Iscariot and Brutus. I forgot the other one. Who's the third guy?" Said Richard.

"I'm the third guy."

Gaius Cassius Longinus. We are intrigued.

CHAPTER THIRTY-SEVEN
The Vote

Highway 287 West
Sinclair, Wyoming

"Aquaman is not a Jedi!" A young man's voice yelled from behind.

"He uses his powers in the sea. He's like the Obi-Wan of *fish*." The other boy scolded back.

"What? Have you even seen the original Star Wars movies?"

There was an innocuous pause. The young boy thought for a moment. "Do you mean, like, *The Phantom Menace*?"

"No I do not mean the damn Phantom Menace!"

"Darth Maul could kill Aquaman," the younger boy said with assurance.

"And you'll hear no argument from me. First chance we get, I'm showing you *A New Hope* and there will be no arguing."

"A new hope for what?"

The response was a beleaguered sigh.

Alex Heton made a concerted effort not to piss on his shoes as Albert and Richie continued to argue in the background. The three had forced Janey to pull over so they could take another Slurpee-fueled piss on the side of the empty highway. He zipped up his trousers and starting walking them back to the old Jeep Cherokee pulled over onto the side of the road.

His hand dropped onto Albert's back as he whispered, "if it makes you feel any better, I feel your pain. Everybody knows *Return of the Jedi* is the best."

Albert pulled his shoulder away and darted angry eyes back at Alex, nostrils flaring, the boy's world in a tailspin.

"I'm kidding. Get back in the car," Alex smiled.

They arrived at the doors and Richie, as usual, jumped in first and went back to coloring on the back of a bland diner menu they had come from earlier that day.

Janey stood in front of the vehicle and stared off into the distance. She made no ruse of her body language; implying, quite blatantly, that something was not as it should be.

"Something wrong, Janey?" Alex called out as he tossed an empty Slurpee cup into the rear window of the car.

"We just wanted a quick word," spoke Albert from the rear.

Alex spun around to make sure the boy was talking to him before spinning back to his girlfriend, aware that something had not gone according to plan. "Did you guys have a secret meeting?"

"No. You watched Bloodsport for two hours and then fell asleep in the car. We did try to talk to you." Janey scolded.

"Whoa, don't bring Bloodsport into this," Alex gave a smile that quickly faded, noticing his charms were not going to be effective. "Seriously, what's going on? We have to get to Seattle."

Albert pushed by Alex and joined Janey, leaning against the hood of the vehicle. "That's what we wanted to talk about."

"About getting to Seattle?"

"About *not* getting to Seattle," Janey said, avoiding his eye contact.

"Okay," Alex trailed off, scratching his scraggly unshaven face.

"Don't do that," she spoke softly.

He swallowed. "Don't do what, *Jane?*"

"Don't get all passive-aggressive for one, and don't drop the 'y' off my name because it's cute and awesome and cuddly *and just don't be a penis to us right now.*"

Albert leaned his head closer to Janey. "I would have stopped after the first point," he whispered dryly to her.

"I got carried away," she whispered back.

"Get back on track," Alex spoke with authority.

Albert turned back, his lips pursing as his jaw lowered, making it clear he was annoyed with Alex. "Okay, no problem." He stepped closer, standing straight and attempting to create height in the presence of a much taller adult. "I wanted to have a discussion about not going to Seattle, so I asked Janey first. I'm not saying we shouldn't go, but I am saying this is something we should talk about and vote on."

No one spoke for a full minute. Richie sat forward in his chair, noticing something wasn't going right outside of the car. The young boy cracked his window to listen in.

"Is that how you both see it? They're counting on us up there."

Janey brushed her jet-black hair away of her face, turning to meet Alex's eyes. "We're getting our asses kicked out there."

"We are up against a lot—"

She cut Alex off. "Let me finish. We're getting our asses kicked and it's not getting any better. *Alex*, John is *dead*—the same John that cooked the worst dinners and was always too cranky in the best way possible." She took a moment to stop herself from crying. "We really liked that man—and he's gone—and he's not coming back. Richard killed him."

"And we're stronger in numbers!" he countered.

Albert stepped in. "I'm not going to pretend that I have any idea how to fight a war—surely, you've got me hands down in that department—but we don't need to be stronger; we don't need to win."

Alex's head coiled back and tilted to the side. "What are you talking about?"

"We need to *live*—this isn't a war," the boy pleaded. "What the hell are we doing, Alex? We go to Seattle—do the Marvel team-up thing and then what?" The boy took a moment to catch his breath. "I don't want to fight a war—I want to live."

Janey joined in. "He's not wrong."

Alex furrowed his brow. "Don't do the teaming up thing."

"It's a discussion!" Janey countered.

"No. It's an ambush." Alex turned out to the horizon, watching the sun begin to melt down the side of the sky. "What about Harriet? What about Eliot? Do we just leave them all to die?"

"In case you haven't noticed, we're not exactly stopping that from happening," Albert spoke in a low rumble, he sounded embarrassed to talk aloud. "We bought some time so maybe," the boy lost his voice. "So maybe we should use that opportunity to disappear—just the four of us."

"We agreed to go to Seattle," Alex said curtly.

"*No!*" The young woman yelled back. "*You* agreed to go to Seattle, cooked a dinner, and figured everything was okay."

"I'm trying to keep everyone alive," he replied softly.

Albert stamped his foot. "Uh, I'm pretty sure that it was Ransic and myself that cooked that dinner."

"Ransic's in Seattle, Albert."

"I know he's in Seattle! He's also with Chloe, Eliot, and Harriet—I'm pretty sure those four can take much care of themselves better than we can." The boy tossed what was left of the Graperang Slurpee into an old barrel on the side of the highway. "How many of us have to die? I mean, what are we even fighting over? Our entire existence is preposterous—we came back, good on us—but have you noticed we returned and became a massive danger to countless millions? A splinter group of people just like us want to kill all of us before that can happen—and they're probably right to do so!"

Alex took a long breath in. "So you're decided then?"

"I vote to find some remote island somewhere and live out our second set of days in peace—at least we'll be together." Albert said calmly, "at least we can make something of *this* life."

Alex turned to the Jeep and saw Richie's bored face pressed against the window, looking bored as ever. "What about him? Does Richie get a vote?"

"No," Janey replied with immediacy.

He recoiled. "Why the hell not?"

"Think about it, genius," she replied.

Alex took a moment to dwell on it. It hit him within twenty seconds. "It's not about him being a kid at all, is it?"

"Correct," Albert replied.

"It's possible that any decision Richie, the kid, would help us make would mean that Richard, the murderer, could make the same decision."

"Precisely."

"Okay then. Albert already cast his vote to not go." Alex looked over at Janey, wanting her to see him say it. "I cast my vote to go to Seattle. We stick together all the way through the end. In the end, that might just mean something"

Albert sighed. "One to one."

"Last vote is up to you, Janey. It's on you whether we keep traveling or turn around and figure out what to do with the rest of our lives." Alex frowned, expecting her to vote against him. "So what's it going to be?"

Janey walked off without saying a word, making her way down the side of the grassy hill—the same hill the boys had walked up as a smiling group, a group now at odds over their futures.

She stopped short, knowing that any further steps might be directly into the distinct urine of up to three different people.

Alex came up behind her. "This isn't me versus you. You can make your own deci—"

"It's not that. I know we sprung this on you, Alex."

"Then what? Just cast a vote to go live on an island and we'll do that." He kissed her on the top of the shoulder. "We'll drink Piña Coladas until we're old—to be honest, I could use the sleep."

Janey spun around and wrapped her arms around him, a tight embrace. "I like Piña Coladas," she sniffled.

"Me too."

"Albert is right, you know?"

He sighed and kissed her on the cheek. "I'm certainly coming around to his way of thinking." Alex laughed onto her shoulder. "Look at me, just some idiot trying to argue with Albert Einstein—"

"We should go to Seattle."

Alex stopped breathing; he could feel his heart struggling in his chest. "What did you just say?" His mouth managed to stammer out.

"We're on borrowed time, Alex." She whispered back into his ear as they swayed together in the light breeze. "We're here for a good reason, a bad one, or no reason at all. I think we owe it to each other to find out."

"That's my girl."

He grabbed her hand and walked her back to where Albert was standing by the car. Alex could see on his face that he knew Janey's vote before they got back to the Jeep. He tussled his hair, much to the boy's chagrin, and spoke one final sentence before he hopped into the driver's seat.

"Let's go, Obi-Wan."

CHAPTER THIRTY-EIGHT
Broken Promises

The Middle of the Night
200 Miles Outside of San Francisco

Cassius glanced up into the rearview mirror of his 1996 Chrysler Le Baron at the man fumbling in the backseat. The chains had been wrapped around the prisoner in crisscrossing patterns all over his body; it would take Harry Houdini four days to get out that, he thought to himself.

The prisoner locked eyes with him as he continued to test the coiling prison for weaknesses. Richard's stare was like ice: frigid and without emotion. "Where do you come from?" The man spoke, never breaking eye contact.

"I'm from Broken Arrow, Oklahoma originally. Weirdest thing, it was destroyed by a tornado when I was like four years old. Seriously, it landed on one end of Main Street and just gutted the entire thing—only structure still standing at the end was a dented Kentucky Fried Chicken bucket. My mom would always joke that it kicked the bucket—still makes that joke, actually. Moms are weird."

The icy stare persisted.

"That wasn't what you were asking was it?" Cassius flashed a shit-eater up into the rearview mirror.

"You know what I'm asking," said Richard, wiggling his right hand under four chains.

"You know, I really don't."

Three plastic crucifixes swung back and forth from the mirror; Cassius had purchased them because he liked the way the colors popped. He took them down and tossed them in the passenger seat. His cracked another wry smile, "don't want them listening in."

Richard showed his dearth of amusement. "The Jesuses?"

"Jesuses can't be the right word."

"Feels right."

Cassius raised an eyebrow. "It's probably weird because you really can't have more than one Jesus."

"There are two that work at my car wash." Richard replied.

"Not what I meant."

"Where are you from?" The man in the backseat asked a second time.

Their eyes met in the mirror once more, "you're asking where Jessup found me? And why you never heard about me?"

Richard Matterhorn nodded and continued trying to uncross his chain-wrapped legs in the back of the old car.

"I was in politics."

The fruitless rustling of chains stopped for a moment. "Say that again?"

"I was in politics, but I guess the more correct way to say that would be 'politically motivated assassinations,' more or less." Cassius flashed another guiled smile. "Ghana, Beirut, Afghanistan, Czech Republic," he took a moment. "*America.* It's all so very *in* right now."

"You don't talk like an assassin." Richard spoke with tension in his voice.

"Oh yeah?"

"You talk like a Disneyland tour guide."

Cassius erupted with a hearty laugh. "Funny you should mention that, I actually did that over a summer when I was a teenager."

"Really?"

"*No,* what a rude thing of you to say. You don't hear me rattling on about you not sounding like a psychopathic serial killer now do you?"

Across Richard's face, the demeanor flashed back to cold. "Watch your step, Cash."

He took his hands off the wheel for a moment and grabbed a nearby bottle of ice tea. Cassius took a few swigs before putting his hands back on the wheel, cool as a bevy of cucumbers. "Uh-huh. Do you need a potty break anytime soon? Gonna have to finish my tea first."

There was a moment of intense silence. Richard let loose a long and purposeful sigh. "You're making what will be a costly mistake."

A hand came up and adjusted the mirror. Cassius laughed dismissively. "For two years, I sat down with African warlords, I'm talking about men that could stack the bodies of children like they were Christmas presents—they all had some version of the angry stare—the hyperbolic threat loosed through clenched teeth. Do you know what I did?"

Richard ignored the man talking in the front seat and attempted to dislocate his shoulder.

Cassius continued. "I took a contract from one warlord to kill this stone cold bastard. His name was Jean-Pilar Akinyemi and he was known for castrating any man that looked at his wives. The surviving wives, I mean—this guy killed six of the twelve of them he had. So this Akinyemi guy, everyone in the Congo wanted him dead, so I took four paying contracts and killed the guy with his own garden trowel—still had soil caked on it." His eyes became distant, staring far off down the road as he made his way through the story. "And I realized something. I could collect on the same morally bankrupt assholes multiple times. Contract-by-contract, I went village to village killing every single one of those bastards. When it came down to the last guy, I put him in the ground on the house."

The silence from the backseat continued.

"So, forgive me if I'm not exactly overcome with fear because you stabbed François-Marie Arouetis in the men's restroom of a Chili's." Cassius turned the radio up in the car. He drove for minutes without talking, constantly drumming on the steering wheel as if the previous conversation had never taken place.

They were good and out in the middle of nowhere now.

"You know they're going to kill you, right?" Cassius spoke up again finally. "You broke the rules."

Richard scoffed from his chains. "There are no rules. You *know* there are no rules."

"Of course I know that, but you don't see me throwing it back in Jessup's face. I just want to live."

"The rules dictate you don't get to," Richard muttered.

"We'll cross that bridge when we come to it." He turned onto a different highway, heading toward San Francisco. "There's a lot of returners left to kill."

"You will be the second person I kill when I escape."

Cassius's eyes flared and lowered the mirror to check that the chains containing Richard were still tightly bound around his person and locked down. For the first time in the entire car trip, his body got a rush of blood and chills went up his spine. "You're going to kill me … second?"

The cold voice in the backseat spoke evenly. "After I escape, yes."

"Yes, sorry." Cassius began. "*After* you escape, you will kill someone else first, and then me?"

"Correct."

"If you don't mind me asking," he wiped a bit of sweat from his forehead. "Who are you going to kill before you kill me?"

Richard managed to lean forward a little in the chains. "I made a promise to someone they would be next and I broke that promise."

Cassius knew they were still quite a good distance from the city and he would have to put up with his passenger's creepiness for a few more hours. "I think you might have to keep breaking that promise a little longer, bud. Who was the promise to?"

"Don't call me 'bud'." Richard snarled.

"*Who was the promise to?*" He repeated.

"Beowulf."

There were signs for restaurants and hotels again crowding the drive down the highway, *back to civilization again.* "Um. You know

Beowulf is a fictional character, right?" Cassius asked with audible confusion.

Richard did not respond. He was too busy dislocating one of his fingers so he could snake his left hand under the chain tightly wrapped around his chest. "I never break my promises."

"I'd hate to have to put you down before we get back to Jessup."

"You won't."

He took a moment to roll his eyes. "We still got a long way to go before San-Fran; think you could lighten up the conversation a bit?"

Richard smiled. "You'll beg me before you die."

"Okay!" Cassius shouted by the front seat. "Let's just agree not to talk then so I don't have to pull over and pummel the crap out of your face."

"Did Akinyemi beg?"

He shook his head for a moment, knowing not to indulge this man. "He never had a chance to."

"Honey, that's the best part."

Cassius coughed a little and glanced into the mirror again. "Did you just call me 'honey'?"

The man in the backseat leaned against the window and pretended to be falling quickly asleep. "In another time, and another place, you could have been my sex blanket."

The brakes slammed hard, sending Richard's defenseless face smashing into the seat in front of him. Cassius turned around for a moment and glared at his prisoner. He did not speak, for there were truly no words that could follow up on that exchange.

Richard closed his eyes again, began going over the math in his head of the chains that ensnared him.

There were fifteen separate bones that he would need to dislocate to get his arm free.

He popped his left shoulder out of the socket.

CHAPTER THIRTY-NINE
Fight Like a Butterfly, Sting Like a Bitch

Early Evening
Poulsbo, Washington

The old tires of the Jeep Cherokee slipped about on the driveway constructed entirely out of tiny rocks stolen from a nearby beach. The drive had been long, too long considering the number of geek-rage arguments that Albert got into with Richie, but they were finally arriving at their destination.

They were finally in Washington and grouped once again with their friends.

Harriet was sitting on the porch, enjoying the last lonesome drag of her American Spirit. The boys hopped out of the vehicle first and ran over to give her a ravenous hug. She patted them both on the head and shared mixed platitudes pertaining to how much they'd grown, knowing they had not.

"What's for dinner?" Richie blurted as soon as he stopped hugging Harriet.

She ran her fingers through her closely cropped hair, "well, I sure don't know, little guy. I know Julius has been in that kitchen all day making all kinds of noise. What say you go have a peek?"

Richie turned to Janey as she closed the driver's side door and yawned. He glared in her direction as he spoke. "We ate at a place where the tacos had a big square piece of cheese in the shell. It was like a grilled cheese but in a taco," he said with his high-pitched and fading French accent. "Where is the cheddar? *Who doesn't shred the cheese?*" He was getting himself worked up.

"Certainly talking a lot more than he was before," Harriet trailed off to Janey as she walked up to the porch and took a seat on the stoop.

"Yup. Can't seem to find something he won't complain about." Janey retorted with a smile.

"I feel like we've spent a healthy chunk of our journey arguing about tacos. Christ, it seems like every time we bring them up someone dies!" Albert half-yelled as he sat down on the stairs, his breathing escaping his control.

For a moment, there was silence.

Albert regained control of his breathing. "That's true isn't it?"

Alex put his hand on Janey's shoulder, gently massaging it. He nodded back to Albert. "Hate to dwell on that one too much."

"You and Chloe had the conversation *in* the Taco Baron," Albert began, "and then Genghis died." He trailed off.

"I really don't think this is a good idea, Al." Alex replied.

"No, hang on!" Albert took a moment.

Harriet stood up and tossed what was left of her cigarette into the grass. She turned and walked back inside without so much as a nod that she was leaving. The screen door slammed against the old wooden frame as she ducked away inside the aging cabin.

"I just stepped in it, didn't I?" Albert whispered as he plopped down on the stoop of the cabin.

Janey sat down next to Albert on the stoop and put her arm around him. "Chloe brought the tacos by the factory in Lawrence, before everything went crazy in Seattle." She ran a few fingers through his hair. "John died right after and that's not a wound that's gonna close anytime soon for anyone—especially Harriet." A lump caught itself in her throat. "You didn't know, buddy."

"I knew. I just didn't think about it." Albert replied.

"We heal at our own pace. Probably not the best idea to try and find superstitious connections between symbolic Mexican food and death."

"To be frank," Alex began, puffing up as if to make a stirring speech. "I think we spend way too much energy discussing Mexican food." He motioned for the group to head indoors and make themselves more comfortable before turning around and heading back for the luggage in the car.

Richie fell onto the couch in a huff, folding his arms over his chest. "You guys forgot that I am hungry still."

Albert flung himself onto the chair next to him and pulled out a half-eaten bag of licorice. "Knock yourself out, Batman."

Julius Ransic came into the room, fake smile upon his face and a towel drying off his hands. "Fantastic to see you all again! I'm still without a job and I spend all my time making food that Harriet pushes around a plate but hey, watching cooking shows in sweatpants I haven't washed in a month makes me feel like my life is really coming together." He sighed and gave Janey a quick hug before heading back into the kitchen, swearing along the way.

"Hey Jules, what's for dinner?" Richie called out as Ransic walked from the room.

"Pizza bagels!"

Richie turned to Albert with a raised eyebrow. "Really?" He called back.

"Yes. I'm making them from scratch and you will love them, got it?" Ransic slammed an oven door closed and it echoed around the living area.

"You can make those? I thought they only came in a box." Richie said to himself inquisitively.

Albert inhaled as if to say something just as Alex burst through the door holding five suitcases and a purse in his teeth. "Any wum wanna gib me a 'and wiffis?'"

The group in the living room jumped to help Alex put down some suitcases. He brushed off his hands and took a number of deep breaths. "We'll worry about sleeping arrangements after dinner." He turned to the kitchen, sniffing the air. "Speaking of, what is for dinner? That smells pretty good."

Richie grinned. "Pizza bagels."

Alex made an exasperated "f-" sound that usually would have been followed by other hard consonants before uttering, "Seriously?"

"I'm making them from scratch. I've been reducing this sauce since this morning!" An impertinent voice called back from the kitchen. "Anyone wanna help me slice some pepperonis?"

Richie turned excitedly and ran into the kitchen. "I do!"

"We sure about giving him knives? I mean, he is, you know…" Alex trailed off as he spoke quietly to Albert.

The thirteen-year-old stared off at his friend. "Yes, *he* is. He's also the kid that saved my life when the groupers crashed my party and brutally murdered everyone there, including my parents." He turned sharply back to Alex. "Do you mind if we have a quick discussion outside?"

Alexander the Great looked down at the little man talking back to him: as an adult, as a friend, as someone who was about to ruin his day. "Sure thing." He said and ushered the boy out onto the porch. He closed the screen door quietly behind them and turned back to Albert. "What's up?"

They kept their voices low.

Albert spoke first. "I get that I lost the vote to come up here." He looked around at the dense forest that surrounded their old cabin. "I like it, I do. We're secluded here and we'll see anyone coming from a mile away."

"I'm glad you like it—"

"But you gotta stop looking at Richie like he's a murderer. He hasn't done anything." Albert interrupted.

There was a moment when Alex looked out among the trees, opting for silence. He took a few solid breaths of the fresh mountain air. "Man, it sure didn't smell like this in Los Angeles."

"Are you ignoring what I'm saying to you?"

Alex rubbed his hair. "I certainly am not. I have to take a moment here and figure out what I'm going to say—because you've already figured out what *I'm going to say*."

A smile crept across the side of Albert's mouth despite his valiant attempts to keep it at bay. "Yes, I have."

"Let's have it then."

"You're going to ask me about the moral imperative again." Albert took his own long breath of the clean air all around them. "You're going to bring up how dangerous it is for Richie to be alive because all Richard has to do is touch him and we'll all be obliterated. "

"This does sound like something I would say." Alex laughed. "So, now that I've theoretically said all of *that*—what, pray tell, is your answer?"

"That even in the face of unparalleled atomic disaster, you cannot justify the killing of an innocent nine-year-old. Not to yourself, not really."

"He grows up to be a killer."

Albert turned and fired back with stubborn brevity. "No. He doesn't."

"I was hoping you'd say that," Alex spoke softly. "Hope for us yet."

The young Einstein smiled. "Hope for the returners."

They turned as the screen door swung open noisily from the other side of the porch. Harriet strolled back out onto the patio nursing a can of beer, another cigarette at the ready. She set the can down on the railing and set a kind hand onto Albert's shoulder. "Didn't mean to walk off like that earlier—still stings." The cherry of the cigarette flashed as she lit the paper and took her first inhale. "I dragged John into this mess. He never wanted any part of it. Old coot was happy enough just drinking himself to death at the same bar on the same dime."

Alex leaned against the rail to her side. "You can't go around beating yourself up about it. It's not like you forced him to come…" He trailed off when he noticed how quickly her eyes had become bloodshot from the moment he began speaking.

"What did you do?" Albert injected.

"I stuffed him in the trunk of my car when he refused to come along," she replied. "Ended up saving his life, actually—grouper chased me down the highway and I took 'em out at a gas station. Bullets through the passenger seat all said and done." Harriet took a moment. "Listen to me try and justify it. I got him killed—it's my fault. He wanted a life of enlightened conversation and soured whiskies and I took that away from him." She trailed off and rested her gaze on the forest beyond the cabin nested among the trees.

The screen door creaked again. Janey was holding the remaining five cans of beers hanging from the plastic rings. "Thought you guys could use some brews," she said, placing a can into Alex's awaiting palm. Albert was surprised as she threw one to him as well, mouthing the words "just one" after the toss. Her dark hair sparkled in the sun as she pulled it off her face. "Did I interrupt you guys? I can go back inside…"

"No." Harriet said over her shoulder before turning around. "Alex was just about to go over the plan."

He gave her a silent nod and set the beer down on a nearby chair. Alex Heton pulled the brim of baseball tightly over his head and took a deep breath. "They're going to come at us shitty."

The group stood in silence waiting for him to say something further.

He did not.

Janey chugged half of the beer and let out a hoydenish belch, wiping her mouth of excesses. "A rousing speech. An instant classic. Ten out of ten. Would rouse to it again."

"Did you—did you just *Amazon review* my speech?" Alex clocked his head to the side.

"I think Amazon uses a five point scale," Harriet added.

"I don't think I know where this is going," he mumbled in response.

Albert said something, but the three adults continued to argue at each other to the point that none of them even knew if they were being sarcastic anymore. The young boy spoke up again and watched it fall upon deaf ears once again. He threw his beer to the ground and yelled, "They're going to hit us at the hospital!"

The adults turned in his direction, mouths slightly agape.

"Grow up, you guys," Albert laughed, now sipping on Harriet's beer. "Chloe is protecting Eliot at the hospital—they know we will show up at some point. They also know trying to take us out in the wilderness is a terrible idea, so they'll hit us there; Richard, groupers, Jessup, everybody."

Alex smiled. "Couldn't have said it better myself, kiddo. We go there and make our stand—force the fight on our terms."

"We'll all be arrested. We don't come back from this," Janey casually mentioned as she polished off her beer and went for another.

"We don't," Harriet offered, holding up her beer in solidarity.

Albert rolled his eyes. "I'm not waiting around to get picked off. You guys seem to believe we're back for some higher purpose—something you know I don't believe in."

Alex glared back. "You out then?"

Albert laughed and crushed the can on the railing. "Nope. I'm in. You think I'm looking forward to going through puberty a second time? I say we do this for John Quincy Adams."

The group nodded to each other in agreement, their smiles genuine but trepidatious. They toasted one another with both full and empty cans as one-by-one they shared memories of John: both good and bad.

This went on for a few wonderful minutes. It was their first good moment in a long time, and they were interrupted by the urgings of Ransic to come try his pizza bagels.

CHAPTER FORTY
Instead of Kisses

Late into the Night
Shipping Warehouse in Downtown Seattle

Wayland Dwight Jessup III mumbled something about fish and went back to scraping up what was left of his microwave dinner. It had been a long few days hiding out in the warehouse. It was more difficult at night, but they were grateful one of their mutual friends in security had helped them get in.

The warehouse was beginning to show its age, passed over by newer and more technological storage facilities. It was in use only a few days out of every month. The rest of the time, it was spacious and devoid of goods, save for Jessup and San Francisco Police Officer, Stephani Turner.

Stephani was beginning to feel the pressures of living her hard-earned vacation in a huge, empty warehouse. She was also growing weary of the way the man chewed—smacking, dripping, with a lack of attention to basic manners. "Close your damn mouth, Dwight."

The portly Police Chief looked up from his dinner. "I'm sorry did you say something, love?"

"Don't call me love."

He wiped the inscrutable sauce from his mouth onto his sleeve. "Posh, I call everyone love."

Stephani rolled her eyes and reached across the table for a half-eaten bag of Doritos. There was a silence in the warehouse that seemed to amplify the guttural mastication of Jessup's dinner like a megaphone. She thought that chewing some chips might help to drown out the noises coming from the narwhal across the table.

She'd really grown to dislike him since San Francisco. To be fair, little had changed in their relationship, save for the fact that they had spent every waking moment together for the past few days. Like any relationship, annoyances were amplified to their breaking point. "I gotta get some air, Chief."

He looked up. "Is it the chewing again? I have sinuses, you know—makes it hard to breathe through my nose."

"Fine," she relented. "Still need some air."

"Cassius will be here soon; best to stay put," the Chief said.

"We gotta get that dude a real name. 'Cassius' doesn't exactly fly under the radar."

Jessup snorted. "It's a perfectly acceptable name."

"If you're a boxer or a Roman assassin!"

"From what I understand, he's quite adept at both." He laughed. "Do keep yourself occupied, love."

Stephani smiled with counterfeit abandon. "As you wish, Bonaparte."

She took her gun out of the holster and looked it over, raising the ire of the Chief sitting not three feet from that happening. The chambers of the revolver were spinning under her index finger, one-by-one.

Click.

Click.

Click.

"It's not time, Ms. Turner." As he finished the sentence, what was left of his dinner was flung across the table, sliding to a stop far on the end. "We had an agreement, if you'll recall."

Click.

"I'm aware of our agreement, Mr. Jessup," she smiled.

"I know you don't want to be here."

Click.

Click.

Stephani lowered the barrel, no longer pointing it at Jessup, but certainly not pointing it away from him either. "What ever gave you that impression?"

The Chief lowered his head and looked back at her with sharp eyes. "You brandished your firearm in a conversation about chewing."

"It isn't even loaded," she said.

Click.

Click.

"Is that so?"

Click.

"*Totally* so."

Click.

She was twirling the gun now, in all manner of styles. Her prowess with a firearm was unmatched on the force, though she was always turning down the invitation to go out for a trick-shooting competition.

"Most impressive," Jessup joked, having seen it all before. He reached for the Doritos she had already given up on.

Click.

"Explain to me our deal again, Chief." There was playfulness to her words, less entertaining than terrifying.

"You know our deal."

"But I wanna hear you say it."

"Annie…"

She stood up from the table, in a huff. "Oh, we're using real names now?"

"If I wanted to use real names, I would have said *Phoebe Ann Moses*. Now have a goddamn seat, Corporal." Jessup barked before continuing, "When the time comes, you'll put the last bullet to me and you'll be the last returner—a privilege you can do with as you please."

Stephani sat back down at the makeshift dining table. "Richard is next."

He bowed his head, his eyes becoming heavy. "Yes. We'll sort out this Richard situation and then we'll get back to business." The Chief took a moment, his eyes searching the room. "Can I rely on you to stay on message?"

"I'm always on message. I come from show business, Chief."

A door slammed open twenty feet behind them. They both turned to the door and drew guns in that direction.

A man with a black bag on his head, surrounded in a litany of heavy chains came through the door with Cassius prodding him in with the butt of a rifle. Cassius kept his gaze on the prisoner, staring intently without looking up.

Officer Stephani Turner looked to Jessup, "Are we doing the right thing, Chief?" Despite all the posturing, there was a vulnerable woman there; it was spelled out across her face. "We're the good guys, right?" She asked with glassed-over eyes.

"We're doing the right thing, Love."

She sniffled a bit. "I hate you."

He smiled back. "I hate you too, Annie Oakley."

Cassius kicked Richard the Lionheart, bag still slung over his head, to the ground with immediate force. He snarled, eyes still on his prey.

"How did you finally capture him, Cassius?" Jessup called out across the warehouse to the man at the door.

"Doesn't matter," Cassius mumbled back, still focused on the prisoner, as if he might run away at any moment. "Just get it over with," he said with an exhausted grumble.

"Take the bag off," Stephani regained herself and called back to Cassius. "We need to know it's really Richard under there."

The man under the bag was shaking, his head turning in many directions. It was obvious he could hear everything being said on the other side of the fabric sack.

Something was wrong.

"Just wait." Cassius grumbled again.

Jessup took a few steps forward, "Don't make us sorry we hired you, Cassius. We had a deal, you bring him in and we let you go on your way."

"The second I hand him over, you'll hunt me down."

The Chief laughed. "When I make a deal, I stick to my word," he said, turning to Stephani as he stepped forward, giving her an inquisitive look.

Cassius took Richard to his feet and concealed himself behind the prisoner before pulling a gun and putting it up to the bag. "Right there is fine."

Jessup stopped in his tracks. "Now, wait a minute."

Stephani zeroed in on the tiniest sliver of Cassius' head.

"I know that Stephani Turner is the only returner that is going to make it out. You guys made a deal—leaving the rest of us to get hunted down like animals!" Cassius barked across the warehouse to the other two.

The man in the bag wriggled in his chains, trying to get free, but it was no use. Richard wasn't going anywhere at the moment.

Jessup turned to Stephani and spoke at a volume no one else could hear. "Cassius couldn't possibly know that. Did you say something to him?"

She took a step backward, offended at the insinuation. "I've never really ever spoken with him. He has to be getting his information from somewhere else?"

Cassius began backing the prisoner to the door, slowly, intently; gun still trained on the bag. As he got within feet of the door, Cassius kicked the prisoner toward both Jessup and Stephani and he began to fall over in their direction.

Click.

BOOM.

Stephani had drawn her pistol and got it into firing position before the man could finish falling over.

The back of the bag, and the man's head, were blown all over the back wall. He fell like a crumpled piece of laundry onto the floor, dead.

The backdoor was swinging on its hinges; Cassius had run out during the gunfire and confusion.

"Don't worry about him. We tracked him down once; we'll track him down again. We got the one we needed to get." The Chief walked slowly to the body in the corner. "Cover the back door in case he comes back."

Stephani did as she was told and trained her gun on the door. There was no one that could move faster than she could shoot.

Jessup pulled the bag up and fell onto his rear, furious.

She already knew what he was about to say.

"No."

"Just say it, Chief." Her eyes did not leave the back door.

"God dammit, no!" He screamed throughout the entire warehouse.

"Chief!"

"It's Cassius! He was under the bag!"

Officer Stephani Turner lowered her gun and catatonically took her seat at the table again. She reached for the bag of Doritos and began to munch on them again.

Within a few moments, Jessup followed suit and took a seat on the other side of the table. His hands were caked in blood and he was trying to wipe it on his shirt. The microwave dinner he had thrown down the table was still there. He grabbed it and went back to shoveling the lukewarm food into his mouth, unable to look up at Stephani on the other side of the table.

She was playing with the chambers of his gun again.

Click.

Click.

Click.

"Did not expect that."

"Nope," she replied without making eye contact.

"He's going to go after everyone at the hospital."

"Yup," she said.

The Chief shoveled more food into his mouth. "Good a' place to end it as any, I suppose."

Stephani Turner tossed what was left of her corn chips across the table to the Chief of Police.

His eyebrow's relaxed. "Wait. I thought you said that gun wasn't loaded."

It took a moment for her to respond. She was thinking about everything that had just happened in that cramped warehouse. After a deep breath, she whispered softly, "I lied."

CHAPTER FORTY-ONE
Light Begins to Fade

The Early Morning
Seattle General Hospital
Private Room #873.B

Chloe Freimont brushed the most unruly hairs from Eliot's eyes, which were just beginning to open in the morning sun. This shift with Eliot had lasted for many days, and she had gotten very little sleep since it started. Though she did not much mind the chore—this was the quietest her life had been in either of her existences.

No voices in her head.

No deception at the hands of men.

No religious persecution; nor fire.

She took a breath and looked out the window at the sun coming up over the parking lot. It was quiet, contained, managed; a simple beauty that was difficult to take her eyes away from.

Eliot squeezed her hand. "You can take a break and go get a coffee, you know."

"Sharper like this," she whispered.

"What's for breakfast this morning?"

Chloe reached across the bed, and Eliot's body, for the menu on the bedside table. "Pretty sure you could have grabbed that yourself, Detective."

"Haven't you heard, miss? I've been wounded—taken by a madman and tortured. Everyone can't stop telling me how sad it all is," he said.

She smiled. "Yes. I have heard that. I'd forgotten your bed rest instructions prohibited the use of end tables."

"It's all so *very* specific," Eliot's eyes flared as he spoke. "Nurses orders, you know how it goes."

Chloe looked over the menu. "Looks like breakfast is a slice of grapefruit, some cottage cheese, and a couple slices of whole wheat toast."

"Animals," he grunted. "How can they expect me to eat that? I'm not sixty-five with a summer home in Miami."

"Your jokes are getting so *very* specific," Chloe winked. "It's good for you, Eli."

Eliot shoved the sliding tray table aside. "No it isn't!" His face got deadly serious. "Cottage cheese isn't good for you! It's not even cheese. And what cottage *hasn't* made cheese at some point? You can make cheese anywhere."

"Slow down there, dude." She put her hand on his forehead and gently rested him back on the pillow. "You're not going to like what I have to say," she paused, as if changing the subject to something dire.

His eyes swelled. "Did you hear something? Are we in trouble?"

Chloe sniffled and turned to the window, her silhouette bathed in the sunrise. "Cottage cheese is a curd." She put her fist to her mouth, her voice cracking. "It's a cheese, I just didn't know how to tell you. God. *Why is it always cheese?*"

He pushed her off the bed.

After landing with a thud, she sprang back to her feet, scratching her head as Harriet and Ransic walked in the doorway with a couple bags of fast food breakfast. They looked puzzled to witness whatever had just occurred on the bed.

"My heroes!" Eliot gasped.

Harriet tossed one of the bags onto the bed, horrified at the speed with which Eliot tore into it. The saltiness of the food filled the room like a smoke bomb. "Don't tell the nurse." She turned to Chloe. "You okay?"

"Tired."

"Take a break," Harriet replied. "Alex, Janey, and the boys are on the lawn. Go get some air and say hello. It'll do you good." She watched as Chloe refused to acknowledge their conversation audibly or in the positive. "They want to see you—even Janey. We're all on the same team, kid."

Chloe gave an unconvincing nod and a slivered smile before heading out into the hallway. She took a few moments, plodding through the maze of endless halls leading to the elevator. "We're all on the same team," she repeated to herself quietly as the elevator dinged on her floor and she got on it, alone.

The phone in her pocket buzzed twice.

She pulled it out and read quietly in the elevator, her eyes glancing up to the ceiling when she'd finished. "i c u..." It read. A sigh broke out, followed by a laugh. There was an irony to how she was now getting pissed off at people texting like that over the phone; the exact same thing she used to do to Alex to annoy him.

A second text from Stephani Turner buzzed in her hand.

As the elevator came to rest on the bottom floor, Chloe ripped the battery from the back of the phone and dropped it into the crack between the elevator and the lobby. She took the rest of the phone in her hand and thrust it onto the ground, her boot not far behind, crushing the plastic into hundreds of pieces.

"Here we go."

Chloe made quick work of the lobby, leaping over whichever hideous 1980's couch dared stand in her way. The double doors to the chilly exterior swung wildly as she burst through them, scanning the parking lot for familiar faces.

Richie caught her eye first. His tiny freckled nose squinting in the cold, his hoarse French dialect like a faint squeal in the wind. "Look, you guys, it's Chloe!" He ran over and gave her the quickest hug he could before turning around and dashing back to Alex and Janey.

He's wearing that ragged-ass fraternity cap again, she thought to herself. For incognito, the four of them were not exactly befitting to any bill. As she looked them over, it occurred to her that Janey could have been wearing a Pocahontas costume from the Disney Store and somehow blended in more realistically. "What's with all the bright colors?"

Alex chuckled sarcastically. "Yes. Hello, Chloe. It's nice to see you too."

Janey laughed in response and caught the dire eye of Chloe, not amused with any of this tomfoolery.

"Oh, where are my manners? Hey dudes, we're all about to die when a serial killer and his limitless cloned thugs descend on us whenever they feel it's a peachy time to do so. Hope you boys said your nightly prayers," Chloe ended with her eyebrows raised. "Is that better, Alex?"

"Much," he winked back. "It's nice to see you, Joan."

Janey shot a sideways glance that Alex did not reciprocate; he kept his eyes squarely on the other woman in the parking lot. "We done with the meet and greet?"

"We are," Chloe said flatly.

Albert stepped forward, flipping his backpack around to the front and rummaging through its contents. "I know I have it somewhere in here," the boy trailed off.

"I saw you put it in there!" Richie added with a giant smile.

The younger boy was shooed away by the older one, still looking through the backpack. "You didn't take it out did you?"

Richie's mouth fell agape. "Why would I take it out?"

"Because you kept telling me you wanted to play with it!" Albert clearly did not believe his young friend.

"What are you guys arguing about?" Alex asked. "Wait. You didn't bring—" He cut himself off.

"I most certainly did," Albert spoke with passion. "We don't know how many groupers are going to come down on us. That's not to mention whatever the hell Richard is planning."

"You're thirteen!" Janey cautioned.

"And I've been married twice! My age is the least relevant factor in this conversation—*where the hell is the damn thing?*" Albert was losing his patience rapidly.

"Guys," Chloe attempted to interject.

Alex leaned over to Albert's backpack and began helping the boy look through the unsorted piles of odds and ends. "Why aren't those gummy worms in a bag?" He asked, holding one of the worms, brushing the crumbs off.

"I didn't have time for a bag, Alex!" Albert yelled in the parking lot.

Chloe spoke up again. "Guys?"

Janey was the first to respond. "What is it, Chloe?"

The fear smattered across her face was unmistakable and Joan turned with Chloe at the mass growing on the other side of the parking lot. They grabbed Alex at the same time and directed his attention away from wayward gummy Annelida and to the men walking across the field adjacent to the parking lot.

At first, it was tough to make out that these men were grouped together at all, but as they stepped into the lot, it was clear that they were all wearing latex masks from a costume shop.

Ronald Reagan.

Mikhail Gorbachev.

Snoopy.

Big Bird.

…Albert Einstein.

Those faces and many others were chambering rounds into various assault rifles and fully automatic handguns as they took the first few strides across the lot.

"Get inside now," Janey called out.

Alex looked over to the doors of the hospital and then back to the group. "No way we can cover that distance. Chloe, take the kids and go!"

"What about—"

He screamed back in her as he checked the ammo in the clip. "This isn't a discussion, Arc. Move your ass!"

He fired twice into the air, trying to clear the parking lot of bystanders before the groupers began their assault. Many were crawling to safety as the men in masks they continued advancing just a few hundred yards away.

Chloe ran with Albert and Richie a few car lengths before as gunfire started popping off from all directions. The two kids slammed into a Prius and began rifling through the bag again. Bullets sailed by on the left side of the car hitting an unassuming blue minivan a few spots down.

"Why is one wearing my face?" Albert screamed as he began to toss old Nintendo Power magazines onto the concrete. "Is that supposed to be a message? I'm next, right?" Albert cried out.

Chloe could barely hear what he was saying over the cacophony of gunfire all around them, but she made out just enough. She gave a firm nod to Albert and tossed her arms flat onto the hood, firing twice before dropping back to cover.

A grouper was struck in the head and fell lifelessly to the pavement.

"Okay, I killed you." Chloe wiped the sweat from her brow and peered around the edge of the bumper at the oncoming mass. "I guess *he* was next."

Albert placed his head sideways on the ground and looked out about fifty yards. He could see that the latex Einstein mask had a bloody hole torn through the forehead. "So it would seem. Why are they wearing masks?"

She took a moment to herself, not wanting to answer the question. "Because they think they're going to get away with it."

"Don't let them," said the tiny French voice to her side. "Shoot them all and *then* shoot some more, okay?"

Chloe gave Richie an agreeable nod and turned back to the fight. "I'm gonna lay down fire! You two have to run two cars down. Can you do that?" She yelled over the noise.

They nodded in approval and set their bodies as if about to engage in a foot race.

"On three!" She scanned the parking lot for the shooters that had the most opportunity to shoot at them. "One!"

Albert zipped his backpack up and slung it back over his shoulder, tightening both straps as far as they would go.

"Two!"

Richie retied both of his shoes as fast as he could: double knots, extra tight.

"Three!"

The boys took off as Chloe fired her Glock-17 as fast as the trigger could cycle. Bullets sailed through the air, missing faux-Gorbachev completely, but providing enough suppression to get the boys safely to a car fifteen feet away. She returned to cover and made a looping motion with her hand, signaling that they were about to repeat the same step.

Albert held up his hand as if to wait, barely visible behind the black Kia Sorento already filled with more than twenty holes.

"He's digging around in the bag again." Chloe sighed to herself before finishing off the clip to keep some of the groupers at bay.

They were amassing less than a hundred feet away and from what she could tell, there were fifteen to twenty in the lot.

They didn't have the firepower to stop an onslaught of this magnitude.

She glanced over to where Alex and Janey were signaling targets to each other at an alarming rate, putting them down as soon as they called them out. But they weren't slowing it enough—the conflict would last less than a few minutes.

In moments, they would all be dead.

This would be how it ended the second time, she thought.

A group of eight of them, one wearing a Charlton Heston mask, sprinted up to a conversion van that shielded them from Alex and Janey's fire.

"Alex, the van!" Chloe shouted, but he could neither hear her nor see the threat. She called out again and again in between reloading, but it had no effect.

Charlton Heston-mask unloaded half a clip, striking Alex in the shoulder and sending him to the ground, his gun sliding under the car.

Janey fired twice more and turned to make sure he wasn't dead.

A grouper at the van raised his hand, signaling to the rest that it was time to make their move.

Chloe slid down the side of the Prius and could feel the world beginning to fall around her. She put the slide of the Glock against her forehead; sweat dripping down the barrel and onto her trigger finger. It was her last clip, and by her count, there was probably around four bullets left in the chamber.

"I'm sorry, Alex," she whispered.

A voice came from the Kia.

She turned, screaming for the children to keep running.

They did not.

Albert yelled it again. "I found it!"

Chloe gasped as the young man with the backpack ran in between the cars toward the van with all the groupers stacked against it.

She couldn't make out what he was holding until he pulled the pin out and skipped the tiny metal grenade twice off the pavement and landed it squarely under the carriage of the van.

The resulting explosion was enough to knock Albert clean off his feet and smash any gummy worms that were still in his backpack. Even with the wind knocked clean out of him, he managed to scramble under a Volvo parked in a handicapped space.

All but one of the groupers was killed in the ensuing explosion and Chloe used two of her remaining bullets to put the last one down, amidst a terrifying amount of fire and black smoke pouring into the air.

Chloe yelled to Richie to stay right where he was and sprinted full bore across the lot to get Albert. On the way, she caught a glimpse of Alex being helped back to his feet by Janey.

Still in this, she thought.

Then she saw a woman on the other end of the lot who was not wearing a mask. Chloe kept running even as she watched Stephani Turner cycle another round into the chamber and take up a firing position.

It was obvious there was nowhere she could get to.

"Al—" she attempted to call out but the bullet silenced her and she fell to the ground. She made eye contact with Janey who looked as rattled as ever.

Chloe rolled over onto her back to stare up at the clouds. The sound of gunfire began to fade—whether the others were no long firing or that she couldn't hear very well was unclear. It was just quiet.

No voices in her head.

No deception at the hands of men.

No religious persecution; nor fire.

Joan of Arc was at peace as the light began to fade from the sky.

CHAPTER FORTY-TWO
Eyes Shoulders Elbows

Moments Later
Seattle General Hospital: Eighth Floor

He hadn't been on his feet for an extended period of time in a long while. Ever since the attacks in Seattle, Eliot would spend long his ample free time looking out the window or staring at the scars where the nails had been driven through his feet. Even though he was under twenty-four-hour-a-day protection, it didn't seem to do much for his rising depression.

Eliot hated the silence, the boredom, and the Mexican soap operas that had no discernable connection from storyline to storyline. For any nurse that would listen, he would go on about the "man in the zebra costume" and how none of his family of friends thought it was odd the overweight grown-ass man gallivanted about in a zebra suit. He really didn't care for Mexican television.

That had been Eliot's demeanor for weeks on end; up until the moment he fired a gun again.

POOM.

The shot echoed down the hallway and a grouper in a Nolan Ryan mask fell to the floor, clutching his chest.

"This is the best!" He shouted at Harriet—whom he was leaning on, as she and Ransic dragged him down the hallway, guns drawn.

Harriet scanned the nurse's station for any stragglers. There were two dead orderlies on the floor and a third clutching many wounds as his bloody fingers struggled to put pressure on the direst of his wounds. She turned back to Eliot. "Probably a messed up time to say stuff like that."

There was cell phone duct-taped to Ransic's shoulder. It had an open line down to Janey in the parking lot. The phone remained connected and on speakerphone so they could communicate numbers, movements, and causalities of the groupers that were currently attacking the hospital. He tilted his chin toward the phone. "We took down three groupers on the eighth floor, but they just keep on comin'. They're killin' everyone, Janey. Nurses; patients…" He trailed off as the three of them stepped over a dead teenage girl.

Janey did not respond.

"We need info here, Ransic!" Harriet yelled as she kicked in the door to the emergency stairwell. "We'll be outside in seven minutes."

They continued to carry Eliot down the stairs as gunfire reverberated through the doors of floors they were passing on the way down.

Janey mumbled something into the phone that the group was having trouble making out. Eliot stopped them on the staircase and took a moment to try and figure out what she was attempting to tell them.

Ransic leaned against the cement corner of the landing between floors five and six. He once more turned his chin to the phone. "Say again, Jay. We didn't catch what you said."

Another few moments passed, the screams of dying patients and doctors bouncing into the stairwell from surrounding floors.

"I—" The phone crackled once more. "Chloe is down."

Harriet put her weight against the rail and slowly lowered Eliot to the ground.

The three of them refused to make eye contact for a solid minute. Eliot let those three words echo around in his thoughts.

Chloe.

Is.

Down.

"We're dying out there," he whispered to Ransic. "How the hell are we getting out of here?"

Ransic leaned in to his phone. "Is she still alive?"

Harriet pushed down on the bullets resting in the clip, checking to see how many rounds were left to chamber. "You really think we're going to get out of here?" She reloaded the pistol. "We ain't getting out of here."

The detective asked again. "Janey, is she alive?"

"Don't know," the phone crackled again. "Doesn't look like she's moving—" Janey's voice trailed off into sporadic gunfire with accompanying screams. She came back, "find the boys—we lost 'em." The other line went dead with a soft click followed by silence.

Ransic ripped the phone off of his shoulder and tried to redial the number, to no avail. He put the phone back in his pocket. "Any ideas, then?"

"Shoot the bad guys; don't die," Eliot laughed to himself.

"Good plan," Harriet agreed.

"Shoot the bad guys," Ransic trailed off as if he couldn't remember. "What was the second part again? I wanna make sure I remember both steps."

"Don't die." Eliot repeated with a smile. He shifted his weight on the railing to check the clip left in his Beretta. "I got five left."

Ransic picked Eliot off the railing and slid his arm over his shoulder. "I got an extra clip in my belt." He looked over to Eliot's gun, dangling within inches of his ear. "Don't fire that right next to my head."

"Wouldn't dream of it," Eliot smiled back. He motioned to the door of the fifth floor from the stairwell. "Let's go get shot already."

Harriet grabbed Eliot's other arm and helped the other two down the stairs. "But don't die. That was the rule." She kicked the door labeled 'POST-NATAL RECOVERY. MIND YOUR NOISE LEVEL' open and led them inside.

The floor was disturbingly quiet. Eliot pulled his arms off the two people carrying him and put his weight on the nurse's station desk. He pulled a stool from nearby and sat near the counter, setting his arms into a firing position. His eyes scanned the area as he aimed into the large expanse that was the fifth floor.

She put her fingers to her lips and motioned to listen to the noise coming from the floor. Harriet looked back at the two men with a puzzled look.

Ransic shrugged and whispered, "I don't hear anything."

"Exactly," she said. "Why don't we hear any babies?"

Gunshots can be terrifying or startling, but the thing about a molten hot piece of metal entering, and subsequently, leaving the body, is that some people won't register that they have been shot. Harriet did not react to the bullet entering her leg until the crack of the bullet awoke the babies on the other end of the floor. Struggling to stand, she keened toward the wall and lowered herself down to the floor, blood pouring out of her leg fast enough that she did not appear to be in any pain. "There they are," she smiled. "They were just sleepy."

A man in a Bill Clinton mask stepped into the hallway holding a massive assault rifle. He was startled to see a woman bleeding against the wall and clutching her thigh to stop the bleeding. The grouper raised the rifle into firing position but she had not even turned to look at him.

Harriet shot him four times without looking in his direction. His body fell lifelessly onto a stack of prenatal magazines with an inglorious thud.

"I just shot Bill Clinton," she drunkenly slurred to Eliot. Her blood-covered finger rose to her lips as if to shush her friends. "Don't tell Hillary, okay? Her finger's on the button—" Harriet passed out against the wall.

Ransic fell into a sprint as he headed around the nurse's station, and a dumbfounded Eliot, to get to the grouper that Harriet had just killed. He slung the Heckler and Koch G3 assault rifle over his shoulder and ran back to the nurse's station. He tossed the rifled onto the counter for Eliot. "Take it."

"I can't even stand, Ransic," he replied, not breaking eye contact with Harriet, still passed out on the floor.

"Then crawl!"

Eliot Ness looked over the massive rifle on the counter, blood still speckling its otherwise pristine surface. He wondered aloud if anyone had ever even fired it before. There was a moment of clarifying silence, as if it no longer mattered what any of them attempted from this moment. "Everyone is going to die."

The force with which Ransic closed the distance between them and shoved the rifle into his hands was enough to make him fall backward to the floor. "Then die last, Eliot," he said and fired twice into a window twenty feet away from them in the lobby. "Everybody dies; sometimes more than once."

His head turned toward the soft bellowing winds coming in from the window and turned back to Ransic. "What are you about to do?"

"You were always the better cop," he put up his hand to stifle whatever argument Eliot was about to make. "Trust me, everyone is a shit cop next to you."

"*What are you about to do?*" Eliot repeated from the floor.

Ransic took a moment. "Die first."

Before Eliot could respond, Ransic took off down the hallway toward more gunfire and left him alone on the floor, wind swirling papers around him.

And then he remembered.

The flood of images that crashed into his mind put him back against the counter. He remembered things that had not occurred to him since the early 1900's.

First, it was the bread. His father, Peter, was a smalltime baker in Chicago when Eliot was a child. The runt of much older siblings, most of which were married before he even got out of primary school. There was something picturesque about how much love he garnered as a small boy. Nothing illustrated it more in his mind than the smell of the bread when he came home from school and closed his eyes to enjoy the aroma. He missed the bread, and he missed *those* parents.

The image of his brother-in-law, Alexander Jamie, came after. It was Alexander that taught him proper gun safety and how to fire it—how to *enjoy* it. There was a particularly memorable day when they went out into a forest and practiced with an old Derringer that they had found beneath some old magazines on a long abandoned farm. His brother-in-law always said that proper firing is done, "Eyes. Shoulders. Elbows." Fix your sightline, lower your shoulders, and lock the correct elbow. It wasn't exactly the most professional of firing techniques, but it was always the thing that stuck out to Eliot.

He put the assault rifle across his arms and began crawling to the window, the wind picking up on his face as he moved closer. Each movement against the broken glass tore into his arms, yet he moved forward without stopping. As he got to the opening, he popped the bipod out of the rifle and took up a firing position.

The chaos below did not seem to be slowing down. Eliot looked out onto the battlefield and noticed Albert running to a car that Richie was hiding under.

Two groupers were closing in on the boys with automatic pistols.

He pulled the bolt back and chambered a round.

Eyes.

He was taught to fire with both eyes open to maintain a field of vision at all time; something he was ignoring as he closed one eye and lined up the rear sights with the front sight.

Shoulders.

Eliot dropped his shoulders, eased in on the rifle and clicked the safety off. "Die last," he whispered as he let out one final breath of air.

Elbows.

He set his elbows against the glass as best he could, each movement sent searing pain up through his arms. Eliot closed his eyes for a moment and opened them again as the grouper in the front jumped onto the trunk of the vehicle that Richie was hiding under.

Albert froze as the grouper pointed the automatic pistol his direction.

Eliot eased the trigger back and exhaled.

CHAPTER FORTY-THREE
A Tale of Two Richards

An Instant Later
Seattle General Hospital Parking Lot

The reality is only two moments in life will be the best or worst of times; a time to live or to die, a time to make a final stand and pray in wanting for the gift of another day, a time to believe that giving up is the enemy and the battle can be won.

In secular terms: shit just got real.

Richie was holed up under a 1992 Volvo 740. He was a nine-year-old surrounded by shell casings and death, and both were beginning to pile up.

He looked up as a figure lofted onto a nearby vehicle and blocked the sun. The shape showed only his silhouette and the gun hanging limply to his side, glinting in the morning light. The head was wrong; it was hung to the side and leaking. Richie watched the man blocking the light fall off the car and slam into the pavement, dead. He covered his eyes from the blinding beams of sunlight.

The second gunman, wearing a mask of some white-haired politician he couldn't recognize, fired into the Volvo's door and tires with his automatic pistol. An errant piece of metal flew past the boy's face, leaving a gash across his cheek. He cried out, "Albert!" But his friend did not appear. Richie inhaled to call out once more.

A bullet struck the second gunman in the chest and put the man to the concrete, gasping, but not yet dead. The mask slid down the face of the dying grouper. His eyes circled to gain a bearing on what had just felled him before returning to the young boy hidden beneath the car. Richie turned, his gaze focused on the upper floors of the hospital to try and find where the shots were coming from. On the fifth floor, Eliot was waving down to the boy. *He looks all happy,* the boy thought as he turned back to the gunman struggling to grab the gun as it slid under the car. The nails of his fingers dug round the pebbles in the cement, desperately trying to grab the firearm.

Richie grabbed a small paring knife from his belt. The adults that lived with him had been careful to keep knives of any shape or size out from his reach. The opportunity to grab a knife had occurred in a soup and salad joint on the way to Seattle. The chef at the restaurant had finished coring a bell pepper when she placed the tiny knife in the expedition window. Alex and Janey were taking a quick bathroom break when he slid it between the leather of his belt and returned to his seat in the eatery. He smiled at the blade in his grasp once more. His eyes fell back to the hand probing under the car for the lost pistol.

The grouper with the chest wound cried out as the paring knife entered the top of his hand between the bones of his index and middle fingers. The man recoiled and rolled onto his back, gripping feverishly at the blood now pouring from his hand.

"Albert!" Richie called out again, hoping his friend was still alive in the chaos pouring out around him.

A pair of legs in uncuffed jeans that didn't quite reach the ankles walked cautiously into view. They stood solemn for a moment; shoelaces untied on the old Airwalks, the right foot tapping on the pavement. It took a moment for Richie to realize that Albert was standing in front of him, his friend staring down at the dying grouper. The man was gripping his wounds in an effort to stop the bleeding.

Albert's left knee lowered slowly and with purpose, coming to a firm rest on the throat of the man on the ground. His right hand followed, carefully placed over the nose and mouth of the grouper. The man reached out again for the gun that was too far away. Albert dropped his weight onto both his knee and hand, causing the man's eyes to bulge with terror and realization that his final breath had already been exhausted.

Richie watched the struggle play out over the next minute and a half as Albert flinched from side to side. The man tried to wriggle free, but the grip was inalienable and he died with his eyes wide with fear.

Albert rose from the ground and called back, "we have to go, Richie."

The boy did as he was told and scrambled out from beneath the car, grabbing the pistol on his way up. "Do you need this?" He asked innocently enough, holding the automatic pistol out to his friend.

"It's empty," Albert replied dryly, "but we'll still need it." He grabbed the pistol from Richie's hand and began to move across the parking lot toward the hospital.

Richie turned back to the car, slowly backpedaling as he talked. "Albert! I forgot my knife!"

"Keep moving toward the hospital," Albert said as he slung his backpack around to the front and began to rummage through its contents. His hand emerged with two chef's knives; one was eight inches, and the other six. "Take these."

"Are you sure?"

"Kill every grouper you see."

Richie put the knives into his hands, flipping them over as he ran. "What about the other guy—"

The two boys were interrupted as a grouper, no longer wearing a mask, stumbled out from behind a tree near the hospital doors. It was clear the man had been involved in some form of physical altercation as he appeared dazed and without a clear direction. He blinked a couple of times and yelled, "They're over here!"

Albert flipped the automatic pistol around in his hand and swung it across the cheek of the man, handle first.

As the man spun toward them, Richie jumped into the air and slammed both knives into the back of the grouper. The knives went in deep near the shoulders, which he used as leverage to pull himself onto the back of the man. He put his weight on the knife in his left hand and pulled the other knife out to stab it again lower.

Richie did this three or four times in rapid succession, pulling one knife out while hanging from the other and climbed down the man like a ladder before dropping to the ground like a monkey from a tree.

The grouper dropped to his knees and buckled back onto the grass of the hospital. His cries caught under the plasma that filled his mouth, choked out; a guarantee of no final words.

The two boys ran across the rest of the lawn and burst through the front doors of Seattle General, falling against the door as they slammed it closed.

"Nice work, Batman." Albert said with a smile.

Richie looked up at the massive atrium, glass artwork spun from suspended mobiles, painting a rainbow of colors across the lobby. "Why do we need a babysitter again?"

Albert wiped the sweat from his brow and laughed. "We don't."

"Damn right we don't," Richie held up his fist. "Blow me up, Bay Wolf."

Seconds After
Seattle General Hospital
Laundry Basement

This mask smells of broken dreams.

Richard straightened the latex Abraham Lincoln mask he had taken off of a grouper he knew as Helio 6. He had not wasted time in killing the straggling grouper. There was blood dripping through the nostrils of the mask, making it difficult to wear comfortably. His hand ran down to the belt at his side, five knives holstered and safe as he ran his fingers across the blades.

He froze.

Someone else was moving in the room. It was a slight scuffle, like someone with a rubber sole trying to move without picking up his or her foot.

Why did you kill Francis Martel?

He breathed in and out quickly, exasperated—already annoyed that the people in his head would choose this moment to address such matters. "Could we not do this right now?" Richard puffed under the mask.

Your love was real; I can still feel it. You hate yourself every day—you think I can't see you hurt, but you wear your pain like an accidental cape. Fluttering; arrogant; meaningless. You pour yourself into murder.

Not the time, Richard thought back. *Seriously, shut the hell up or we're both dead.*

His eyes welled.

Richard Matterhorn; manufactured boyfriend of the recently deceased Francis Martel, indifferent murderer defaulting into moral bankruptcy, elder reincarnation of Richard the Lionheart, and caretaker of multiple personality disorder; stalked slowly through the laundry room of the hospital. It smelled of bleach and slow, agonizing death—a stench he had intimate familiarity with. His thumb slowly raised a seven-inch blade from the holster to his side, keeping his eyes fixed on a shadow moving beyond a hanging sheet.

Flutter on, Richard.

He inched toward the sheet, answering back in his head. *Okay. Okay—he found out who I've done; who I am. I—I put a bullet in the back of his head. I loved him but it was already lost.* He paused shy of a white divider between predator and prey, taking a moment to savor the kill to come. *I loved him and I had to let him go.*

It was quiet in his mind for a second.

Finally. *Then make it quiet,* his other personality spoke softly in the back of his mind.

He brought the knife up to his chin-level and slowly pulled the sheet back, revealing a terrified hospital patient still rolling his IV around on the rack. The man was on too much medication to notice his presence. Richard slid his shoes across the cement of the basement and found himself breathing inches from the man's neck.

The knife rotated with purpose and silence toward the small of the patient's back; he stopped it half an inch from the flesh, the gown tearing against the blade. With his other hand, he cupped the man's mouth and pulled backward.

Richard slid the blade in slowly, as if the knife were a teenager attempting to parallel park their hand-me-down automobile for the first time; he needed it to happen with deliberation.

The patient convulsed in Richard's arms as the blade mutilated recklessly through the man's nervous system.

It took few moments for the man to stop dying.

Richard tossed the corpse carelessly onto a pile of freshly cleaned linens but slid his blade back into his belt with care and precision.

We need to find him.

His eyes rolled back into his head. "I know," Richard offered quietly.

If we get our hands on the boy, this can all be over.

"I know!" he screamed furiously in the deserted laundry tunnel. "We will get our hands on him and then we can rest." His boot stepped over the bloody laundry and tried to avoid the IV bag shooting all over the cement floor nearby. "We just need the rest," he trailed off.

Richard's head fell silent and his thoughts were his own again. He dropped his eyelids for a welcome moment of peace as dryers continued to tumble unattended sheets all around him.

The sound was asymmetrical, yet, welcome and soothing.

THUMP. THUMP. *CLINK.* THUMP.

THUMP. THUMP. *CLINK.* THUMP.

Someone accidentally dropped coins in the dryer; he smiled, alone in his thoughts once again. Richard collected himself, taking one last look around the area before proceeding. His feet lumbered up the stairs leading out of the laundry dungeon. His boots slipped on many of the metal steps, blood still fresh against the tread.

The door in front of him had a sign that read, 'LOBBY ENTRANCE 2A.'

The voice in the far corner of his mind spoke up again, this time more direct, intensified.

Kill anyone that so much as staggers into our path. There is only one task now.

Richard Matterhorn secured his knives and pushed through the door into the lobby where the faint sounds of two boys could be heard arguing as they made their way through the atrium.

He spoke to himself as he gently closed the heavy door behind him, "some were not meant to return."

After

The End of the Seattle General Lobby

Richie twirled the knives in his hands in an ornate manner, not unlike a Benihana chef would do prior to blowing a train whistle and making an onion turn magically into a volcano before the eyes of children.

This child could no longer experience the palpable extraneous nature of youth.

This child was a soldier now.

This child was no child anymore.

The lobby was filled with the piteous whimpers of men and women, both good and bad, so close to the edge of death that the two children could hold their breath and exhale to a chorus of perfect silence; the whimpers now dead alongside the people making them.

The battle had been costly; it reminded Richie and Albert of the people that the groupers and Richard killed at his thirteenth birthday party—old wounds; new cuts.

Richie had not been with Albert and his family for too long before the day he was thrust into a war—a concept he understood in his previous life but was not yet old enough to understand in this one.

"I'm tired," Richie whined, bending over once more to tie his shoes.

Albert tightened his backpack and looked at all the different doors and hallways coming off the main lobby. "We need to find somewhere to hide, Richie."

"Let's hide under that counter."

"I think we're going to have to be more adept than that," Albert responded without looking.

"What about a closet?"

"Just shut the hell up for a second, Richie. I'm trying to think," Albert yelled.

Richie dropped his chin to his chest and tried to find a spot on the carpet that needed a firm gaze placed upon it. A lump stuck in his throat that could not be swallowed away. "Sorry," his voice squeaked as he took a seat on a nearby couch.

Albert took a knee and rummaged through his bag. He pulled a piece of paper from the pack and unfolded it across the swirling earth tones of the lobby's carpet. For what felt like minutes, he ran his fingers up and down the map, trying to find the best route out of the lobby and into safety.

"Got it!" He realized with hushed exasperation. "We can take the side hallways on the left there—deep into Radiology. It's nothing but a maze of CT scanners, MRI machines, and tons of rooms for X-Rays. It's all connected too, so we can move around if the need arises." He jumped back to his feet and looked over to Richie who was quietly stabbing tiny holes into the fabric of the couch.

The other boy did not look up, his mind preoccupied on *appearing* preoccupied.

"We need to go now." Albert scolded, to little effect.

Richie continued poking holes amidst the sound of distant gunfire. If he had a care in the world, it appeared to be ensuring that hideous couches were in need of a good goring.

Setting his pack down on the ground, Albert walked over and took a seat on the couch. "Batman," he began in a much softer tone.

Richie looked up; his eyes had turned a shade of light red, clearly on the verge of tears for any number of reasons.

"Batman, we need to hide from Mr. Freeze—"

"Poison Ivy," Richie cut him off.

Albert laughed. "Okay, Poison Ivy is after us because she wants to turn us all into plants for her garden—" He took a moment, cocking his head to the side in confusion. "Poison Ivy doesn't make any sense."

His young friend shushed him. "Neither does Clayface. Some of the Batman villains are magic. Just like it, okay?"

"But Batman isn't magic…"

Richie jumped to his feet and grabbed Albert's bag, thrusting it back into his arms. "Batman is the *most* magical."

The bag slung back onto his shoulder and Albert began the walk across the lobby to the hallway at the end. "Can't argue with that logic now can we?"

The two ran hand-in-hand down a maze of hallways and ascended numerous staircases before pushing through the door leading to Radiology. It was pin-drop quiet and most of the lights were out. The gunfire had become almost inaudible this deep into the hospital, behind so many thick metal doors. It looked abandoned.

"This will do nicely," Albert announced, still careful to keep his voice down.

Richie tugged on Albert's sweater. "Where do we hide in here?"

"I don't know, buddy. I imagine we find the deepest room and hang out there until the gunfire dies down."

"What if the gunfire stops because all of our dudes got shot?"

Albert rummaged once more through the backpack, this time into the front pocket. He pulled back a new phone, purchased on the way from Kansas. "If we get a text on this, we know it's safe to head back outside."

"And if we don't get a text on that?"

"We don't go back outside."

The way Radiology was laid out took a moment to decipher. The hallways ended in weird ways and the number of swinging double doors made it easy to be completely turned around. There were many moments when Albert would stop and check over the map again, trying to get to the deepest and most difficult place to find in the hospital.

Seven minutes later, they found what they were searching for.

The two of them pushed through a thick wooden door, ordained with all sorts of family photos of a doctor with his wife and kids. This was a personal office, and would do nicely as a hiding spot.

Albert took a single step into the room before freezing in place, blocking Richie from what he just uncovered in the room. His arms were trembling and his breaths became so short, they were almost non-existent.

Richie stuck his head under Albert's arm and got a look at what made him stop so suddenly after all of that searching. His eyes grew and he brought his head back behind his older friend, hiding like a small child hides behind their mother's leg.

In the middle of the doctor's back office, sitting in an office chair, was Richard Matterhorn.

"I was wondering when you two were going to show up. I must say, it took you a bit longer than I expected. Albert, I thought you were supposed to be some kind of genius." He took a sip of coffee he'd clearly had time to acquire before hiding out in the office.

Everyone in the room said nothing; the only sound in the room was the hum of a computer and Richie tightening the grip on his knives.

"I won't let you take him—" Albert began.

"Send the boy away." Richard interrupted him.

"What?"

"Unless you want to detonate a decent portion of the state of Washington, I'd suggest you send that boy as far from here as possible." Richard spoke evenly, devoid of any emotion.

"I thought—" Albert tried to speak, but stopped himself.

Richard stood up. "You thought wrong, *boy*. Now send him away."

Albert spun around to Richie, his voice already cemented into the middle of his throat. He took a knee and put a hand on his friend's shoulder. "You need to go back to the lobby—you need to try and find Alex, okay?" Tears had already started falling down his cheeks.

Richie threw his arms around Albert and dropped his knives to the ground. "No! I want to stay with you, Bay Wolf!"

Albert brushed the back of his hair between his fingers. "I gotta go for awhile, okay?"

"I will go with you!" Richie screamed, his accent and emotions making his words borderline incomprehensible.

It was becoming difficult for Albert not to break down completely. He spoke in broken sentences, as he dug through his bag and pulled the map out again. "Take this." Three breaths followed just to calm himself back down. "Take this and get back to the lobby."

"No!" Richie screamed at the top of his lungs. "I have to stay with you, Albert!"

Albert pushed Richie so hard he fell into the thick wooden door and some of the pictures of the doctor and his family fell to the floor. "Go, now!"

It took a few seconds for Richie to realize that the situation would not be changing in any way. He collected himself from the floor and shambled over to grab the map. "Are you coming back?" He sniffled.

Albert shook his head, no. There were no words he could force out of his mouth as Richie pushed open the door and walked into the hallway, leaving Albert alone with Richard.

Without wasting a moment, Richard put his hands on Albert's shoulders. "They don't know it yet."

His teeth clenched together, but Albert did not bother to turn around and look at his captor. " They don't know what yet?"

Richard Matterhorn exhaled with laughter. "That the thing they should be fighting over," the hum of the computer grew louder, "is you."

CHAPTER FORTY-FOUR
March of the Arrow

Seven Minutes Later
Seattle General Hospital Parking Lot

Unfortunately for Alex Heton, one could not simply *will* the flow of blood to slow or dissipate from a freshly born gunshot wound. His breathing had become shallow. Not that he was dying; he was actually quite sure he *wasn't* about to die, but the pain in his arm and the shock of the wound were enough to keep him down.

Where the hell is Chloe? He thought silently, not brave enough to ask Janey verbally, despite the fact that they were all under sporadic gunfire. *I haven't seen Chloe since the boys ran off inside.*

Damn.

The boys! I hope they're okay. His thoughts were running away with him.

"Drink this, Alex." Janey barked with force, holding a water bottle that was swirling on down to its final third. He took a sip and watched her pour the rest onto his blood-caked arm. "You're going to be fine," she said; her voice exasperated but her demeanor truthful.

Her hair was cute when it fell into her eyes. Alex knew that delirium was only as serious as the amount of gunfire that was heading in their direction. In his previous life he was known to make a mockery of anyone that placed too much fear into someone falling into a delirious state—people did that on purpose all the time with alcohol and controlled substances to air grievances or stress. The only time to fear delirium was when an enemy was within striking distance.

"How many are left?" He spoke abruptly, trying to get a better handle on his breathing patterns.

Her head popped up over the car, eyes scouring the battlefield with efficiency. "Sniper's still in place; probably a hundred meters. Looks far enough out there that she won't fire on us with other options on the table." Janey returned to sitting on the cement.

Alex glared. "How do you know it's a woman?"

"Because a ponytail changes shape when the head turns from left to right."

"Could be a guy with a ponytail," he corrected.

She laughed. "You find me the guy with *bangs* and a ponytail!"

Alex relented. "Okay. Sounds like we have a lady-sniper laying down the relevant fire. What about groupers?"

"I haven't seen any in a while; there's some inside." Janey took a moment to catch her breath. "We don't know who's still alive."

"And we can't worry about it right now."

Her glare flashed over to maternal. "They're just kids, Alex."

He did his best not to put too much weight on the injured arm as he peaked around the side of the car in the direction of their sniper. "You know on an airplane—they always tell you that in the event of an emergency to put the mask onto yourself before you assist those around you?"

"Yes."

Alex adjusted his ballcap. "We gotta get our mask on. Thoughts on the sniper?"

The sigh was loud enough that he caught her meaning before she spoke the sentence. "You got a shit arm, so cover fire at this distance is suicidal."

"We're gonna have to make a move on suicidal options pretty soon."

Janey placed her head upon Alex's shoulder. "We don't have to discuss them yet. I'd guess we have four entire minutes before we go full-on Butch Cassidy mode."

He stroked her hair with his good arm and gave her a simple kiss on top of the head. Alex knew that there was very little they could do; at any moment, a grouper would walk past and kill both of them without a second thought. He picked up the walkie-talkie that had been completely silent for going on ten minutes and held down the talk button. "Ransic, come in. Ransic, are you still alive?"

The soft rustle of static on their airwaves did not alter in any way. The other end of the line remained dead for thirty seconds before a voice crackled back.

"Alex! Alex, is anyone else still alive?" The voice on the other end of the line sounded terrified.

"Eliot!" He answered back into the handset; happy to hear anyone had made it out. "Janey and myself are still alive. I'm hit but I can still move around okay," Alex trailed off.

"I can't get a bead on your sniper, Alex," Eliot replied through the walkie. "Looks like she's got a nest in between two eighteen-wheelers that are pointed right at you."

Alex ignored everything that Eliot had just said. "Any word on Ransic or Harriet?"

The other end was silent for a few seconds. "Harriet's down. We need to get her to a hospital."

Janey laughed. "We're *at* a hospital."

Eliot did not seem to be enjoying her ill-timed sense of humor from the other end of the line. "Hardly the time for jokes, Janey. We have to get out of here, guys."

Alex took another peek around the side of the vehicle. "Workin' on it," he spoke into the walkie. He came back around the bumper of the vehicle and looked up to Eliot, still perched in the shattered window many floors above the parking lot. A smile crept across his face and he held his thumb up into the air. In response, a tiny hand stuck out of the window and replied in kind: a thumb's up for the soldiers still standing.

The static on the end of the radio crackled to life again, but whoever it was did not speak up. Alex knew that the person trying to speak wasn't Eliot. "Say again?" He quickly spouted into the walkie.

Once more, the radio crackled, this time with the faint sound of breathing before it fell back into silence.

Alex and Janey exchanged shrugs and turned their attention back to the sniper on the other end of the lot.

It reminded Alex of a battle in his previous life. Out-manned, wounded and dying, there was a single archer bringing a grievance to bear on Alexander and his small contingent of soldiers. The men had to remain pressed into the muddy bank of a ravine, lest one of the arrows came arcing into the pit and through one of them. Alexander the Great took hours to divine a solution where he, and all of his men, would be able to walk away with their lives.

No archer could carry any more than twenty arrows that far from a battlefield, and they knew that their assailant had already exhausted five. They put helmets on swords to draw a few more arrows off into the forests. When the enemy no longer fell for that, they took turns sprinting from tree-to-tree and pulling whatever arrows toward them that they could. With each arrow the archer fired, his hesitancy increased to fire another. When they were sure the archer was down to a single and final arrow, they took up shields and began marching up the hill as slowly as possible: *painfully* slow. Years after, men would tell campfire stories of that moment; they called it "the March of the Arrow."

Alexander had to convince his men that the archer would not fire, that if they gave him enough time, he would not take the final shot and simply abandon his post. Sure enough, they marched up a hundred-foot hill over the course of twenty minutes to find that the archer's nest had been vacated and the plan had worked.

A sniper with a high-powered rifled would inevitably be able to last longer and carry much more ammunition, but the ideas were similar in principle. Alex turned to Janey. "We gotta do something kind of stupid, okay?"

She smiled back at him. "Thought you'd never ask."

"Take off your shirt."

Janey's face changed. "I thought you meant the other kind of stupid."

Alex smiled. "I mean *exactly* that kind of stupid."

She shrugged and pulled off her shirt revealing a camisole underneath. The purple top landed in Alex's lap. "This better impress me, Alexander."

Alex smiled. "This is gonna be *great.*" He grabbed the shirt from his lap and felt around under the car they were behind.

"What are you looking for?"

He yanked toward the pavement and caused a piece of folded metal to pop loudly into view. "A jack!" Alex held up the black metal carjack and began to fully unwind it in his hand. When it was fully unwound and vertical, he carefully wrapped the shirt around the metal as if it were a mannequin. His fingers pulled on the shoulder of the shirt to make sure it fit well enough, and he set it back on the ground.

"I think that your carjack-person needs a head," Janey said flatly, unimpressed.

"No need." Alex smiled and jumped to his feet, careful to keep his head under roof-level of the car. He tore his own shirt as well, tying it carefully around his wounded arm in a makeshift sling. It was crude, but effective enough to break into a run across the parking lot.

Janey did not have an opportunity to say any last-minute goodbyes as she watched Alex run off with the jack toward another car. A bullet ripped past him, smashing through a mini-van a few rows behind them.

His hat flew off while he was sprinting between a pickup truck and an economy sedan; he slid along the concrete into a Cadillac, fraying his jeans and grinding his skin in the process. It took a moment to rip off the rest of his shirt and wrap it tightly around his hand. There was a fleeting glance back toward Janey. He exhaled with a smile before smashing in the driver's side window and popping the lock on the car door. Careful to remain unseen, he pulled a knife and crawled on his back to a position under the steering wheel. The knife popped the key guard with little effort and he took a few cracks at cycling the engine. On the fifth try, it whirred to life.

The jack wearing Janey's shirt fit perfectly in the driver's seat. Alex carefully put the car into drive to start it idling across the lot.

A shot ripped through the windshield, but missed both of the front seats. It would be much more difficult to make out what was in the car for further shots. "Here we go, Sacagawea," Alex sighed to himself as he jammed the knife into the accelerator pedal and sent the car screaming off toward the pair of eighteen-wheelers.

Four more shots pegged the car in different places, but the vehicle continued to hurtle forward.

Alex was running as flat out as he could, crouched between whatever automobile provided cover, and lost track of how far he had to sprint before he got to the sniper. His shoulder crashed into the side of one of the eighteen-wheelers and he knew immediately that the collision had given him away.

The firing had stopped, in its place, a light patter of footsteps before they went silent.

He crept around the side of the truck cab, sliding his feet to create as little sound as possible. His head remained on a swivel, checking behind every second to make sure the gunman wouldn't get the jump on him.

A four-inch shard of glass caught his eye glinting on the ground. He bent over and picked it up, holding it with his the hand that was still wrapped in what was left of his t-shirt.

A popping sound spun him around, but there was no one there. Alex turned back to front and received the stock of a sniper rifle to the face.

His body violently flew back into the driver's side door, leaving a sizeable dent before colliding hard with the pavement. The blood flowing onto the cement was coming from his nose he thought. *Or maybe that's from my eye.* He touched his face, still not sure how many places the blood was coming from.

A female leg came into view.

The shard of glass had shattered in the palm of his hand, but he still had a tiny sliver resting there. There was not a hesitation as he sliced through her Achilles; an anarchic screaming sound followed the snap of the flayed tendon.

Officer Stephani Turner fell to the ground next to Alex. They rolled around in confusion and pain, bleeding and unable to return to their feet.

Alex heard the click of a pistol cocking. His glance returned to the truck they were laying in the shadow of.

Jessup closed the door on the truck and stepped down onto the ground, hovering over Alex.

Three gunshots followed in close succession.

Alex felt one of the bullets go into him.

CHAPTER FORTY-FIVE
This, the End?

After
Seattle General Hospital Parking Lot

He clutched his wounded abdomen, his eyes fluttering with dizziness as he attempted to account for the second shot. *Janey couldn't have crossed the lot in time*, he thought.

Jessup fell to the ground a few feet to Alex's right. There was blood coming from his mouth and he made no effort to stop his face from smashing into the pavement. The second bullet was now accounted for.

Are we both about to die? Had it already come to this, the end?

Alex Heton grimaced as the bullet, still lodged in his side, scraped against his organs with every beat of his heart. He tried to roll over but the pain was too fierce. Every few moments he would black out, only to come to as a result of the pain. Once more, he attempted to roll over onto his side, his mouth agape in a silent screech, only to slam back to the concrete.

He could tell there was some confusion on the radio, though; he was struggling to hear or make sense of any of it. The sounds of the world grew dim; the sunlight less brilliant and the sensation of life fell into numbness. There was little doubt that Alex was dying, that much he was aware of. Perhaps Jessup would die too, the only two bodies left at the scene of the crime that weren't exact biological replicas of each other. He could just make out Jessup yelling to someone over the radio.

The effort commenced again. Alex flung his left arm over his chest to roll onto his side. Just as he was to give up and fall back to the ground, a pair of hands caught him and gave a push to roll him over. The landing was perfectly centered on his wound, the pain so searing he *couldn't* pass out. He screamed for mercy but a pair of hands appeared on his shoulders and calmed him. These hands were not a mystery, but they were also not Janey's.

Alex had not noticed that the blood dripping onto the ground belonged to the person holding him. A cobalt-blue Glock bounced off the cement with an audible crack. Chloe's exhausted knees dropped into Alex's eyeline. "I think we might all be dying here," she spoke with a raspy voice that was barely there.

"I see you copied me," he coughed and laughed. "I go and get shot so you do the same."

Chloe Freimont curled down on the ground beside her former boyfriend. "Dude, hell no. *Hell* no—I took a seven-six-two from Annie Oakley over there an hour ago…" her voice was fading.

With great effort, he was able to adjust his head enough to see the police officer whose Achilles tendon he had sliced ninety seconds before. She was passed out from blood loss. "That's Annie Oakley?" Alex's words were beginning to slur.

"Yup." She used his shoulder to pull her body closer to his. "I don't think we're walking out of the Taco Baron this time, buddy. You were right, Alex."

Chloe started crying in a way that Alex did not immediately recognize. This was because he had never seen her actually cry for real. He wiped a tear before it could drip from the bridge of her nose. "I was right about what, Joan?"

"I hate that—*hate* that name," she stammered.

"I don't care."

She tried to cough out some blood that had since coagulated in her throat. It took a few tries. Barely able to speak, she pulled out her phone and scrolled through her saved messages. Her hands trembling, she turned the phone around to show a message that read: 'Okay, apologies. Seriously, I need you to get here as soon as possible. We're in—'

"I meant to write danger, but I accidently hit send instead." Alex smiled. "Why did you save that?"

"*Because*, stupid."

"I see we haven't changed," he said, holding out his hand for hers.

Chloe placed her hand into Alex's and closed her eyes. He was about to do the same when a striking pain shot through his hand and up his arm. She was squeezing his hand as hard as she could, keeping Alex awake. "Find out why we're here, Alexander. You don't get to go yet." Chloe had just finished speaking her peace when she passed out and let go of his fingers.

His eyes drifted over to Waylan Dwight Jessup III, coughing and sputtering on the ground six feet away. He dug his fingers into the cracked cement, the fingernails on his right hand forming white lines where they began to bend back. Alex pulled his body forward across the lot. The left hand followed, blood coming from under the nails of two fingers as they slid over the tiny rocks.

Alex kept pulling.

Within three minutes, he had pulled himself all the way to Jessup. "Wake up, Napoleon." Alex slapped the man across the face.

The man abruptly awoke and his eyes swelled with terror as he realized that Alex was on top of him. "Don't do it," the man said limply.

Alex put his forearm over Jessup's mouth. "Why are you killing us?" The force of his voice was surprising at first; he didn't know he had the power to scream at that moment. He repealed his arm to allow Jessup to speak.

"You know why, Alexander. There is danger where there is miracle."

"I want to hear you say it, Napoleon," Alex growled.

Jessup grimaced, trying to catch his breath. "And if I refuse?"

Alex scraped Chloe's pistol from the ground and slowly shoved it into Jessup's mouth. "Then we'll have a shorter conversation."

The shaking lips smiled around the pistol. Alex removed it from Jessup's mouth and placed it instead to the man's forehead.

"The next thing you say to me will be denial with a sarcastic flare." Jessup was rattled and going into shock as he slowly bled out on the ground.

"So get started. We need to know how we came back." Alex could feel himself beginning to pass out again, holding himself up with one arm on the ground. He fell to the side, making sure to keep the gun and his right hand trained on Jessup.

"Do you believe that reincarnation is possible?"

Alex scoffed. His laughter hurt like hell, but the reaction was unavoidable. "Are you asking me if I believe in Hinduism? Now I *am* going to shoot you."

The dying police Chief rolled over onto his back, trying to take short breaths as the clouds moved by overhead and sirens were heard echoing off hills in the distance. "Told you." The man took a few inhales to try and ease his archaic breathing. "I'm not speaking of religion, no. I'm speaking about science."

"Science?" The gun was beginning to waver in Alex's hand.

"Reincarnation is not impossible, at least, in a purely numerical sense." Jessup's breathing was becoming shallower by the minute. He would not last much longer. "You were born from the matter in millions of different stars in as many galaxies—that you exist at all is infinitely less possible than simply duplicating that recipe a second time."

"How?" Alex repeated, his voice also beginning to shake.

"Did you know that a flipped coin will land on its edge every one in six-thousand times?"

"Is that what they teach you in cop school?" Alex whispered.

"Harvard." Jessup said flatly, gently closing his eyes. "If you had infinite time and infinite mothers, eventually a genetically exact person would be born a second time. We enjoy thinking of ourselves as snowflakes, but the reality is we're blueprints." He coughed, grimacing with every word but tried to continue anyway. "Anything is *possible*. You can duplicate anything, but it's the memories that defy reason—are you cold? Is this all we can ever be," the man trailed off. He was thinking of too many things to say at once, and they were beginning to collide.

Alex could feel his eyes becoming heavy as his heart rate slowed. He bit down hard on his tongue to try and stay awake. "Where do our memories come from?"

"There is a man." Jessup was beginning to seize.

"I need a name!"

"Duplicates," Jessup said slowly and sleepily.

"You mean the other Janeys?"

"Yes—and, there are more. Duplicates can't exist." He took a long and gaspy breath. "Paradox." Another breath. "It's a side effect of his work. Kill all duplicates." His eyes were beginning to spasm as the color drained from his skin. "The memories are pulled from time. There is a machine…"

There was an attempt by Jessup at further speech but his heart had already stopped beating. Alex stared at his lifeless enemy, now devoid of any threat, save for that of confusion

Alex Heton had been shot twice, once in the arm and once in the stomach. His head was spinning and his arms could barely pull him. Despite this, he was already heading toward Officer Stephani Turner. It looked like she was still breathing. He could get more information from her, he thought, pulling himself across the lot to her now.

Her body seemed to get further and further away with every drag of his palms across the pavement. His eyes were heavy. Alex knew that closing them could be the end, but they were just *so* heavy.

His arms gave out and his cheek fell to the concrete; he was out within seconds.

This would be a peaceful end, he thought.

The questions about reincarnation played out slowly again and again as his consciousness faded.

Why would someone bring us back on purpose?

Will anyone get out of the hospital alive? Would it matter if they did?

What is the machine?

Alex Heton came to in the back of a van, a makeshift IV in his arm, and numerous wounded surrounding him on all sides. He could see Harriet and Chloe, laying together, same IVs in their arms. Janey was attending to them both, checking the fluid in the IVs and trying to keep their wounds neatly dressed and clean.

Behind her, it appeared that Ransic was driving and Eliot was giving him directions into the forest. They were heated as always, but civil.

At his feet was Stephani Turner—he could not make out if she was still alive or not.

"Alex!" a young French accent announced from behind. It took a moment, but he managed to turn over to see Richie's face, excited by him waking up but sad all the same.

"What's wrong?" Alex whispered.

Richie lowered his head, trying to ignore the arguing between Eliot and Ransic in the front seats. "He was there. The bad man."

Alex had just noticed that Albert was nowhere in the van and began to panic. "Where's Albert? Eliot, where's Albert?" He screamed, "Turn around, Ransic! He's still there!" They were listening when he started yelling, but they quickly ignored his request.

Richie had tears in his eyes and was unable to say it.

Alex screamed again. "Richie, where's Albert!"

"The bad man took him away," Richie whimpered. His eyes were almost completely red from all the crying he must have been doing, nestled in the back of a van filled to capacity with gunshot victims. His best friend kidnapped by a psychopath and a murderer.

Alex placed his bloody hand on Richie's shoe; he gave a little squeeze. "We'll get Bay Wolf back." The words hung in his throat. "I promise."

The van became dark as it pulled into a cave deep in the forests around Seattle. Ransic killed the engine and said to Eliot, "we'll have to stabilize them here."

"There's a mass—" Alex's eyes rolled back into his head. He tried again. "There's a m—" He could barely put words together.

The backdoors of the van burst open and Ransic jumped up next to Alex. Janey followed and came over to be next to him, her hand gently stroking his forehead. He pushed it away. "There's…"

Janey put her finger to his lips. "Sweetie, it's okay. We got you."

"There's a *machine!*" He screamed. "It isn't supposed to create duplicates, but it does!"

"Alex, please," Ransic said sternly. "Don't yell, there are probably police less than a mile away."

Eliot pulled himself closer; his arms looked like they had dug into the broken glass something fierce. They were bandaged up hastily, blood seeping through the cracks in the fabric. "Let him speak," he said.

"Some were not meant to return!"

The entire cab fell silent in response to Alex's words. No one said anything as they took a few breaths in the back of a cramped van.

Richie slid off his chair and onto the floor. He tiptoed between the wounded masses spread out across the cold metal of the van's floor. His hand grabbed Alex's and pushed him up against the metal wall on the inside of the van. It took all the strength the boy had. "Alex. What are we supposed to do?" he asked politely.

Alex took a moment.

"We have to destroy the machine."

About the Author

Mikey Neumann lives in Plano, Texas,
where he makes video games at Gearbox Software
and writes books about reincarnation or
Apocalypses. This is his first novel.

Check out other novels he is working on at:
www.bozpublishing.com